A Cafe Christmas

A Pine Valley Christmas Novel

Vanessa E. Kelman

WORD COLLAGE PUBLISHING

ISBN 978-1-961761-25-4 (print edition)
ISBN 978-1-961761-26-1 (ebook edition)

To Carrie and to Paul, without whom this book would not exist.

Carrie, I hope this one has enough romance for you.

Chapter 1

Natalie Mitchell turned the cafe's open sign to closed and locked the door. It had been a good day, busy. Now that the weather had grown colder, it seemed everyone in town was craving baked goods, toasted sandwiches, and warm beverages. And Natalie was not complaining. Combined with the pastries and cookies she was now providing to the motel, the increased business had been very good for her bank account. If it kept up, she might have to hire another employee.

Stifling a yawn, Natalie joined one of her current staff members, Chloe, in the kitchen. Though they tried to keep up with cleaning throughout the day, last-minute customers always left them scrambling, especially on busy days like today. They tidied the kitchen, then moved into the dining room.

"When did you want to decorate for Christmas?" Chloe asked as they wiped down tables.

Natalie sighed. "It is getting to be that time, isn't it?" November was already half over, but she hadn't given it more than a passing thought.

"Yup. The holiday lights have already gone up along Main Street, and some of the other businesses have started decorating. The cafe will be looking pretty naked soon."

"I suppose you're right. I'll try to dig out the boxes tonight. Maybe we can start this week."

They finished the cleaning, and Natalie said goodbye to Chloe before climbing the back stairs to her apartment above the shop. She had been up since four and was exhausted, but if she didn't dig out the holiday decorations now, she would probably forget. Besides, it was much too early for bed. She had to keep herself awake.

Natalie dragged her personal decorations into her living room and brought the cafe's decorations downstairs, then she grabbed her purse and keys and headed outside. She had to pick up a few groceries for dinner, and she was hoping a brisk walk in the cool air would perk her up.

The air was chillier than she had expected, and Natalie was soon wishing she had worn something warmer than a sweatshirt. Working and living in the same building made it easy to misjudge the weather. But the sun felt heavenly on her face, and she breathed in the crisp air. This was her favorite time of year.

Since the cafe closed at two, Natalie got out of work earlier than most people, and the streets were relatively quiet. Holiday shopping hadn't started in earnest yet. But she smiled at the few passersby she encountered. Pretty much everyone in town frequented the cafe, so all were familiar faces, even if she didn't know their names.

The grocery store was only a few blocks away, and soon Natalie was stepping into its warmth, rubbing her arms to escape the chill. She greeted Sandy, a cashier who stopped by the cafe nearly every morning for coffee before work. Then she grabbed a basket for her shopping.

Living alone, she didn't go through much, but she preferred to shop regularly rather than stock up. Technically, she could purchase items from the cafe and never have to leave her building, but she needed to get out into the town, stretch her legs, and escape the little bubble that was her daily life. She needed the fresh air, and, just as importantly, the reality check. Plus, it helped her feel connected to her community. If she had remembered to dress more warmly, she likely would have taken the opportunity to wander Main Street, stop by the park, and enjoy the beautiful fall day. Maybe tomorrow.

It didn't take long to grab her few groceries, pay, and step back into the world. Natalie closed her eyes, smiled, and breathed in the air. Yup, her favorite time of year.

She loved Pine Valley. It was a small town, with friendly residents and plenty of charm. She had grown up here, and, though she had gone away for college, she couldn't imagine living anywhere else. She loved her neighbors, her fellow businesspeople, and the building she called home for both her cafe and herself. Life was good.

Natalie climbed back up to her apartment, put her groceries away, and grabbed the stack of mail that had been delivered earlier that day. Since they had been so busy, she hadn't had the chance to give it more than a quick glance. But there had been something sent from her landlord, and she was curious what it had to say. She hoped the rent wasn't going up, though she knew she could cover it if it did.

She slid the letter from the envelope and skimmed its contents. It wasn't about the rent, at least not directly. Apparently, Mrs. Malloy had decided to sell.

Pine Valley might be small, but it wasn't immune to drama. Just over a year ago, an apartment building had collapsed. The owner of the building had skimped on safety and repairs, and the building had become unstable. Its collapse had thrown the entire town into upheaval. Fortunately, that shady property owner was now in jail. But the collapsed building wasn't the only one he owned, and when the owner went to jail, his wife had taken control of the properties. Natalie's building was included in his portfolio.

Natalie was grateful that she and the other tenants in the building hadn't experienced the same issues the apartment residents had, and Natalie was savvy enough to handle most small repairs on her own. The property owner's wife, Mrs. Colleen Malloy, had put a property management company in charge. The company seemed on top of things, and they hadn't had any issues up to now. Natalie hoped the new owners, whoever they ended up being, wouldn't change that. She supposed only time would tell.

Christopher Parker rolled his chair behind his desk and picked up the phone receiver. The flashing light told him he had a message, and he was hoping it was someone either looking to sell or looking to make an offer. As a commercial realtor, he thrived on the constant flow of traffic. And, with his stellar reputation in the state, it wasn't uncommon for people to call him out of the blue to hire him, bypassing the main office he worked for.

A while back he had considered going out on his own, since he knew the clientele would follow, but the overhead for real estate was ridiculous, between the office space, the software, the staffing. He would much rather just deal with the clients.

Christopher pushed the voicemail button and punched the air as he heard the message. Not just one listing, but four. Four new properties to sell. In Pine Valley.

Chris wasn't too familiar with Pine Valley, but what he had seen he liked. That summer a friend and client of his had expressed interest in purchasing a motel in the town. It was a small community, tight knit, friendly. Well, mostly friendly, he thought, as he remembered the initial reaction of the motel owners' daughter. But the sale had gone through with few issues, and everyone seemed happy.

Now he had four properties to sell in the town: three commercial buildings near the center of town, and one land property that was zoned for residential, the site of a former apartment building. Now that he thought of it, he remembered seeing something about that on the news. He would have to get all of the details when he called the current owner back.

Yes, this was good. He was heading back to Pine Valley.

Chapter 2

"So, what's going to happen with the building?" Chloe asked Natalie the next morning as they prepped for the breakfast rush.

"I guess it depends on who buys it and what they decide to do with it."

"Do you think they'll kick us out?"

"I really hope not."

Natalie had filled Chloe in on the details of the letter, though there hadn't been much to go with yet. It had basically been the owner giving them a heads up.

"Where will you go if they kick us out?"

"I think you may be jumping the gun a bit. The most likely thing is that the rent will go up. And even that would take a while. It didn't sound like a buyer had been found yet."

"But it could happen. And what if the rent goes up so much you can't afford to keep the cafe?" Chloe seemed on the verge of full-on panic mode.

Natalie shot her a look. "Chloe. Settle down. We have to take things one step at a time. And right now, all we can do is keep doing what we've been doing. We have no idea what will happen until the building sells." Despite her assurances to Chloe, though, Natalie had to admit to herself at least that she was slightly worried. Not about increased rent, but what would happen if the new owner decided to do something drastic, like kick all of the tenants out and bring in new businesses. She would have to discuss it with her neighbors and fellow business owners.

Fortunately, the cafe was busy enough again that she was able to push the concern from her mind for the time being. But shortly before closing a sharply-dressed man Natalie did not recognize stepped into the cafe, sporting a grin she supposed was meant to be charming. Hoping it wasn't a prospective buyer, she greeted him with a somewhat-forced smile of her own.

"Hello, there, how can I help you?"

"Hello. Wow, this is a great place you have here."

"Thank you. Was there something I could get for you? We'll be closing shortly."

"Oh, uh, sure." The man's grin faltered, and he browsed the glass display case quickly. "I'll have one of those chocolate croissants."

Natalie placed the croissant in a to-go bag. "Will there be anything else today?"

"No, I think that will do it. I really just came in to get a look around. Are you the business owner?"

"I am."

The man grinned again. "Great!" He stuck out a hand. "I'm Christopher Parker. I'm a real estate agent. Did you receive a letter from your landlord?"

Natalie took a deep breath. "I did. Will you be handling the sale of the buildings?"

"Sure am. And from what I've seen, they look like great buildings. Good bones. You mind if I take a look around, take a couple of pictures for the listing?"

Natalie made a show of looking at the clock. She was not looking forward to having this guy poking around. "Uh, sure, I guess, as long as it doesn't take long. As I said, we will be closing soon. So we'll need to clean up and prep for tomorrow."

"Oh, I won't be long. And I'll stay out of your way." He paid for his pastry, left the bag on the counter, and wandered around the dining room, taking the occasional picture with his cell phone.

Natalie had made the place her own over the years, with cozy furnishings and artwork from local artists. She had been one of the first to purchase one of the community murals painted at The Art Spot in town. The space felt welcoming, like her second home. And having a stranger walking around taking pictures of it felt wrong somehow, like he was invading her space. Which was ridiculous. They were open to the public, after all. She had people come in all the time.

Giving herself a mental shake, Natalie helped the last customer who came through the door, then began closing procedures. She definitely needed to talk with her neighbors.

The walk around Pine Valley had been productive, Christopher mused as he slid back into his Mercedes. He had gotten a feel for the buildings he would be selling, the site of the apartment building, and the community as a whole. He would have to discuss with Mrs. Malloy the status of the apartment site. It would be difficult to sell it as it was; it really should have been cleaned up months ago. But the others were in decent shape, and all fully rented. He just needed to find someone who was looking for a commercial investment. Ideally, they would buy it all and make it an easy transaction. But the owner seemed willing to separate the properties for individual sales if necessary. He would have to see who he could find.

Having been in the business as long as he had, Chris had a list of investors he regularly worked with, but most of them were drawn more toward bigger towns and cities, looking for nearly guaranteed income from the higher traffic. Zachary White, the investor who had purchased the Pine Valley Motel, had been an exception, but he looked for hospitality projects, not retail. Chris wondered if he might want to try his hand at the apartment building, though. That might be up his alley. He would have to give it some thought.

Chris looked around Main Street again as he backed up and drove off. This place would be too small for most of the people he knew, but he kind of liked it. While he lived in a large suburb himself, small communities like this had a certain charm that he found appealing. Maybe someday when he retired he would settle in a place like this. But that was years away, and he had a lot of selling to do before then. Starting with these buildings. Maybe Zach White would have some contacts for him.

Natalie watched Christopher Parker's fancy car drive away as she wiped down tables. There was something about him that rubbed her the wrong way. He seemed too cocky, too sure that he would be able to get what he wanted. Would whoever he found to buy this place be the same way? Would they come in and try to change things? Bring in a Starbucks or something to replace her?

With a sigh, Natalie straightened and returned to the kitchen. Everything looked ready for the following day.

Chloe had left early that day, needing to pick up her parents from the airport, so Natalie was alone with her thoughts. Never a good thing. What she needed to do was take a walk and talk with her neighboring business owners.

With a curt nod to herself, Natalie grabbed her purse and keys and headed out the door, locking it behind her.

The cold wind blew into her, and Natalie kicked herself for forgetting her coat again. But she wasn't going far. Less than a hundred feet away was the entrance to the business next door: a boutique that carried mostly clothing but also sold some small home decor items. The shop smelled deliciously like cinnamon, courtesy of the candle sitting on a warmer behind the checkout counter.

"It always smells so good in here," Natalie said as she greeted the boutique's owner, Courtney.

Courtney grinned. "You know I love my candles."

"Yes, you do." Natalie walked around, brushing her hand against a soft sweater and cozy wool skirt. The boutique wasn't very big, but Courtney had filled it with a wonderful assortment of clothing for men, women, and children. Though she hadn't grown up in Pine Valley, Courtney was very in tune with the needs of her clientele, and the rotating stock ensured her regulars could find just what they needed. "I love this outfit. Remind me to try it on before I go."

"You could just try it on now."

Natalie sighed. "I know. But I need a serious gab session first. I assume you got the letter from Malloy?"

Courtney returned the sigh. "Yeah, I got it. And met the agent selling the place. What did you think of him?"

"A bit too self-assured for my taste."

"Same. But he *was* really cute."

"Courtney!"

"What? He was."

"Priorities, please. What are we going to do to make sure the building doesn't fall into the wrong hands?"

Courtney shrugged. "The way I see it, we don't have much say. Unless you know someone who wants it. Or we buy it ourselves."

"Aren't you worried the new owner will kick us all out?"

"It's possible. But the business is doing well, and I pay my rent on time. It seems like more hassle than it's worth for them to start from scratch. I just think Chloe's doomsday mentality has been rubbing off on you."

"Maybe." Natalie slumped against the counter, but then stood up when a customer walked through the door. She watched as Courtney helped the woman pick out a dress for an upcoming function and thought about what Courtney had said. It was probably pointless to worry about something that was out of her hands. Maybe she should start looking for a new space as a backup plan. But where would she go? Businesses didn't usually leave Pine Valley, so available spaces were pretty much nil. And she did not want to leave town.

Courtney finished up with the customer, rang her up, and bid her farewell. Natalie hadn't moved an inch.

"Maybe we *should* buy the building ourselves."

Courtney laughed. "I was kidding. Business might be doing well, but it's not doing that well. There's no way I could buy this building."

"But what if we all did, pitched in for it all together?"

Courtney looked skeptical. "I don't see that working out. I get along just fine with you, and Josh next door and I get along okay, but I barely know the people who rent the apartments upstairs. I certainly wouldn't want to get into business with them, which is basically what that would be. Do you really want to rely on other people to make sure the bills get paid on time and maintenance is done promptly? Especially when we don't even know if they're reliable?"

Natalie sighed. "No, I guess not. But we wouldn't have to involve the apartment people. It could just be you, me, and Josh."

"Have you ever been a landlord?"

"No."

"Have you ever *wanted* to be a landlord?"

"Not particularly."

"Exactly my point. Look, the situation isn't ideal. But maybe the new owners will be great. Maybe we can sweet talk that realtor into letting us vet them before they buy."

It was Natalie's turn to look skeptical. "Yeah, I don't see that going over too well."

"You never know."

"Well, I'm going to talk to Josh anyway, see what he has to say on the matter."

"You do that. And bring me back an ice cream cone."

"You seriously want ice cream when it's forty degrees outside?"

"It's always a good time for ice cream."

Chapter 3

Natalie pushed open the door to the ice cream shop and greeted Josh. The shop was empty, as she had expected.

"How's business?" she asked as she approached the counter.

Josh shrugged. "Going okay, I suppose. It's the slow season."

"Have you ever thought about closing for the winter?"

Josh chuckled. "Every year."

Natalie laughed. "Then why don't you?"

He shrugged again. "It gives me something to do, and it brings in enough income to keep the lights on. I have some regulars who keep things going."

"That reminds me: don't let me leave without a cone for Courtney. I forgot to ask what kind though. Do you know what she likes?"

"She always gets the same thing: whatever flavor I just made. I've got a great one this time, too. Pumpkin with a caramel swirl. You want one, too?"

Natalie shivered. "Too cold for me, but thanks."

"So you just stopped in to get a cone for Courtney?"

"No. I came to talk about this whole building business."

"Ah."

"What do you think about it?"

"Well, it's not ideal. I like stability. But I suppose we'll just have to wait and see how it goes."

Natalie sighed. "That's basically what Courtney said. Actually, she said we should buy the building, but then she said she was just joking. But why does that have to be a joke? I can't stand the idea of waiting around, not knowing what's going to happen."

"So you don't know what's going to happen, and that means you should buy the building?"

"I just think we should look into all possibilities. And maybe if we all pitched in, we could afford it. But I take you think I'm crazy, too."

"Not crazy. It would be tempting to have more control. And to know that my rent isn't just going to someone else. Or that I could be kicked out at any time."

"Exactly!"

"But who exactly would be buying this building?"

"All of us. Or it could just be you, me, and Courtney. Whatever."

"Hmm. Not sure about that."

"Okay, fine. I'll count you out, too, then."

"I get where you're coming from. And maybe I'll feel differently when we find out who's buying the place."

"Mmhmm. I won't count on it." She sighed. "Well, just get me Courtney's cone, then."

Josh scooped out a heaping cone and handed it over.

"How much do I owe you?"

"Don't worry about it. Tell Courtney I'll see her tomorrow."

"You got it. See you later."

Natalie waved goodbye and left the shop, then went right back to Courtney's boutique and thrust the cone into Courtney's hand.

"Josh agrees with you. And he says he'll see you tomorrow. What's tomorrow?"

Courtney blushed. "Nothing special. I just usually stop in on Thursdays after I close up."

"I see." Natalie grinned. "Well, then, enjoy your cone." She winked. "I'll catch you later." And she went back to the cafe to get ready for the next day.

By the time she made it back to her apartment, Natalie was feeling somewhat discouraged that her friends weren't as inclined to take charge as she was. There had to be something they could do. She was not one to just sit back and wait for things to happen. She needed to minimize the potential damage. But how?

Her thoughts returned to the conversation with Courtney. No, she hadn't ever wanted to be a landlord, and no, she didn't necessarily want to get into business with her fellow tenants, but would it be so bad to look into buying the property? How much did this kind of building go for, anyway? Business was doing well. Really well. Aside from general overhead, she didn't have many expenses. She didn't have a frivolous lifestyle, despite the occasional new outfit she bought from Courtney. She had a good amount set aside for a rainy day or whenever she decided to retire. Would she be able to do something with that money? Use it as a downpayment on a commercial property, perhaps? After all, she would have income from the other tenants coming in. And she would save on her own rent – for both the cafe and her apartment. That had to count for something. Could she get a mortgage for the rest?

Okay, she had to think logically about this. It wasn't just the money thing. Even if she could get a mortgage tomorrow for the full amount, it wasn't about the money. Would she seriously want to be a landlord?

But, then again, she could hire a property management company like Mrs. Malloy did. The company had seemed decent, and, except for the letter informing them that oversight of the building had changed and the letter about selling the property, they had never even interacted with Mrs. Malloy, despite her being the owner. Any maintenance issues went to the property management company. Sure, it could take a little while to get someone out, but it all worked out okay.

But being their landlord could affect her relationships with Courtney and Josh. Business relationships always did. They would no longer be colleagues or peers. Suddenly she would be in charge of the building, and if anything went wrong, she would be to blame. Did she want to put that kind of pressure on herself? Was she willing to take the risk of her relationships imploding?

Yes, she would have to give it some thought. But at least it was something to think about other than impending doom.

Chapter 4

Christopher pushed open the door to his apartment and tossed his keys on the table in the entryway. He loosened his tie, kicked off his shoes, then went into his bedroom, where he promptly changed into sweatpants and a t-shirt.

While he thrived on the hustle, the research and details, and matching sellers with properties, there were definitely days when he wished he didn't have to be so buttoned up to do it. He believed in looking professional, and he was willing to wear a tie to give the impression that he was in charge, but some days he envied his friends who worked from home and could live in sweats. Fortunately, though, he had no other commitments tonight and could just lounge in front of the TV, put a movie on, and eat junk food.

He thought back to his trip to Pine Valley earlier that day. He had stopped into the local real estate office, out of professional courtesy. They handled mostly residential properties and the occasional rental, so they hadn't been upset about his handling the sale of commercial properties. But the vibe in the office had been completely different than what he was used to. The staff had looked professional but not uptight, and the atmosphere had been friendly and welcoming, not the modern chrome aloofness he was used to. While he was treated well and made plenty of money where he was, it got him thinking about the possibility of a middle ground. Could he do what he loved and still feel comfortable doing it? Sometimes his face felt like it would crack from all the smiling he did. And the sucking up to corporate investors? Not his favorite part of the job. What would it be like to work in a place like Pine Valley? Would he still have to deal with the fakeness, the confident show? He supposed with commercial properties it was inevitable, regardless of where you worked.

It was funny, though, he thought. The big, confident grin and charming attitude didn't seem to work when he was in Pine Valley. It hadn't worked with the motel, and it hadn't worked when he was walking around today. The business owners he met had been indifferent at best, and scornful at worst. Maybe they were scared about losing their livelihoods. Or maybe they saw through the cockiness. Hmm. He would have to give that some thought. Maybe he had to change his approach for this sale, with the community at least. And if that was how the community was, how would the investors who were interested in this kind of community be? Would they want the buttoned-up charm or a more natural, easy-going professional?

He might have to change his whole persona. He might even be able to let some of his actual personality show. Imagine that.

The next morning, Chris was back at his desk, and getting frustrated. He was getting nowhere with his contacts. Despite his specialty being somewhat small-scale retail properties, some of his investors had nearly laughed in his face when he mentioned Pine Valley. It was too small, not enough profit to be had. Even Zach White hadn't offered any inspiration. His contacts were all hotel people.

But there had to be someone. Someone had to be able to see the charm and appeal of a small town. After all, Don Malloy had bought the properties originally. And if he hadn't been such an idiot about safety, he could have had a comfortable life. Reliable, long-term tenants. It seemed ideal.

Despite his profession, Chris had never given much thought to the flipside of things. Once the sale of the property was done, the rest was out of his hands. He knew most of the investors he worked with hired property management firms to handle the day-to-day operations of the properties while they just signed paperwork and cashed checks. But he couldn't imagine not wanting a hand in what you had just spent millions of dollars on. Sure, they had a say in any renovations or large projects that needed doing, but everything else? They hardly even stepped foot on their own property.

A knock on his office door disrupted Chris's musings.

"You busy?" his coworker and friend Eric asked.

"Not really. Just pondering the intricacies of being a landlord."

Eric laughed. "You thinking of switching sides? Buying instead of selling?"

Chris shrugged. "Nah. Just trying to find a solution for my current listings. Small town. None of my regulars are interested."

"Such a shame. You won't be able to sell it in record time. There goes your streak."

Chris grinned. "Nah. Where there's a will, there's a way. Just need to change tactics, that's all."

"Good luck with that. I'm running out to grab lunch. You interested?"

"Sure. Grab me my usual from that sub place."

"You got it."

Eric headed out, and Chris resumed his musing. What would it be like to be a landlord? he wondered. Surely, he would be able to do a better job than that idiot Don Malloy. Reliable, long-term tenants. Regular income that didn't require hustle to keep coming in. Hmm. Maybe if he couldn't *find* an investor, he could consider *becoming* an investor. He had some savings. And his commission checks were nothing to sneeze at, with enough consistency to be somewhat reliable. It could be a retirement plan of sorts. Hire one of those property management companies. Heck, he could even just keep the one Colleen Malloy had in place. Easy peasy. And it would give him an excuse to spend more time in Pine Valley. Hmm.

Chapter 5

Natalie had always been a morning person, and she truly didn't mind waking up before dawn to start baking. But lately she had been finding it harder and harder to get enough made before the morning rush, especially since she also needed to have the order ready for the motel. While Lindsay was willing to pick things up, they needed to be baked and cooled in time. She was going to need to either start waking up even earlier or bring someone else in to help with the baking and prep work before Chloe arrived.

The trouble was, she was starting to feel reluctant to hire someone else. While she certainly had the room in her budget, she had started consciously putting more into her savings account. Or, as she had started referring to it, her down-payment fund. She hadn't decided anything, but she wanted to be ready if it came to it. And hiring another staff member would seriously cut into what she would be able to save. So for now, it looked like getting up earlier was the best course of action. She just hoped she could stay awake for the rest of the day.

By the time the first loaves of bread were rising and the first batches of cookies and pastries were in the oven, Natalie was already tired. Maybe if she did more of the prep work the night before she wouldn't have to get up as early. Or maybe one of her existing staff members would be willing to come in an hour or two early so she wouldn't have to do it all herself. It was worth a conversation, at least.

Natalie sighed as she mixed the batter for a batch of chocolate chip muffins. She loved her job. She did. But she suspected if she tried to keep going at this pace she would end up burning herself out, and that didn't help anyone, even if it did save her a few bucks. She was going to need to make some decisions, and soon.

Maybe it would help if she had an idea of how much the building would even cost. Maybe it would be completely out of her reach and she was wasting her time – and stressing herself out – over nothing. The listing had to have been posted by now, right? Maybe that would be her project for the afternoon: find out how much the building would cost, and then crunch some numbers to find out if buying it was even feasible. Or, if she was set on buying but this building didn't work out, maybe she could look into other properties. Sure, commercial spaces didn't come up too often, but maybe she could find a nearby residential space and see if she could get it zoned for mixed use. Then she could own without having to be a landlord.

But then she would lose her perfect space, right on Main Street. And the building would likely need total renovation to get it to where she needed to be. That could cost just as much as buying this place.

Natalie sighed again and rocked her head back and forth to stretch her neck. Just a couple of days ago she had been happy, thrilled with the increased business and content with her cozy little life. Why did everything have to get thrown off kilter?

By the time Chloe arrived to get the cases and equipment ready for the morning rush, Natalie was ready to call it a day and crawl back into bed. Not only had she gotten up earlier than usual, but the stressful introspection of the last two hours had done nothing to ease her anxiety or nerves.

"You look like hell," Chloe said by way of greeting as she hung her jacket in the staff room behind the kitchen.

"Gee, thanks," Natalie replied. She was sure it was true, but that did little to help her mood. "Let's just get ready for the morning."

Chloe washed her hands, then tied an apron around her waist as she assessed the state of the kitchen. "Wow, you were busy this morning."

"Yeah. I decided to wake up early to make sure we had enough. With the increased business lately, we've been running out of some of the favorites. And if Mrs. Jackson doesn't get her blueberry muffin one more time, I think we'll have a riot on our hands."

Chloe grinned. "She could totally take you, too. That purse of hers must weigh a ton."

"Yeah, well, I'd rather not find out."

The cafe officially opened at seven, but if everything was ready in time, they opened the doors early. Chloe had the routine down pat, and the doors were usually unlocked by six thirty. As she crossed the dining room to unlock the door, Chloe called over her shoulder, "you might want to run a brush through your hair or something. Maybe splash some water on your face. Increased business won't be an issue if you scare all the customers away."

"Ha ha," Natalie said, rolling her eyes. But she went into the bathroom to see what she could do.

The regulars started strolling in, Lindsay stopped by to pick up the motel's order, and Natalie found her groove. Once she had small talk to occupy her mind, thoughts of buying a building disappeared. Another staff member, Joey, started his shift at eight, just in time for everyone to grab coffees on their way to work. The first half of the morning passed in a blur.

When they finally had a moment to breathe, Joey went to wipe down tables in the dining area, and Natalie turned to face Chloe.

"Hey, Chloe."

"Yeah?" Chloe was restocking the cases.

"Would you be interested in picking up a few more hours? Come in an hour or two early to help with baking?"

Chloe paused her task and stood up, releasing a breath as she leaned against the edge of the case. "Maybe. I wouldn't mind the extra hours, just not sure I could get myself up in time. Some days it's a struggle getting here for six."

"I get that." Natalie worked on slicing bread in preparation for the lunch crowd. She should stick a couple more loaves in the oven.

"Let me think about it."

Natalie nodded. "Okay. Just let me know as soon as you can. I had hoped getting up early would help fill the gaps, but I am exhausted. I'm not sure how long I can keep it up. If you can't do it, I'll probably have to hire someone."

Joey tossed the cleaning rag into a bucket as he returned to the counter. "I'll do it."

Natalie turned to look at him. "Seriously?"

"Yeah. I love to bake. I make all the birthday cakes for my family, and my turnovers are to die for."

Natalie and Chloe shared a look. Natalie paused her task and leaned against the counter. "How did I not know that?"

Joey shrugged. "Dunno. You never asked. Just assumed I was another beautiful face eager to serve coffee to the masses."

Natalie laughed. "Can't argue with that, I guess. Could you get here by five? Or even four?"

He shrugged again. "Sure. I'm up super early to walk and feed the dogs anyway."

"Huh. I didn't even know you had dogs."

"Guess you should take more time to learn about your employees, then." He gave her a wink.

"Guess I should. Okay, Chloe, you're off the hook. Joey here is going to be my baking sidekick."

"Thank God," Chloe said. "I really wasn't looking forward to losing more beauty sleep."

Natalie grinned at Joey. "Start tomorrow?"

"Sure thing."

Relieved that at least one thing was decided, Natalie felt lighter for the rest of the day. At least until one o'clock, when Christopher Parker strolled in.

"Back again so soon?" Natalie asked.

"What can I say? That was a delicious chocolate croissant." He flashed her a grin.

"Yeah, well, sorry, but we're out of those today. Can I get you something else?"

"No problem." He glanced through the cases. "Let's go with one of the candy cookies."

Natalie raised her eyebrows. "Seriously? I did not take you for a candy cookie kind of guy."

"I'd be willing to bet there are a lot of things you don't know about me."

Natalie couldn't tell what he was trying to accomplish here. Was he flirting? Threatening? Just stating a fact? She was too tired to read his tone. But he definitely had a different vibe today than when he had been in the other day.

She rang him up, and he was out the door soon after. Huh. Maybe he really did just want a cookie.

Christopher sat on a bench outside the cafe and took the cookie out of its bag. Taking a bite, he looked around the center of town. The location of the building really was ideal. The other commercial buildings weren't too far, either. Even if the current tenants left, it wouldn't be hard to get new ones, even in a town this small. Any of the buildings – or all of them – would make excellent investments. Maybe not the same caliber as his typical clients were used to, but nothing to sneeze at, either.

The listings had gone up a couple of days ago, and so far he hadn't gotten much interest. He had had a few inquiries, but nothing that seemed serious. He knew it could take time, so he wasn't worried about that part. But he had to make some decisions of his own. Something about the spaces, and this town, made the idea of purchasing his own investments very appealing. But if he was seriously considering purchasing one or even all of them, he would need to relinquish the listings, hand them to another realtor. He hated to lose out on the commission, but it would be a serious conflict of interest. So what did he want more: commission or property? Would he regret buying the buildings? Would he regret *not* buying the buildings?

That was why he was in town. In addition to getting some paperwork from Colleen Malloy, he had to figure out if this was a passing interest or a serious consideration. He also needed to check on the site of the apartment building. Cleanup was supposed to have started the day before. He needed to make sure it was on track. It would be hard enough to sell the space as it was. A pile of rubble with remnants of crime scene tape strewn about would be even harder. Of all the properties, that was the one that worried Chris the most. But if Colleen was willing to go down on the asking price, it could be sold as typical residential space, not as a potential apartment building. The parking lot would have to be ripped up in that case, but it would be an easier sell. He suspected she wouldn't be willing to do that anytime soon, though; the selling price would likely be considerably lower.

So much to think about. But he had time. Commercial spaces could take a while to sell. And with no other interested parties, there was no rush. He had plenty of time.

Chapter 6

Natalie checked out the property listing and gulped. She was sure for many people it would be a drop in the bucket. But for her, it was a serious chunk of change. Over a million dollars for a building in little Pine Valley? Sure, it was a good-sized building, with space for three businesses and four apartments, but seriously. Even if she decided she wanted to go for it, who would possibly give her a loan to cover that?

At least now she could understand why Mrs. Malloy wanted to sell. If she could get this amount for each of the three buildings in town, plus money for the land that used to have the apartment building on it, she would be set. And considering the tough spot her husband had put her in, Natalie couldn't really blame her. A fresh start in a new place, with a few million dollars in her pocket to tide her over? Yeah, that sounded like a pretty sweet deal.

But if Natalie didn't go for it, who would they get? What kind of person takes a chance on a building in a dinky little unknown town? What kind of person would be able to spend that kind of money and not even blink an eye? And how long would it take to find that person? Would this building start deteriorating like the apartment building had in the meantime? At least then she might be able to get a good deal on it, Natalie half-joked to herself.

Could she even swing it if she wanted to? If someone gave her a loan, would she be able to cover the payments? Sure, the rent from current tenants would go a long way toward covering any expenses, but some of that would go to the property management company, and Natalie had no idea what the payments would be. She had good credit, but she couldn't even imagine.

Okay, but what if she *did* imagine? What would it be like to own this building? To know that she couldn't get kicked out, that she could ensure her friends didn't get kicked out? Would they try to take advantage? If she were the landlord, she would have to make sure they kept up with their payments. That could cause some animosity if they found themselves in a tough spot. Could she keep a professional distance? How would that affect their relationships?

And what about the maintenance, repairs, taxes? Her rent currently covered all of that. Was she prepared to take it all on? More expenses, possibly big ones. What if the building needed a new roof? Or furnace? Or any of the million and one other things that would need to be replaced at some point?

And what about her own stuff? Sure, it would be great for her budget to not have to worry about paying rent, but it would probably make good financial sense to still pay rent, for the business and herself. Keep the budgets separate. The cafe could pay its way, and that would help pay the mortgage or whatever. She would have to handle the building like its own business. After all, it would have expenses and income, hopefully eventually a profit.

So much to think about. No wonder Courtney wanted nothing to do with it. Natalie should probably just forget the whole idea.

Something wasn't letting her go, though. Ever since Courtney had gotten the idea stuck in her head – however unintentionally – Natalie had felt a strong pull toward making it happen. It couldn't hurt to at least find out if it would be possible, right? She could check with at least the local bank to see if they would be willing to approve her. They could at least tell her if she was way off base for even considering it. Then maybe she could get this ridiculous idea out of her system.

Before she could talk herself out of it, Natalie visited the bank's website and sent off a quick message requesting an appointment. It didn't hurt to find out.

Of the three retail buildings for sale, Chris was most drawn to the one housing the cafe. It had the greatest potential, he felt, since it had the apartments above the retail spaces. The other buildings just housed the commercial spaces. While residential tenants could pose problems, they also offered greater opportunities for income. More tenants meant more rent. It was a no-brainer, really. Even if the other buildings were less expensive, he wasn't worried about it. His income gave him the opportunity to live a lavish lifestyle, but he was actually pretty low-maintenance. His car was the most expensive thing about him, and he drove that mostly to impress his clients. If he didn't have to show off, he would probably still be driving around in the Toyota Corolla he had owned in college.

He would still need a business loan, he mused. His savings wouldn't quite cover the cost. But would he just go for the one building? Or would he try for all three? He really wasn't feeling up to tackling the apartment property. That was a bigger project than he felt equipped to handle. But he could do commercial. He could probably do commercial in his sleep.

He still hadn't decided if he wanted to, though.

Then there was the question of the current tenants. The boutique owner and the ice cream shop owner had been pleasant enough, if a bit cool. That was un-derstandable. But his interactions with the owner of the cafe had an undercurrent of hostility he wasn't quite sure he understood. It wasn't like he was kicking them out. Heck, it hadn't even been his decision to sell. He was just the one facilitating the transaction. For now, at least.

And whoever bought the property – whether it was him or someone else – would likely just keep things as they were. Why mess with it if it was working? Based on the financial records Colleen had provided him, all of the tenants on all of the properties paid their rent on time. A hiccup here or there perhaps, but overall very consistent, conscientious tenants. Who would mess with that? Well, if he was honest, some of his regular clients probably would. They would jack up the rent or bring in bigger companies. But in a small town, that was less likely. Most big companies couldn't be bothered with little towns like this. Not enough profit.

Maybe she was just upset at the situation in general. Or maybe someone had soured her on the whole business. Or maybe she was upset at something that had nothing to do with him.

Maybe he needed to turn on the charm. Not the sucking-up-to-clients charm, but the real charm. He would kill her with kindness and see if he could turn that pretty scowl into a smile.

Chapter 7

Having someone else in the kitchen took some getting used to, but Natalie and Joey soon found their rhythm. And Joey turned out to be a whiz in the kitchen. Not only did he know his way around a stand mixer, but he could knead bread to perfection, design picture-perfect cookie icing, and create a flaky pastry that melted in Natalie's mouth. She practically swooned when he handed her the first turnover.

"Where have you been all my life?"

Joey grinned. "Right under your nose, being the best barista in the northeast."

"So you're just good at everything, then."

He sighed. "Well, not everything. I have not once made a perfect souffle."

Natalie feigned disappointment. "That's it. You're fired."

"We don't even serve souffle!" he yelled in mock outrage.

Natalie scowled. "You're right. Fine. You can stay." Then she grinned. "As long as you keep making these." And she took another bite of turnover.

"You got it, boss."

The morning passed quickly, and by the time Chloe arrived, the counters were full of delicious everything.

"Wow, you guys have been busy," Chloe responded as she peeked into the kitchen.

"Joey is a genius," Natalie replied.

"You can say that again!" Joey called from where he was placing cookies into a case.

"I'm glad it's working out," Chloe said as she hung up her jacket. "Maybe it'll help soften the blow."

Natalie turned to meet her gaze. "What blow?"

Chloe sighed and leaned against the doorframe. "I need to request a leave of absence."

"What? No! Why?"

"My dad got hurt when my parents were on their trip. He's going to need surgery. And there's no way my mom can handle taking care of him by herself."

"Oh no! What happened?"

"He lost his balance when they were walking down a steep hill, and when he fell, he landed on his hip pretty hard. He already had trouble with that hip, and it looks like that was the last straw."

"Oh man. I hope he's okay."

"They're pretty confident he will be. But it will be a while before he can do things on his own, at least a few weeks."

"When's the surgery?"

"In a couple of weeks. So we have time to get someone in here if you want, train them to take over. I mean, no one could possibly replace me," Chloe said, attempting a smile.

"You are irreplaceable. But I'll definitely need the help, even if it's just temporary. I'll put together a job posting."

"Sorry to leave you in the lurch, especially with the holidays coming."

"We'll figure it out. Family comes first."

"Thanks."

Just when one dilemma got solved, another had to rise up to replace it. What next?

Christopher walked into the cafe, eager to see if he could win Natalie over. He was disappointed to find another woman at the counter. A quick glance at her name tag told him her name was Chloe.

"Good afternoon," she greeted him with a smile. "What can I get you?"

"Hmm." He took a look inside the glass display case. "Let's go with one of those turnovers."

"Good choice," Chloe said as she placed one in a bag.

"Natalie isn't in by any chance, is she?" he couldn't help but ask as Chloe rang him up.

"She's in the back taking care of some paperwork. I can get her if you need her, though."

"No, no, that's okay. Maybe next time."

"Okay. Have a good day."

"Thanks. You, too."

He paid for his purchase and headed back outside. Disappointing, but there was always tomorrow. At this rate he was going to need to get a place in Pine Valley just to save on gas. Or he could just not worry about it. After all, what difference did it make if the cafe owner liked him or not? If he ended up buying the building, they could cross that bridge then. Or not. Landlords should probably maintain a professional distance anyway.

But there was something about her that made him want to put in the effort. Was it worth the time and expense of driving into Pine Valley every day, though? At this point he had no other reason to come into town. And it was taking time away from his other clients and listings. Maybe seeing him too often would make her more upset. Would he wear her down or piss her off? Was there any way of knowing?

Okay, he had to settle down. This whole Pine Valley situation was getting him way too wound up. What happened to his simple life? Go to work, sell some property, make a bunch of money, hang out with friends or chill in his apartment. Why did he have to suddenly get ideas about buying up investments and getting hung up on someone who most likely would have no effect on his life?

No, he had to take a step back. He had to work on finding buyers – other buyers, *real* buyers – to take the properties off the table. Then he could get back to his real life. His empty, lonely real life. No...his lucrative, secure life that brought him fulfillment. These buildings were just more listings to sell. This town was just another town. And Natalie was just another woman.

But there was something about her...

Chapter 8

Christopher decided the best thing to do was avoid Pine Valley for a few days. He had been fixating too much. He needed to let it simmer for a bit and see how he felt after stepping back. It was a big decision, after all. He needed to be sure.

In the meantime, he would work on finding investors for the Pine Valley properties, and properties elsewhere for some of his other clients. He had plenty to do. His schedule would have been tight if he tried to drive over to Pine Valley. And he had no actual reason to go.

He still found himself driving there Saturday evening. Which was ridiculous, he told himself. The cafe would be closed. What on earth would he accomplish?

He pulled into a parking space in the lot across the street from the cafe and took a look at the building. The cafe was dark except for a single light that shone by the entryway. It gave the space an otherworldly feel, like an old movie. He had never visited Pine Valley at night. The whole town felt like a step back in time, with streetlights illuminating the brick buildings and town green. Holiday lights were hung off the streetlamps, wreaths adorned many business doors. It was quaint, soothing in a way.

Near the parking lot was a diner that, though obviously modernized, still felt old-fashioned. And, now that he thought about it, he should probably stop in for a bite to eat. This impromptu visit had happened before he had even thought about dinner.

Luck must be on his side, for just as he stepped through the front door, he spotted Natalie sitting on a stool at the counter, chatting and laughing with an older woman holding a pitcher of water. There happened to be an empty seat beside her. Would that be presumptuous? Could he play it cool, make it look like the accident it actually kind of was?

"Hello, sir. Table for one?" A young woman greeted him, interrupting his musing.

"Uh, maybe. Is it actually possible to just sit at the counter?"

"Of course. Grab a seat, and someone will be right with you."

"Thanks."

He felt surprisingly nervous as he approached the counter and slid onto the seat beside Natalie. The older woman she had been talking with turned to face him and greeted him with a smile.

"Hello there." She snagged the menu resting between the napkin dispenser and sugar packet tray and handed it to him. Then she grabbed a glass from under the counter and in one smooth movement flipped it and poured him a glass of water. She had obviously done it a time or two before. "My name's Maggie. I'll give you a minute with the menu, and then I'll be right back." She turned to Natalie and winked, then walked off to greet other customers.

Chris was perusing the menu, trying to decide what to try, when Natalie's voice broke his concentration.

"What are you doing here?"

Chris looked up to meet her gaze. She wasn't exactly happy to see him. "Um. Eating?"

"So all of a sudden, you – who, to the best of my knowledge, has never spent any time in Pine Valley before now – finds a reason to be here all the time?"

"I do have business in town, you know."

"Trust me, I know. Does the fact that you're in town on a Saturday night mean that you've found a buyer?"

"No, not yet."

She gave him a pointed look. How could he possibly defend himself when he didn't actually have a reason for being in town?

"I...wanted to take some pictures of the town at night, and get a feel for the place, you know? So I can give potential buyers the rundown on how the town feels in terms of safety and whatnot."

He didn't think she believed him, if the skeptical look was any indication. But she didn't press the issue.

"Any suggestions on what I should order?"

"Everything is delicious, but the open-faced sandwiches are my favorite. I could be a little partial, though. They use my bread."

"Open-faced sandwich it is, then." Maggie returned, and he gave her his order, then turned back to Natalie.

"So you support the competition?"

Natalie shrugged. "We're not really competition. People in this town like to work together, help each other out. We each have our regulars, and, like I said, they buy some things from me to serve here. And I've referred plenty of people over here or to the other restaurants in town. Last year, when the diner had a fire, Maggie and Richard even used the cafe to try some things out. They held an event to try to bring in some money and get their staff some pay. It didn't hurt my business any, and I'd like to think it made a difference to them."

"I'm sure it did." Chris took a sip of water and observed Natalie for a moment. She was definitely still guarded, defensive, but she had said more to him in that one short speech than in both of their other meetings combined.

She looked at him in a way that made him feel he was being judged. "So why are you really here?"

It was Chris's turn to shrug. "I don't know." If that wasn't honest, he didn't know what was.

"You just decided to take a drive and somehow ended up in Pine Valley? We're a little off the beaten path."

"No, I meant to come here. I'm just not sure why. There's just something about this town. I told myself I wouldn't come back for a while, and yet here I am."

She examined him again. It made him want to sit up straighter, run his fingers through his hair, straighten his silverware – anything. "All right, Mr. Christopher Parker. You eat your open-faced sandwich. And then you have a piece of Maggie's pie. And then you and I are going for a walk."

"We are?"

"Yes."

"Isn't it a bit cold out for a walk?"

"You afraid of a little cold?"

"No, ma'am."

"Good. I'll be back in half an hour."

Natalie didn't know what she was thinking. She had been thrown off seeing Christopher at the diner. It was supposed to be a relaxing evening after a long week, a time to unwind and forget about the drama with the building. The diner had always been a warm, inviting place, and she felt comfortable there, chatting with Maggie, ignoring her troubles for a bit. And then *he* had invaded.

She didn't know why she let him get to her so much. It wasn't his fault the building was being sold. But something about his smugness, his fake smile, just rubbed her the wrong way. It was like he didn't care what happened to her or the other tenants, or the building, or the town, as long as he got his commission.

But maybe that was unfair. What he had said about being drawn to Pine Valley struck a chord. She understood that draw. It was what had brought her back after college. It was what brought new residents to town, like Addy over at The Art Spot and Courtney with her boutique. So maybe she would give him a shot and see what he had to say.

Chapter 9

Christopher was standing outside the diner when Natalie returned. She had really just wanted to grab a heavier jacket and collect her thoughts, but seeing him standing there, looking uncertain, made her pause. He looked so different from the first time they'd met.

"I hope that jacket is warm," she said by way of greeting as she approached.

"Hopefully warm enough. I wasn't expecting to go for a walk outside tonight."

"Well, if you get too cold, we'll come back."

"Where are we going?"

"Don't know yet."

"You don't know? This won't be one of those drag-me-into-a-dark-alley things, will it?"

Natalie gave him a pointed look. "Pretty sure I wouldn't be able to overpower you."

"I bet you're stronger than you look."

"Are you saying I look weak?"

Chris didn't seem to know how to respond to that one, but Natalie let it slide. If she was honest, it had been fun bantering with him.

"I thought I'd give you more of an introduction to Pine Valley. I'm going to guess that you've been focused on the numbers. How much can I get for this property? What are the maintenance expenses? Are tenants paying their rent? Am I right?"

Chris shrugged. "In part."

"Anyone you get to buy those buildings – and especially whoever you get to buy the land for the apartment building – has to understand the town. It's like what you said at the diner. You saw Maggie and me as competitors. But that's not how this town works. Sure, we have friendly little competitions once in a while, but nothing serious. We respect each other and look out for each other. We know that helping each other succeed helps the town as a whole."

"Okay. I get that."

"I hope so. Because if you have someone come in here and raise all the rents or try to kick out the people who have been here for years to put in big companies who are willing to spend a fortune to be here, that won't go over well with the townspeople."

"I get it. I do."

"Good. Let's go this way." They started walking down Main Street, moving away from the diner and toward the library and community center. "We are a small town, as you know, but we have great public facilities. Our library is very well-utilized, and the community center houses both the senior center and the parks and recreation department. This building might be unassuming, but it has a full gymnasium inside, plus meeting rooms, plus a cafeteria for the seniors. And during the day it's usually bustling, with programs and sports events and all kinds of things going on." Natalie gestured across the street. "We have businesses for just about everything in town. People could technically never leave Pine Valley and have all of their needs taken care of right here. Maybe not a lot of options, but if you're in a pinch or short on time, we've got you covered. We've been lucky in recent years that some newcomers have fallen in love with the town and filled in gaps. Courtney, the person who owns the boutique next to the cafe, she didn't grow up here. She was visiting a friend and decided to stay. So now we have a clothing store. Addy, who owns the art store that I think is also in one of the buildings the Malloys own, her car broke down outside town. She planned to move to Boston, and actually did for a bit, before realizing that this was where she belonged. Now we have art. And not only that, but she was able to recognize what this community meant. She introduced a community art project that anyone can participate in for free, just as a way to bring people together."

Natalie realized she'd been talking for a while, so she decided to stop talking and let Christopher just take in the town. It was peaceful, walking in the chilly air with him. It had been a while since she had walked the town at night, since her early mornings usually had her in bed by eight. She closed her eyes for a moment and breathed in the fresh air. It was quiet, still. Businesses were closed, so there wasn't much traffic. Lights were still on in houses, but everyone was inside. Some people had started decorating for Christmas, and she saw the twinkling lights shining down side streets and in the distance. It was beautiful.

"Did you grow up in Pine Valley?" Christopher's voice broke the silence.

Natalie nodded. "Yup. Went away to college, but then came back. That feeling you mentioned, back at the diner? About there being something about Pine Valley? We all feel it. It's what keeps us here. It's what makes us love living here. And it's what makes us reluctant to let outsiders who don't understand it intrude."

"Well, from what you've said, you've had outsiders move here."

Natalie nodded again. "Yes, some have decided to move here. But they understood the town. They wanted to make it better, not change it." She stopped walking and turned to look at Chris. "That's why it's important to get the right person to buy the property. Actually, I —"

She was cut off by the ringing of Chris's cell phone. The sharp noise pierced the stillness of the night.

"Sorry. Let me just..." He took the phone out of his pocket and looked at the screen. Wincing, he said, "I have to..." and answered the call.

Natalie wandered a short distance away to give Chris his privacy. Maybe it was good that she had been interrupted. After all, she wasn't sure if she was interested in buying the building. Or, more accurately, if it was even an option at the moment. She had an appointment with the bank on Monday to go over the financial stuff, and she had a sneaking suspicion they would laugh in her face when they saw the numbers.

After a few minutes, Christopher disconnected the call and walked over to Natalie. "Sorry about that. It was an important client who had questions about a listing."

"They call you on a Saturday night?"

Chris shrugged. "They call me whenever they want. With the amount of money these guys spend, they expect people to be available whenever they are."

Natalie shook her head. "That is exactly what we don't want here. I hope they weren't asking about one of the properties in town."

Chris shook his head. "No, something up in Hartford."

"Good."

"So, where were we?"

"Actually, let's just head back. It's getting cold, anyway."

They walked back to the diner in silence.

"Thank you for showing me around town," Chris said as they approached the parking lot beside the diner.

"No problem."

They said their goodbyes, and Chris walked to his car. Natalie watched him climb in and drive off before crossing the street to the cafe. She wasn't sure what to make of the evening. Just when she thought he was becoming more human, more real, he went and did something that made it apparent making money was the goal. Was it just because it was his job? Or did he really feel that way?

Chris slammed his hand on the steering wheel in frustration. Stupid Jenkins. Just when he felt like he was getting somewhere, really getting to know Pine Valley and Natalie's place in it, Jenkins had to call. And not even with something important. Info that was in the listing. He just couldn't be bothered to read any of the paperwork Chris had given him.

Chris sighed. What was he even doing? Even if he decided to buy the property, it wasn't like he was moving to Pine Valley. He would just be investing. He supposed Natalie had a valid point about whoever bought the property needing to know about the town. And, if it didn't end up being him, he needed to make sure it was the right person. But beyond that, there was little sense in connecting with the town, getting to know its residents, and feeling like he belonged. He was just passing through, or throwing some money at it at best.

Maybe that was the problem. Maybe that's what Natalie was trying to get him to see. He had been treating it as merely a business transaction. Buying and selling. But it was more than that. Chris had looked up articles about the apartment building collapse the previous year. Poor real estate decisions seriously affected people's lives. It wasn't just about money, even if Malloy had based his choices on that. And, while that had been people's homes, businesses were just as important. They were people's livelihoods. And the people who owned and ran these businesses, worked at these businesses, lived in town. This was their home, too. It was a community.

Okay. So maybe getting to know Pine Valley wasn't a bad idea. And, on a somewhat unrelated note, maybe getting to know Natalie better wasn't a bad idea, either. He liked her spunk. He liked how protective she was of her town and the people in it. He liked how the holiday lights hanging from the streetlamps had reflected in her eyes. And if he let her teach him about the town – or, more accurately, convinced her to teach him about the town – he would get to spend more time with her. Maybe she would warm up to him. Maybe she would even give him a chance. What did he have to lose?

Chapter 10

Chloe usually ran the cafe on Mondays so Natalie could have some time off. While Natalie still did the baking in the morning, having the rest of the day to herself always felt like a vacation. Today, however, she had her meeting at the bank, and she was nervous.

She had done her best to compile all of her financial documents – tax returns and profit sheets from the business and even bank statements, though her accounts were at the same bank. The more she looked at everything, and the more she thought about it all, the more she was convinced that it wouldn't be nearly enough. Even with the practically guaranteed rent from the building's current tenants.

But she had to know.

She had printed out the real estate listing with the asking price. She could probably offer less, but she figured it was best to start with the full amount. And as she waited to be called in for her appointment, she read over the listing again and again. It looked like Chris had added some details about the community, which was nice. Maybe he had taken what she said to heart.

"Natalie?"

Natalie looked up to see Linda, the bank manager, smiling at her. She gave a nervous smile back and stood up, gathering her paperwork as she did.

Linda led her into an office, then gestured to the seat in front of the desk while she sat behind it. "I understand you're here to inquire about a business loan."

"Yes, um. I own a business, but, um, the building it's in is being sold. So I wanted to see if it would be possible to purchase it."

"You own the cafe, correct?"

"Yes." Natalie gave another tentative smile.

"Love your sandwiches."

"Thanks."

"You're not the only one in that building, though, right?"

"No. There are two other shops, and then four apartments above the shops. I actually live in one of the apartments, as well."

"Okay. That can certainly be taken into consideration. But that being said, it's not a small building. What is the asking price, and how much would you be able to put down?"

Natalie went over the paperwork with her, showing the listing and then the bank statements. The growing savings she had been so proud of looked tiny next to that huge number.

Linda took a deep breath and raised her eyebrows. "You would be taking out a considerable loan."

"Yes, I know. But I figured the shops and the apartments are all rented, so there would be income from those that could be applied to the loan payments, and, of course, income from the cafe."

"That can all be taken into consideration, but rented spaces are not guaranteed income. If a tenant were to leave, that income would leave, too, possibly for a considerable length of time until the space could be rented again. Do you have anything to offer as collateral other than the cafe?"

Natalie sighed. "No." She didn't own her apartment, and she had never needed a car in Pine Valley. All she had was her cafe, her furniture, and her savings.

"Would you be acting as landlord or hiring a property manager to oversee the property?"

"Probably hiring a property manager, since I don't know much about being a landlord."

"That will eat into the income, as well."

"I know. I don't have to hire them if that would be better."

Linda leaned back in her chair and examined Natalie. "I'm not going to lie, Natalie. This would be a very hard sell. May I ask why you want to purchase the property?"

Natalie could think of a hundred reasons, but none of them seemed good enough. What would make a bank want to put their faith in her? Their money on her? "When I got the letter saying the building was being sold, I tried to look at all the options. We both know what happened with the apartment building last year, and the same people own my building, too. I worry that the new owners will look at the building as a cash cow and skimp on safety just like Malloy did with the apartments. I also worry about them evicting myself and my neighbors, or raising the rent so high that it pushes us out, just to bring in fancy stores or businesses. Pine Valley is special, and I don't want that to change. One of my neighbors, the boutique owner, Courtney, mentioned as a joke that we could buy the building, and it got me thinking."

"Had she wanted to purchase it with you?"

Natalie shook her head. "No. She's not interested in that. She said she was joking and tried to talk me out of it."

"But you still want to do it."

Natalie took a deep breath and met Linda's gaze. "I'll be honest with you, too, Linda. I really don't know what I want. Part of me wants to have the security of knowing that I own the building I live and work in, that I can control what happens to it, that I can keep my neighbors safe and prevent them from being evicted. Part of me is scared about that kind of pressure, and the kind of money that's required. Could I do it? Yes, I think I could. I'm smart and resilient and savvy. I know my way around a socket wrench, and I can read contracts, and I can use spreadsheets as well as anyone. Is that enough? I don't know."

Linda evaluated her for a moment in silence. "I like your spirit, Natalie. So here's what I'm going to do. Give me all of your paperwork. Let me go over all the numbers, see what I can figure out. Do you have rent numbers for the other tenants?"

"No. I could probably get them, though. Courtney and Josh, the other shop owner, probably wouldn't have a problem telling me what they pay. I think the apartments are all the same size, so they're probably the same as mine, which is in the file."

"The listing agent should also be able to provide that information if you reach out to them."

Natalie nodded. After her confession the previous night had been interrupted, she wasn't sure she wanted to tell Chris she was thinking about buying the building. Would he judge her? Belittle her? Laugh at her? Or would he think it was a good idea? She would see what she could find out without him.

"Get me those numbers when you can, and I'll see what I can do. I'm not making any promises. These are tough numbers to work with. But I'll discuss it with my underwriting team and see what we can determine. Just be forewarned, you may only qualify for part of the asking amount, if that. So if you decide you want to purchase the building, you would have to find another way to come up with the rest of the money."

"Okay." Natalie handed Linda the rest of her paperwork. "Thank you. I appreciate any information you're able to provide."

"My pleasure. Get me those numbers, and I'll be in touch as soon as I can."

Natalie stood up, and she and Linda shook hands. "Thanks again." Then Natalie walked out of the bank.

Well, it wasn't a total loss. She still had a chance, however small. But what would she do if she was approved for part of the amount but not all of it? Would she walk away? Take it as a sign that it wasn't meant to be? Or would she try to find another way to come up with the money? And what on earth could that other way be?

And what was she hoping Linda's answer would be?

Chapter 11

Chris saw Natalie approaching just as he was about to enter the cafe. She looked distracted, deep in thought. He hoped everything was okay. He waited at the door, then held it open for her. She looked up, gave him a small smile, but didn't say a word. Chris followed her inside.

"How'd it go?" he heard Chloe ask as he entered.

Natalie shrugged. "Okay, I guess. It's a long shot."

"You knew it would be."

That was it. Natalie walked through the cafe and out the back door that led to the hallway where the staircase to the apartments was. Apparently, she wasn't working today.

Chloe greeted him then, as if just realizing he was there. "Oh, hello. How can I help you?"

He ordered a coffee and a cookie, but his mind was still on Natalie. He wondered what had been a long shot. What was she trying to do?

He wanted to help her, but he wasn't sure how. He didn't even know how to get in touch with her. Knocking on her front door would definitely be crossing a boundary. And if he wanted to get closer to her, that was not the way to do it.

Had she even realized it had been him holding the door open for her? That smile, however small, had been the first one she had ever given him. It had made his stomach flip. But it may not have even been intended for him.

He was being ridiculous. His being here at all was ridiculous. But he had hoped to pick up where they had left off on Saturday. Apparently, that wouldn't be happening today.

Chris sat at one of the tables by the front windows and watched people go by. He sipped his coffee and broke pieces off his cookie and ate them. He saw smiling people, and people in a hurry, and people lifting faces to the sun, and people bundling themselves against the cold. He didn't notice Chloe sitting next to him until she spoke.

"Hey."

Chris jumped. Chloe chuckled.

"Sorry. Didn't mean to scare you."

"It's okay. Just off in my own little world I guess."

"Must be. The cafe's closed."

Chris looked around him. "Oh, geez. I'm sorry."

"That's okay."

He moved to get up, but Chloe put a hand on his arm.

"It's Chris, right?"

"Yeah."

"You've been coming in here a lot lately. Either you really like our stuff or you have a thing for Natalie."

"Can't it be both?"

Chloe grinned. "Aha! I knew it! Does she know?"

Chris shrugged. "Probably not. She obviously does not feel the same. I'd go so far as to say she outright dislikes me."

Chloe's face took on a skeptical expression. "I wouldn't say that," she said. "I think she's just preoccupied with this whole building thing."

"She and I both. There's a lot up in the air right now."

"Have you found a buyer yet?"

Chris shook his head. "Not yet. Commercial property can take a while to sell, especially in a small town like this."

"So no idea on timeline."

"Not really, no. Sorry."

"It's okay. Just trying to get the latest info for Nat. I'm going to be taking a leave of absence soon. I need to make sure she's taken care of."

"You're a good friend."

"She's a good friend. And a good person. You'd better not break her heart."

"I will do my best not to."

"I'm going to hold you to that. But for now, I'm going to kick you out so we can close."

"Yeah. Got it." Chris stood up and handed Chloe his mug and plate. "Thanks. Sorry for holding you up." And he left the cafe.

Natalie watched Chris walk across the street to the parking lot. He had spent a while in the cafe today. She wondered what he had been doing. She was actually surprised he hadn't tried to engage her in conversation earlier. Not that she had given him much of a chance. Her mind had been swimming after the bank meeting.

She wondered if she should try to catch him to ask about the rents in the other spaces. But doing that would make it all real, and she wasn't sure she was ready for that yet. Better just to ask Courtney and Josh.

She was being ridiculous. She knew that. If the building was all her, it would make sense that she wanted to buy. But it wasn't. She would have to take charge of other people's space, their homes. And she didn't really want to do that. But what were her options?

Natalie sighed. Part of her would love a building of her own, that she owned, that she would only be responsible for herself in. But there wasn't anything like that available in Pine Valley. She could probably find something in another town, but was she willing to leave her home over this? Over something that might not even end up disrupting her life after all?

If only she knew who would end up buying the building and what their plan for it would be. Then she would at least have some guidance. Maybe she should talk to Chris. Maybe he would have an idea of who or at least when. Or she could really drive home the importance of getting the right person in.

She hated the idea of her livelihood being in the hands of an unknown entity. But she hated just as much how this was quickly becoming an obsession. Maybe she needed to just take a step back.

But then what reason would she have for talking to Chris again?

Chapter 12

"Alright, Joey, we need to talk," Natalie said Tuesday morning.

"Uh oh. That sounds serious."

Natalie sighed and leaned against a counter. "Kind of, I guess. You heard that Chloe's going to be out for a bit, right?"

"Yeah."

"That's going to leave me seriously short-handed here. She's my only full-timer. Well, besides myself, of course. I have Sylvie helping out most days at lunch, and you're here for breakfast and now baking, but Chloe's here five days a week open to close. And with business how it's been, we need the help. So. We need to talk. Are you up for more hours? Or do you know anyone else who might want a temporary part-time gig? I know you have your other job, too, so I don't want to stretch you too thin."

Joey thought for a moment. "I don't think I could handle open to close, especially not with coming in early to bake. It's a lot of hours, especially since I have to be at the florist by three to do deliveries. I could do maybe until one?"

Natalie thought, then nodded. "That would help with lunch, at least. I'll still need to figure out morning. I don't know if Sylvie is up for more hours. Or maybe McKenna, though she has so much other stuff going on. Normally I'd say we can just do what we have to do, but we're going into the holidays. As it is I know I'll be working extra hours after we're closed to get all the cookie baking in."

"Oh, that's right! I forgot about your holiday cookie boxes."

"Yeah. The sign-ups for that will be going up soon, and they keep me hopping even with a fully-staffed shop. Okay. I'll have to see what I can come up with."

"I'll ask around."

"Thanks, Joey. And if I haven't said it yet, thanks for coming in to help with the baking, too."

"Are you kidding? I'm loving it. I wish I could help with the cookie baking, too, but Sasha can't run the shop and make deliveries, too."

"I get it. I know she appreciates the help. How's she been doing over this whole building-being-sold thing?"

Joey shrugged. "She hasn't really said, but she doesn't seem worried. Business has been good, so I guess she's just focused on that right now."

"That's good. I hope it all works out for her."

"It'll all be fine. For you, too. I know you've been stressed, but I'm sure it will all work out."

"I really hope so."

Chris stared at his computer screen, but he wasn't taking in the calendar in front of him. His mind was elsewhere, thinking about a certain cafe owner in a little town. It didn't look like he would be able to get there for a few days. He had meetings with clients, showing properties and discussing wants and needs, then sweet-talking a couple of prospective clients to see if he could become their agent. Most of his regular clients were set with properties for now. He needed to bring in more clients if he wanted to keep his momentum. And, since he hadn't made any decisions about his own interest in the Pine Valley properties, he really needed to start looking for buyers for those spaces, as well.

The phone rang, startling Chris out of his reverie.

"Christopher Parker," he said by way of greeting.

"Mr. Parker, my name is Matthew Townsend. I came across a few of your listings, and I was hoping to discuss them with you further, perhaps arrange a time to see them."

"Of course. Which properties are you inquiring about?"

"There were four, I believe, in Pine Valley. Three commercial and a lot zoned for multi-unit residential."

"That is correct." Chris swallowed. "Were you interested in all four properties?" Colleen Malloy would be happy with that, but his heart sank at the thought of missing out on what he was starting to want.

"Possibly. I deal primarily with retail spaces, but I've been considering diversifying. Being able to start from scratch with a residential building could be a good start."

"Of course. I would be happy to go over the specs, answer any questions you may have."

They chatted for several minutes before setting a time to visit the spaces the following day. By the time they hung up, Chris wasn't sure what to make of Mr. Townsend. He had been professional, civil. He was definitely an investor who knew what he wanted. But what that was was hard to say. He had held his cards pretty close to the chest. Would he be a good fit for Pine Valley?

Chris chuckled to himself. Natalie was definitely rubbing off on him. A couple of weeks ago, he would have been chomping at the bit to get Townsend signed and properties sold. Now he was worried about the impact on the town. But ultimately, the choice wasn't his. If Townsend put in an offer, he was obligated to tell the seller. It was up to her if she would accept it or not. The most he could do was get a read on the potential buyer and dissuade him if it looked like he wasn't a good match.

Maybe he should do a little research on Matthew Townsend. It never hurt to be prepared.

Chapter 13

Ever since her evening walk with Christopher, Natalie had felt the urge to spend time outside, breathing in the fresh, cold air and exploring the town she loved. It helped clear her mind and reconnect her with what was actually important. As long as she could keep doing what she loved, sharing her love for good food with the people she loved, it didn't matter who owned the building. She needed to remember that.

The sun was setting as Natalie stepped out of her apartment to take a walk. The streetlights were turning on, as were the holiday lights wrapped around their poles. Courtney's shop was still open, but not for long. Same with the ice cream shop, though Josh seemed to be a little busier than usual. Not surprising, if the scent of waffle cones baking had made everyone else in town as hungry as it had made her. He didn't usually make waffle cones once business slowed. Maybe he was hoping for a boost in business. And maybe if he was still open on her way back, she would stop in, though she didn't really see the appeal of ice cream when it was cold out. Did he sell the cones by themselves?

Giving herself a mental shake, Natalie continued on her walk. She had remembered to bundle up this time, knowing the temperature would dip even lower when the sun went down. She wondered when they would get the first snowfall. She loved snow. Seeing the trees around town adorned with white, having the sound of cars muffled by the blanket of snow, hearing excited children laughing and shouting on the town green as they took advantage of the hill that led down to a soccer field – it was all so magical, joyful. It filled her heart with peace. Looking back at the cafe, Natalie's heart sank. The windows were still dark, the door unadorned. She had been so worried about who was buying the building she hadn't even decorated for Christmas yet. The boxes of decorations still sat cluttering her office. Technically she still had time. But it was a week until Thanksgiving, and then the holiday season would really be upon them.

Thanksgiving wasn't a big holiday for her. Her dad had passed away when she was in high school, and her mom had followed shortly after she graduated college. She had one younger brother who lived in Massachusetts, and they sometimes got together for the holiday, but he had his own family now, and Natalie wasn't always up to making the trip there and back in one day. She supposed she could go up the day before, but figuring out a way home after the festivities was never fun, and she had to be up early on Black Friday to serve coffee to the early morning shoppers. So it would probably be a quiet day on her own. Maybe she would see if some friends wanted to get together. They could play board games or watch cheesy movies, make a turkey, and just enjoy a day off from work. That could be nice. Or she could head to the diner for Maggie's annual holiday dinner. That could work, too.

Then it would be Christmas. Customers had already started asking about her cookie boxes. Every year she made a variety of classic holiday cookies and packed them in assortment boxes for gift-giving or entertaining. They were very popular, and the profit margin was pretty good. But they were a lot of work. She could usually prep some of them ahead of time, making dough and freezing it, then thawing and baking as needed. But she still had to do all the measuring and mixing and rolling and packing, then all the clean-up that went with it. Chloe usually helped, particularly with the clean-up. With her being away, Natalie would be on her own. She wasn't looking forward to it. She and Chloe would usually close up the cafe, then crank up the Christmas songs and get to work. What could be tedious turned out to be fun, and Natalie had plenty of happy memories of those times. While Sylvie had agreed to help when she could, and Joey had seemed interested in helping whenever he could fit it into his schedule, it wouldn't be the same.

What a Christmas this was turning out to be. The future of the cafe was up in the air, her good friend and coworker would be gone for who knew how long, and she was feeling more bah humbug than jolly elf. And it wasn't even really Christmas time yet.

She had to turn things around. No matter what happened with the cafe in the future, it was hers right now, and she had to do what she could with it. Tomorrow she would start decorating, open registration for her cookie boxes, and come up with a game plan for the rest. She could do this.

Deciding she had walked enough, if her frozen toes were any indication, Natalie headed back toward the cafe. Courtney's shop was closed now, but Josh was still open. It looked like he only had one customer: Courtney. Interesting. They looked cozy, chatting together with wide smiles. Maybe she would skip that waffle cone tonight. But she was definitely stopping by Courtney's tomorrow to find out what exactly was going on there.

She hadn't seen Chris that day, Natalie mused as she climbed the stairs to her apartment. Not that he had to visit every day, of course, but she had started getting used to him being around. Maybe she had scared him off with all her talk about Pine Valley solidarity. She did tend to get overprotective.

Natalie sighed. Nothing had really been resolved. But at least she had gotten some fresh air and exercise. And if she could get things going tomorrow as she had decided, maybe she could start feeling more like herself. All she could do was hope for the best.

Chapter 14

"Okay, spill it." Natalie had taken advantage of a lull in customers to head to Courtney's shop as soon as it opened.

"Spill what?"

"What's going on with you and Josh? I saw you last night in his shop. You looked awfully cozy in there."

Courtney looked like she was going to deny it, but then her shoulders sagged and she pouted. "I don't know."

"You don't know?"

"Well, I've been going in there every week for a while now, and we've gotten to be good friends. And then last week he kind of asked me out, but we didn't set a date since he had a customer come in, so things were kind of up in the air, and I had hoped that when I saw him last night he would say something, but he didn't, so now I don't know if he's actually interested after all."

"Oh geez. Are you interested in him?"

Courtney blushed and gave a little nod.

"And I don't think he would have asked you out if he wasn't interested."

Courtney shrugged.

Natalie rolled her eyes. "I feel like I'm in high school. Would you like me to say something to him?"

Courtney looked hopeful but didn't say anything.

Natalie rolled her eyes again. "You are ridiculous. I'll try to stop in after work and see what he says. Okay?"

Courtney grinned. "You're the best."

"And you're a chicken."

"Maybe. But I'm a chicken with the best friends." And she grinned again.

"Yeah, yeah. I'll see you later."

Natalie left the shop and headed back to the cafe, shaking her head as she walked. She knew Courtney wasn't that experienced when it came to guys, but she and Josh had obviously gotten to know each other. How hard was it to just ask?

As Natalie pulled open the door to the cafe, she looked up and happened to see Chris walking with two other men down the street. Uh oh. While Chris had become something of a fixture in the town, the guys with him definitely weren't. Walking with purpose, dressed in designer suits, one with eyes glued to the phone in his hands, the other talking intently to Chris. Not from around here. Natalie ducked into the cafe before Chris could see her.

"Everything okay?" Chloe asked as she walked in.

"Yeah. Just saw Chris walking around with some new guys. I don't have a good feeling."

"You knew it would happen sooner or later."

"Yeah, but I was really hoping it would be later."

"Well, it's not too busy now. Why don't we start working on the decorations to get your mind off it? You said you wanted to tackle them today."

"You're right. Let's get decorating."

Natalie was hanging garland when the door opened and Chris and the strangers walked in. Her eyes went to Chris's, and his gaze softened before he turned to the other men. Natalie almost fell off her stepstool.

"Natalie, I'm glad I caught you," Chris said. "This is Matthew Townsend and his realtor, Art Hudson. Mr. Townsend may be interested in the building. Okay if they take a look around?"

What could she say? She didn't like the looks of this Matthew Townsend. But she hadn't liked the looks of Chris at first, either, and he had grown on her. Maybe this Townsend guy would surprise her. "Sure."

"Great."

Chris walked around with Matthew and Art, pointing out details occasionally, then led him to the back hallway. She could hear them walking up the stairs, voices fading as they climbed. Natalie wanted to know what they were talking about. Was this guy serious about the building? Was he looking at the other buildings, too? What were his plans? Would he kick her out?

Natalie felt like she couldn't breathe.

"Nat, you okay?" Joey paused in his decorating task to look at her. "You don't look so good."

Natalie stepped down off the stepstool and pulled out a chair from a nearby table. "I'll be fine. Just having a mild panic attack."

"Need a paper bag?"

Natalie shook her head. "No. I'll be fine. Just need to calm myself down." She needed to stop letting this consume her. She had been on track for the day, working to think positively and focus on the good stuff. She couldn't let this derail her. It was out of her hands anyway.

After a few moments she felt herself relax and started to breathe normally. Just in time to hear the men coming back in through the back door.

"I would want a full building inspection, of course. Especially with the track record of the previous owner."

"Of course. I can get that scheduled for you, if you'd like, or if you have someone you usually work with, feel free to pass along their info, and I'll line something up."

"I have a guy. I'll be in touch."

"Great. Let me walk you to your car."

Natalie watched them as they left the cafe. Her shoulders sagged in defeat. It didn't matter what the bank said now. It didn't matter what she wanted. This out-of-towner was going to come in and buy her building and probably kick them all out. She sniffled.

Joey pulled out the chair beside her. "You know, until the paperwork is signed and keys handed over, nothing is final."

Natalie attempted a small smile. "I know. But it doesn't sound good."

"I didn't like the look of the guy."

"Me neither."

"Maybe he'll change his mind. Or the inspection will bring up something that's a dealbreaker for him. Oh!" Joey got a mischievous gleam in his eyes. "Want me to bribe the inspector to say he found termites or something?"

Natalie laughed. "No, no bribing. I appreciate the thought, though."

Joey patted her arm and gave her a sympathetic smile. "Let me know if I can do anything."

"Thanks. For now, we'll just focus on the decorating."

"You got it, boss."

Natalie took a deep breath and stood up. If this was going to be her last Christmas in the cafe, she was going to make it the best one yet.

Chapter 15

Chris waved to Townsend and Hudson as they drove off, then sighed. He was torn. The guy seemed interested in everything. It could be a good, easy sale. He had the credit; he had the drive. He was the perfect client for Chris. Or, at least, the old Chris. And anywhere else, he wouldn't have had a problem with it. But Pine Valley had gotten under his skin.

And Townsend would ruin it all.

He had said in no uncertain terms that he worked as a middleman, investing in properties so his clients – most of them regionwide or nationwide companies – would be able to expand. Many of his clients were looking for spaces in this part of the state. That meant he would be working on getting the current tenants out as soon as possible, to move his clients in.

It would destroy so many businesses, ruin so many lives. But what could he do? It wasn't his call. He had to remember that. Ultimately it was up to Colleen Malloy. If Townsend put in an offer, he had to pass it along.

But what if he put in an offer first?

The thought hit him like a punch in the gut. He hadn't decided yet about buying the building. But if he got an offer in before Townsend did, that would at least protect Natalie's building.

But this was about more than just protecting Natalie. What about the other buildings? The other business owners? If Townsend still proceeded with the sale of the other properties, the effect would be almost the same. Buying one building might protect a few of the business owners, but not all of them.

Unless he bought all of them.

Okay, that was biting off way more than he could chew. Not only would he lose out on all that commission, but he would be in a much bigger financial hole than he felt comfortable with. One building he could probably handle. More than that was asking a lot. Even if he didn't consider the residential land, he would still be looking at three commercial buildings. Nine retail spaces and four apartments. That was a big responsibility, and a lot of money. Who knew if he would even get approved?

He had to think rationally about this. He had at least a little time to think about it. The inspection would take time to set up and take place. And he would want an inspection anyway, so it made sense to wait until that went through. In the meantime, he could meet with his financial advisor, talk to a bank, and figure out what made the most sense. Even if his emotions were telling him to jump in with two feet, this was not the kind of decision to take lightly.

Chris really wanted to talk to Natalie. Even if she was upset about the building selling and mad at him for bringing in Townsend, he really wanted to get her take on everything. She seemed to be his voice of reason, the one who took him out of his privileged little bubble and connected him with the real world.

He crossed the street again and entered the cafe. Natalie was still hanging up decorations and didn't see him right away. He watched her for a moment, appreciating the care she took. She was an attractive woman, but when she turned to smile at a customer, that's when he realized he was a goner. This wasn't the small smile she had given him. It was a full-blown expression of joy, shared with someone who was obviously a regular. And it lit up her face. But when she saw him, the smile faded. Chris took a deep breath.

"I didn't expect you to come back," Natalie said as she approached him.

"I wasn't sure if I would be welcome. But I wanted to see you. Any chance we could talk?"

Natalie seemed to consider for a moment, then she cocked her head toward the back of the cafe. "Come with me."

He followed her past the kitchen into the office. It was a small space, but there was a desk with chairs both behind and in front of it. Natalie sat behind the desk and gestured toward the chair in front of it. "What did you want to talk about?"

Chris took another deep breath. "Townsend isn't right for this place."

Natalie's shoulders sagged in apparent relief. "Well, on that we can agree."

"But if he puts in an offer, it's not my decision. It goes to Colleen Malloy, and she has to decide. She seems eager to sell, so I suspect she'll take any reasonable offer."

"So it doesn't matter if he's right for Pine Valley or not."

"Exactly."

"So it's hopeless. Any idea what his plan is?"

"From what he said, it sounds like at least a few of the tenants will lose their spaces."

Natalie closed her eyes and sighed. "I was afraid of that."

"I don't know what to do."

"Me neither. This is going to sound silly, but I had actually been looking into buying this place myself, to prevent this kind of thing from happening."

"Seriously? That's not silly at all. Real estate is usually a good investment, and it's obvious you've got a good head on your shoulders."

"Yeah, but I'm a long way from being able to afford it, and being a landlord wasn't exactly on my bucket list."

"You can get a property manager. And a business loan."

Natalie shook her head. "I tried. Technically, my application is still pending. But the bank manager said it was a long shot. She didn't seem hopeful I would get much if anything approved."

Ah, so that's what had been the long shot. The pieces were starting to come together.

"And I don't know if I would want it anyway. The only reason I was even considering it was for the security bit. My business and my apartment are both in this building. If we get some crummy owner in here, I could be kicked out onto the street and lose my job and my home in one fell swoop. Malloy had his issues, but he was a hands-off kind of landlord. He didn't bug us as long as we paid our bills every month." She paused. "But buying it myself? It's a lot of money. And being responsible for other people's homes and businesses is not something I take lightly."

That was something he would have to consider, too. He was so often focused on just the money side of things. Was he willing to not only be a responsible member of the community but a responsible landlord, too? Would he be hands-off like Malloy? Would he want to be?

"I, uh." Chris cleared his throat, then tried again. "I was actually considering buying the building, too."

Natalie's wide eyes met his. "Seriously? You buy buildings, too? I thought you just sold the things."

"I do. I've never bought anything before."

"So why would you start now?"

"Well, like I said, real estate is usually a good investment. And when my clients didn't immediately jump at the chance to buy what seemed like no brainer opportunities, I got to thinking. But it was just a passing thought until I started spending more time here. We discussed it before – there's just something about this place that draws me to it. And, if I'm being honest, something about you, too."

Natalie could only stare at him.

Chris cleared his throat. "But, as you well know, it's a lot to consider. I had never really considered being a landlord before, either. And I could hire a property management company, too, but part of me wouldn't want to. Though, of course, that opens up a whole new can of worms. But even if I decided to buy this building, there are still the others to consider."

"You wouldn't want to buy them all?"

Chris laughed. "I may be doing pretty well financially, but that's a lot of money. That might be biting off more than I could chew. But if I don't, and Townsend puts in an offer, my buying one building won't have made much of a difference. He'll still come in here making waves."

"It would make a difference to some of us."

Silence fell as they gazed at each other.

"I don't know what to do," Chris said after a while. "I'm an outsider, too. Maybe I wouldn't be welcomed as a landlord any more than Townsend would. And maybe I would do a horrible job."

"When you first came here, with your big flashy grin, I would agree with you. But now? I don't know. I guess that would depend on what you wanted to do with it. Would you make waves like Townsend or preserve what we have?"

"Definitely leaning toward preserving. Why mess with a good thing?"

"Hmm. Then I guess it just comes down to if you want it or not."

"If I did, would you back my decision?"

"I'd consider it."

"I'll take what I can get."

Silence fell again. "Wait," Natalie said, sitting up straighter. "Can you even do that? Buy a building you're selling?"

Chris sighed and leaned back in his chair. "No. That would be a serious conflict of interest. So I would have to surrender the listings to another agent."

"So not only would you be going into debt buying properties you may or may not want, but you would lose out on all that commission?"

"Yup."

"Geesh." Natalie leaned back again. "You must really like it here."

"Yeah," Chris agreed. "I really do."

Chapter 16

By the time Chris left, Natalie's head was swimming even more than it had been that morning. Not only was there a potential buyer on the scene, but now Chris was thinking of buying the building, too? If he did, that meant she would be off the hook, but was that what she wanted? She didn't want to be seen as some damsel in distress. And it would be weird having Chris as a landlord. Just as she had been concerned over how Courtney and Josh would look at her, she wondered how she would start looking at Chris. Not that she was as close to him as she was to Courtney and Josh, but it would still be weird. She would be paying him every month. That definitely put a damper on any romantic feelings she may or may not have been starting to feel toward him.

But if Townsend bought the building, or buildings, as the case may be, she and lots of other business owners would be out on the streets. Where would they all go? And what kind of businesses would he be bringing in with him? How would that change Pine Valley?

Change was inevitable; she knew that. But some change was definitely more positive than others. How could she know which change was for the best?

Natalie thought back to the conversation with Chris. He had basically admitted he had feelings for her. Or at least that he was attracted to her. How did that make her feel? If she was honest, somewhat giddy. But she had way too much going on right now to even think about being in a romantic relationship. Especially with some city guy who might end up becoming her landlord.

What a mess.

Okay, so worst-case scenario: Townsend bought the buildings, kicked them all out, and Chris left town. Where would she go? What would she do? Would she try to start the cafe up again somewhere else? And where? There wasn't exactly an overabundance of commercial space available in Pine Valley. Would she have to move? Or, heaven forbid, try to find a job in one of the new businesses? And would she be kicked out of her apartment, too? Would she be homeless on top of everything else? Maybe Courtney would let her crash with her for a little while. But that wouldn't work if she had to get a job somewhere else. She didn't have a car, and she wouldn't be able to afford a car if she lost her job.

She was spiraling now, which was never a good thing. She needed to get her mind off of things. Which reminded her: she needed to talk to Josh. It was almost time for the cafe to close, then she could head on over to the ice cream shop. Better to worry about someone else's life than her own mess.

As she walked a couple of doors down a half hour later, Natalie was feeling at least somewhat better. No, her problems hadn't magically disappeared. But, as Chris had said, she had a good head on her shoulders. She would figure it out. And in the meantime, she could at least figure out her friends' love life.

Josh was alone when she walked in.

"Hey, Natalie. What brings you in on this chilly day?"

Natalie had once again forgotten her coat, so she stood rubbing her arms in the middle of the shop. "Two questions: can I get a waffle cone without ice cream, and are you still interested in going on a date with Courtney?"

Josh just stared at her and blinked. "Okay, two answers: sure, and absolutely."

"Great. Then get me a cone to go and just go tell her, for crying out loud. You are two grown adults. The least you can do is tell each other you like each other. Geesh."

Josh grinned sheepishly. "I can do that."

"Good."

Five minutes later, Natalie was walking back to the cafe with a delicious waffle cone, pleased with herself for accomplishing at least something that day.

Chapter 17

Chris felt like he went over every possible scenario a hundred times as he drove back to the office. If Townsend made an offer, he had no doubt Colleen Malloy would accept it. So he either had to make an offer first, accept that Townsend would buy the buildings, or somehow find another buyer – the perfect buyer – before Townsend put in an offer. Much easier said than done.

Then, of course, if he decided to make his own offer, he had to decide what that offer would be, and for which properties. He couldn't handle the residential space. That project was just too much for him at the moment, and he didn't think he would want to tackle a project of that size anyway. Townsend could have that one if he wanted it. But the commercial spaces?

Part of him just wanted to say screw it and buy them all. Pine Valley was a thriving community, with loyal residents and business owners. They would be solid investments if he maintained them properly and didn't scare off his tenants.

Of course, the thought of maintenance brought to mind the possible laundry list of issues the inspector might find. With Malloy's less-than-stellar track record of upkeep, it was possible one or all of the buildings could have major concerns. Maybe Townsend would be scared off. But even if he was, another buyer was sure to come along once the issues were taken care of.

And then, of course, was the issue of money. He was pretty confident he could get approved for the remaining amount required to purchase Natalie's building. But tacking on the others would be stretching him thin, even if he did get approved. And if he decided to be more hands-on as a landlord, he would likely be spending less time on his actual job, which meant his income would be lower. Would the income from renters cover whatever loan payments he ended up needing? And if not, would he have enough income to cover the rest?

While the thought of purchasing all three buildings was incredibly appealing, Chris was concerned it would be too much. The stress alone would make him uncomfortable, even if he was able to make the payments. And that's assuming he would even be approved for a business loan that high.

So where did that leave him? Right back to square one.

Chris greeted the receptionist and a couple of coworkers on the way to his office. When he saw Eric was at his desk, however, Chris headed to Eric's office, instead.

"Hey," Chris greeted.

"Hey," Eric said, still staring at his computer screen. "Give me one second."

Chris waited until Eric looked up and grinned.

"What's up?"

"I'm trying to wrap my head around something and figure out what I should do."

"Sounds serious. It's not like you to be unsure about something."

"I know. And I don't like it. But first, a question: if I had to surrender the Pine Valley properties, would you want the listings?"

"Seriously? Why would you just give them up?"

"Because I'm thinking of buying them. The commercials, at least. Or maybe just one? I don't know."

"I take it that's what you're trying to wrap your head around."

"Yeah. I have a potential buyer. Just waiting on inspection."

"If someone else is buying them, what's the problem?"

"He's not a good fit."

"For what? Can't afford them? Think he'll run them into the ground? Hate to break it to you, but that's not our problem. Once the sale's done, it's out of our hands."

"He's not a good fit for the town. He'll go in there and kick out business owners and make big changes, and I don't think it'll go over well."

"So? Since when do you care about that? Your job is to find a buyer. And it sounds like you did. So congrats, you did your job. Take your big fat check and be happy."

"I know. I should. But there's something about this town, man. I can't explain it. It feels...right."

Eric laughed. "Right? For what? For you? You are getting way too sentimental."

Chris sighed. Maybe it had been a mistake to discuss this with Eric. He and Eric had been friends for a while now; he had thought he would at least hear him out. But Eric only knew him as the man-about-town, dressed to impress and bringing in the big clients. He never saw him in his t-shirt and sweats, eating Doritos straight from the party-size bag as he played video games or binged a TV show on Netflix. Come to think of it, Chris couldn't think of anyone who had seen that side of him. At least, not since he was a teenager playing video games in his parents' basement. His buttoned-up ready-to-impress persona was the only one he had shown others for years. So of course it would sound strange to hear him waxing poetic about a little town in the middle of nowhere.

"Maybe I am," he finally said. "But either way, if I decide to surrender the listings, would you want them?" At least he knew Eric would handle the sale properly, thoroughly and ethically.

"With a buyer already lined up? Absolutely."

"It would probably only happen if the buyer was me." *Or if I can't stomach the idea of selling to Townsend,* Chris added to himself. "Conflict of interest and all that."

"Sure thing. Just let me know. I've got a couple of other clients, but not much happening right now, so I got time."

"Thanks."

Chris put one hand up in farewell and headed to his office. Now he had to figure out what he wanted to do. First, though, he should probably set up a meeting with his financial advisor. Better to have all the info before making any final decisions.

Chris groaned. He also had to touch base with Colleen Malloy, let her know the status. She had checked in the week before, but he didn't have any updates at that time. Might as well get that over with before he went down his own financial rabbit hole.

"Hello?" The woman who answered sounded hopeful but a little annoyed, if that was a possible combination. It was unsettling.

"Hello, is this Colleen?"

"Yes."

"Hi, Colleen. It's Chris Parker, from Ryker Commercial Properties?"

"Yes, hello, Mr. Parker. Have you got an update for me?"

"I do. I have a couple of parties interested in the properties, but they are both interested in having inspections done. No offers yet. We'll have to see what the inspection returns."

"Okay. Sounds good."

"I do need to discuss one other thing with you, though, since we're at the inspection stage."

"Okay..."

"Since the properties are not listed as-is, you would need to decide how to proceed in the event the inspection brings up concerns. Some buyers want issues taken care of before the sale is completed, and some will be content with money taken off the asking price to cover the costs of getting the issues taken care of."

"Do you expect there to be issues?"

"I haven't seen anything glaring, but there's no way of knowing for sure until the inspection is completed. But, not to sound insensitive, your husband doesn't have the greatest track record, so it would not surprise me."

Colleen sighed. "It wouldn't surprise me either. I will be so glad to get rid of those buildings."

"There's no need to decide right now, but I wanted to give you a heads up in case the inspector finds something."

"Thank you."

"No problem. I expect the inspection to take place sometime next week, so I'll keep you posted when I have more information."

"Okay."

"I'll talk to you then."

They said their goodbyes, and Chris hung up the phone. Well, that was done. And, as suspected, Colleen Malloy was anxious to be rid of the properties, so she was likely to accept any reasonable offer. Suitability didn't matter. Chris had a feeling she would be leaving Pine Valley as soon as the buildings sold.

But what did that mean for him?

Chapter 18

Thursday began with a light tinkling of freezing rain against Natalie's window. As if getting up before four in the morning wasn't bad enough. Natalie turned off her alarm and lay in bed for a moment, listening to the sound. These were the kinds of days she was grateful she didn't have to leave her building to go to work. And the kinds of days that brought in less customers, but customers who were more likely to linger, craving the warmth.

As much as she loved the space she was in, with its cozy seating and friendly artwork, in the dream space in her mind, she would have a fireplace along one side. Or maybe in the middle, with welcoming seating around it, perfect for days like today. She'd been to cafes like that, and it was always so inviting to see a fire flickering in a hearth, even on days that weren't quite as chilly. Maybe someday. Though not if she ended up buying the building. Then she would definitely be here for the long haul.

With a sigh, Natalie pushed herself out of bed. Joey would be arriving soon, and they really had to get moving. Even if they had less customers, the customers they did get would want warm comfort food. Their breakfast sandwiches would be popular. And maybe they should go with some more savory options this morning, like cheese scones or something. She would have to see what they had on hand.

Soon she and Joey were busy mixing, folding, and baking. They had gotten into the habit of turning on upbeat music as they worked, which had taken Natalie some getting used to, but she now enjoyed, especially since it woke her up and got her blood pumping and ready for the day. The morning passed in a blur, with the regular greeting and serving of customers. Their first lull didn't come until shortly before lunch, and Natalie and Chloe chatted as they refreshed the cases and got ready for lunch.

"So," Natalie said as they worked, "since I only have you for another week before you abandon me."

"Not my fault!" Chloe protested.

"I know, I know. I'm just giving you a hard time. Anyway, since I only have you for another week, I was thinking maybe we could get a head start on the holiday cookie prep. I freeze the dough anyway, so a couple of weeks early won't make a difference. And I could use the help."

"Maybe. When were you thinking?"

"Since you're not in tomorrow, maybe this weekend? We could put in a couple of hours each day?"

Chloe thought for a moment. "That should be okay."

"I'll pay you overtime."

Chloe grinned. "I'll make it work."

Natalie returned the grin. "I thought that would convince you." She turned back to the bread she was slicing just as her cell phone rang. Wiping her hands on a dishcloth, she pulled out her phone. It was the bank. "Be right back. Hello?" she answered as she walked toward the back office.

"Hi, Natalie? It's Linda at the bank."

"Hi, Linda." Natalie swallowed. After everything that had happened the last couple of days, Natalie had almost forgotten about the loan application. Almost.

She heard Linda sigh. "Okay, so here's the deal. The building itself seems like a sound investment. The bank would want it appraised, but just from running the numbers, the asking price seems very reasonable."

Reasonable? It had seemed insanely high to Natalie. But what did she know?

"The rent income aligns well with the projected payments and expenses."

There was a "but" coming. Natalie could feel it.

"The concern lies in the requested loan amount in relation to the proposed downpayment. With commercial properties, we usually look for at least a twenty-five percent downpayment, and the amount you indicated you have available is significantly less than that. If you were able to acquire a larger downpayment, we could re-evaluate your application, but as things stand, we are not able to approve you for the requested amount. I'm sorry."

Natalie leaned against the side of her desk. It wasn't a surprise, not really. But to hear the words hurt. So much for that idea.

"Now, if you can either save up a larger downpayment or find a less expensive property, we would be happy to work with you. The rest of your paperwork was in order. You have a reputable business history and credit history, and I see no other concerns. It really is just the numbers. It's too big a risk for the bank to take on at this time."

"I get it," Natalie finally said. Her voice felt hoarse. "Thank you, Linda. I appreciate you calling."

"I'm sorry, Natalie. Really, I am. I know it wasn't what you wanted to hear."

"No, but it's not a surprise. I knew it was a long shot."

"Good luck."

"Thanks."

Natalie disconnected the call and put her phone back in her pocket. She had known it was coming. And at least now she knew. She took a deep breath and went back to the front counter.

"Everything okay?" Chloe asked.

"That was the bank."

"The loan?"

Natalie nodded, then shook her head. She could feel tears welling in her eyes.

"Oh, Natalie." Chloe went over and put her arms around Natalie. "I'm sorry."

"I knew it was coming."

"Does this mean we're going to get stuck with that horrible guy who was here the other day?"

Natalie shrugged. "Maybe." She didn't want to mention Chris. That was too much of a question mark.

"Oh, man. I didn't like that guy. Just the vibe, you know? He'll kick all of us to the curb and not even care."

"Not helping, Chloe."

"Oh. Sorry."

"Let's just get back to work."

Natalie washed her hands, then resumed cutting bread. She was feeling pretty defeated at the moment, but there had to be something she could do. She refused to be kicked to the curb, as Chloe so elegantly put it. But what were her options?

Chapter 19

Chris had other clients. Really, he did. And he put forth a valiant effort to focus on them Thursday morning instead of Pine Valley. He even set up some meetings with potential new clients. But after his last showing, he found himself at loose ends. He wanted to go back to Pine Valley, but, really, what was the point? The inspection was scheduled for the following Tuesday. The meeting with his financial advisor was scheduled for Wednesday. And until both of those meetings took place, he was no closer to figuring out what to do. So he waited.

He waited until Saturday afternoon, at which point he could no longer hold himself back. He wanted to go to Pine Valley. He wanted to see Natalie.

But, of course, the cafe was closed. He had waited too long, and now he wondered why he had even bothered. He parked in the parking lot across the street, peeked into the diner to see if Natalie had by any chance stopped in there again, then figured he might as well take a walk and see if he would run into her somewhere else.

As he passed the cafe, he glanced inside, and, noticing lights on in the kitchen, took a closer look. Natalie was still there, moving around doing something. He knocked on the glass panel of the front door.

Natalie looked up, then walked to the front door. She unlocked the door and opened it partway, sticking her head out to greet him.

"Hey, we're closed."

"Yeah, I know. I just saw you moving around inside and wanted to say hi."

"Did you need something?"

"Not really." How could he say that what he needed was to be here, with her?

"Okay. Well, I'm kind of busy right now, so I can't really chat."

"Oh, okay. No problem. Anything I can help with?"

She paused at that, as if debating whether or not to take him up on his offer. "Actually..." She pushed the door open all the way and beckoned him inside. "Chloe was supposed to help me, but she got called away." After locking the door again, she led him back to the kitchen. "How are you at baking?"

"Um..."

She met his gaze then, and Chris lost his train of thought for a moment. "I'll take that as a 'not good.'" And she grinned.

"Yeah, no, I've, uh, never really done any baking."

"That's okay. Chloe doesn't usually help much with the baking, either. Can you wash dishes and wipe counters?"

Chris nodded, eager to agree to anything that would keep him in close proximity to her. "Sure."

"Great. I'll make the dough, and you do the grunt work." She looked him up and down. "Though you will definitely need an apron. Don't want to mess up your suit."

"I didn't expect to be baking today."

Natalie cocked her head to one side. "What did you expect to be doing?"

He shrugged. "Honestly, I had no idea. I didn't have much going on today."

"So you decided to take a drive? And you wore a suit?"

"Never know how the day will end up. And I just...felt like I needed to be here."

"Hmm." She paused for a moment, assessing him. "Well, I could certainly use the help."

"What are you making, anyway?"

Natalie sighed. "Christmas cookies."

"Isn't a little early for that?"

"I was hoping to get a head start. Every year I make boxes of assorted holiday cookies. They've become so popular I've been taking orders for them the last few years, and I can't really keep up with the demand. So I started making the doughs ahead of time, freezing them, then thawing and baking for fresh cookies as needed. I usually start after Thanksgiving, but Chloe's taking a leave of absence, and she usually helps me, so I figured we could get an earlier start."

"But she abandoned you."

"Not intentionally. Her dad needs surgery, so she's taking time off to help her parents. The surgery is next week, but I guess her dad had a rough night, so Chloe went to help them."

"They live far?"

Natalie shook her head. "No, just a couple of hours away. But far enough that she won't be able to juggle both."

"Gotcha. So I'm Chloe for the day."

"You're Chloe for the day." She grinned again, and Chris's breath caught.

"Okay. Just tell me what to do."

Though it was an awkward start, Chris seemed eager to please, so they soon found their rhythm. Natalie pulled up a Christmas music playlist on her phone to get them in the mood, and she actually started enjoying herself.

When Chloe had called that morning to say she wouldn't be able to make it in, Natalie had almost abandoned her plan for the afternoon. But she had already gotten her order of supplies in, and she wanted everything to be as fresh as possible. Besides, she didn't have anything else going on. So she had started measuring and mixing on her own, accepting that she just wouldn't be able to accomplish as much as she had hoped. Chris seemed like the answer to her prayers, though she did wonder why he was there.

After a couple of hours of working, Natalie decided it was time for a break. She wrapped the last batch of dough tightly in parchment paper, then bagged it and stuck it in the freezer. She was pleased with the stash that had started to accumulate. If they could get a couple more hours in, she would have an excellent start. And if Chris was willing to help her again...

Natalie made them both mugs of coffee, and they sat in the dining room.

"Thanks for your help today."

"No problem. Are you done for the day, or are we getting back to work after our coffee break?"

Natalie stared into her cup of coffee. "Well, I would like to get a bit more done, but you don't have to stay if you don't want to."

"I wouldn't mind."

Natalie looked up to meet Chris's gaze. She couldn't quite interpret the look in his eyes. Did he just want to be helpful, or was there something more? She thought back to their conversation the other day, when he had essentially admitted he was attracted to her. Did he have an ulterior motive for helping her? Was he trying to get on her good side? And for what purpose? Maybe she should tell him to leave. But she had so much to do, and it really did go much faster with two people working. So she settled for "thanks."

They lapsed into companionable silence as they drank their coffees. Natalie pulled out a couple of leftover cookies from the display case and handed him one, then sat and ate while staring out the window. The sun was starting to set. They probably should have stopped for dinner, not just coffee and cookies. But that brought up a whole slew of other questions. Would they go out for dinner, or would she just whip up some sandwiches here, like she usually did with Chloe? Did she want to have dinner with him? That seemed to be a step farther than she intended. But they had to eat. Maybe the cookies would tide them over long enough that she could whip up another batch of dough, then they could go their separate ways.

What did she want their relationship to be? They seemed to have settled into an awkward friendship, but there was an undercurrent of something more, and she didn't know if she liked it. He was attractive, yes, and certainly more amiable than she had originally thought. But, despite the pleasant chatting they had done while she prepped her cookie dough, she got the impression they didn't have much in common. The only tie they had was the building, and if he ended up buying it, that would make for a very awkward relationship. She should probably tell him she didn't get the loan. But was that admitting defeat? She hadn't come up with another plan yet, but she wasn't ready to give up.

What a mess.

They finished their coffee and cookies, then headed back into the kitchen.

"So," Chris asked as they paused in the doorway. "What's next?"

"I think I'll make the dough for candy cane cookies."

"Okay. Tell me what you need, then I'll wash out our mugs."

Her love language was acts of service, Natalie decided. It had to be. The simple matter-of-fact way he pitched in without complaint, ready to help however she needed, made her stomach flutter. She could only stare at him for a moment, unable to move or speak.

"Natalie? You okay?"

"Yeah," she said, smiling quickly and shaking her head. "Yeah. Just got lost in thought for a minute."

He grinned. "No problem. Let me see if the measuring cups are dry."

Something in the way she had looked at him made Chris feel like something had shifted. She had seemed startled, almost, like a thought had caught her off guard.

He had been right to come to Pine Valley. Spending this time with Natalie had only cemented the knowledge that he wanted her in his life. Was it too much to hope she was starting to feel the same?

They spent another hour together, but the air felt heavier somehow, not as lighthearted and jovial as before.

Yes, something had shifted. But Chris could only guess what that shift would bring.

Chapter 20

On Sundays, the cafe was closed, and Natalie usually took the opportunity to sleep in, lounge around in her pajamas, and binge a show on Netflix. It was the one day of the week that she rarely had commitments, and she took full advantage of it.

This week, however, Natalie was having difficulty enjoying her time off. Not only did she wake up much earlier than she would have liked, but she felt antsy, unsettled. She had planned on prepping cookie dough today, too, but Chloe was still away, and there was no way she could ask Chris to help again. Not after what had happened last night.

The last hour they had been working the night before had felt awkward, and they hadn't been able to find the rhythm they had settled into before their coffee break. While she had been considering starting a new batch after the candy cane cookie batter, she instead only made half of the candy cane batter and wrapped things up early. She couldn't get Chris out of there fast enough.

What was the matter with her? It wasn't like she had never been attracted to anyone before. And it wasn't like he was a bad guy. But he wasn't from here. This wasn't his life. And once this "feeling" or whatever he had been experiencing passed, he would move on and forget all about her. No, it was better to just push down the feelings, figure things out one step at a time. And she had to focus on the business right now, anyway. That was her top priority.

She should just work on making cookie dough herself today. That would be the smart thing to do, and it would definitely help the business. But she wasn't feeling very Christmassy. And cookie making was a happy activity, full of hope and cheer, and she was definitely not in that frame of mind.

Natalie looked at the boxes of Christmas decorations she had pulled out ages ago. She should work on those, too. While she had pushed herself to finish the decorating in the cafe, she hadn't gotten around to decorating her apartment. She sighed. She usually loved Christmas, couldn't wait to decorate. But it would have to wait.

Natalie made herself a cup of coffee and brought it over to her sofa. The sofa sat in front of a window overlooking Main Street, and it was Natalie's favorite spot in her apartment. She loved to curl up and watch the people go by. Sundays were usually pretty quiet, but she saw a burst of activity at the diner after church let out, and if the weather was nice, she would see couples or families taking leisurely strolls. Most of the businesses on Main Street were closed on Sundays, but the playground on the town green was open, of course, and when the weather warmed up, Josh had his ice cream shop open. Sundays were lazy days, a time for people to relax and get together and enjoy their time.

Natalie had never felt so alone.

She didn't often mind living alone. She spent her days surrounded by other people, so she appreciated the quiet solitude. But every once in a while, she wished she had someone to share the everyday bits of life with. What would it be like to curl up on this sofa with someone else? To have someone to bicker with, laugh over shows with, or share a meal with? It had been so long since she had been in a relationship, she could barely remember what it felt like. And that had been a disaster. Better to be alone than with someone who didn't want to be there.

Maybe the building was just an excuse. Maybe she was just scared. Living alone in this little apartment was her comfort zone. And breaking out of that was intimidating.

Natalie sighed. She didn't want to dwell on her love life. She had to figure out this building situation. But the building and Chris were intertwined in her mind, and every time she tried to brainstorm, her mind kept veering back to Chris and the way he had looked washing dishes in Chloe's apron. Maybe she should give it a shot, however intimidating it might be. But what if he left her, too?

She needed a break. Reaching for her TV remote, Natalie decided to get her mind off it all. There was plenty of time to figure out her life later.

Chris wasn't sure exactly what had gone wrong the night before, but he hated leaving things unsettled. With the cafe closed, though, his hands were tied. Besides, he had plans to get together with some guys from work to watch football at a brewery nearby. Since he had become obsessed with Pine Valley, he hadn't spent much time with his friends, and he needed to take a break, think about what had happened, and come up with a game plan.

He had enjoyed spending time with Natalie. Conversation had flowed easily between them, and they had worked well together once they learned each other's quirks. And he had enjoyed watching her work. She was at ease in the kitchen, whipping up cookie dough with practiced efficiency. She didn't even need a recipe, though she did have a binder with recipe cards open just in case. He could have watched her all day.

Chris looked around his apartment. He couldn't picture Natalie here. It was too modern, too sterile. He thought back to her cafe, and how warm and inviting she had made it. Was her apartment the same? What would it be like to be in her space, sharing what he imagined to be a plush couch covered in throw blankets? What would it be like to curl up with her, share a bowl of popcorn as they watched a movie? Did she like action movies or comedies? What did her laugh sound like?

There was so much he didn't know about her, and yet he felt like he knew her pretty well. Maybe it was because they had already talked about some of the important stuff – hopes and dreams and worries. Though, he realized, he hadn't shared much of his own with her. While the building situation brought her concerns to the forefront, he hadn't had to open up nearly as much as she had.

He couldn't remember the last time he had opened up to someone. Sure, he had dated. But aside from a long-term girlfriend in college, most of his relationships had been superficial, inconsequential. He hadn't felt any real connection, and he hadn't found it necessary to share more than the bare minimum. They were companionship, someone to pass the time with, a way to stop the comments from his coworkers. He felt the potential for more with Natalie.

But she had pulled away from him the day before, and he didn't know why. Was she still upset with him? Angry about Townsend? Worried about her building? Or was it actually him that she couldn't stand?

Chris sighed. He would just have to keep trying.

Chapter 21

*O*ne more day until the inspection, Natalie thought. And then what? If all went well with the inspection, did that mean Townsend would buy the buildings? And if he did, did that mean she and her fellow business owners would be evicted? Or had Chris been reading the situation wrong and they would all be fine?

And what was Chris's plan? Was he still considering buying the building? Or buildings?

Natalie paused from kneading bread dough and took a deep breath. She hadn't gotten much sleep the night before. While she had been able to distract herself with television and miscellaneous tasks around the apartment for most of the day, as soon as her head hit the pillow, the questions and worries had started up again. She yawned. She hadn't heard from Chloe, so she really hoped she would come in to work today. Natalie needed a nap.

Joey nudged her from the side. "Hey."

"Hey."

"Go upstairs and lie down. I got this."

Natalie met Joey's gaze. "Are you sure?"

"Of course I'm sure. We've been doing this for the last week and a half. I can handle the rest on my own."

Natalie sighed. "Thanks. But if Chloe doesn't show, wake me up."

"You got it, boss."

She gave Joey a few last instructions regarding items she had already started, then went upstairs. She only hoped she was exhausted enough to actually fall asleep.

One more day until the inspection begins, Chris thought. And then what? With so many properties, it would take a couple of days to complete all of the inspections, then it would likely take at least a couple of days for the inspector to write up his report. But, barring anything major, he expected an offer from Townsend to follow shortly thereafter. That didn't give him a lot of time.

Regardless of what had happened between him and Natalie on Saturday, Chris knew that Townsend was not suitable to purchase the properties, especially not the commercial spaces. And, while he would hold out on making any final decisions until he met with his financial advisor, Chris didn't think he would feel comfortable purchasing them all. Even if his advisor said it made sense, and even if he was approved for a business loan large enough to cover them – both of which were not very likely – he didn't think he could take on that much right now. It was better to start small, maybe a single building, to get his feet wet as a landlord. So, if anything, he would probably want to buy the building with the cafe. Nothing new there.

But if Townsend put in an offer, and it was at all reasonable, Colleen Malloy was incredibly likely to accept it. And if Chris didn't put in an offer himself, there wasn't much he could do at that point. So if he was going to do something, it had to be now. And if he didn't intend to purchase the other commercial spaces or the residential land, he needed to find someone who would, and that someone had to be a better fit than Townsend.

Chris had no problem with research. He ran reports and crunched numbers all day, running specs for his clients, arranging inspections, and searching properties. If he hadn't let his personal feelings get in the way, he could have been researching more suitable investors this whole time. *That* was how he really could have helped Natalie and the other business owners. Not by making cookies and dreaming about being a landlord.

It wasn't too late. He had the resources. He still had time. Surely there had to be someone out there who would be interested in buying up commercial property and actually helping a community. But who?

He needed to reach out to Zach White again. Zach specialized in renovating hospitality properties in small towns, revitalizing them and helping the towns in the process. Even if he didn't know anyone directly, he had to have some leads that could get him started in the right direction.

Chris had known Zach for years. They had met fresh out of college at a real estate seminar. And even though their careers had gone in drastically different directions, they had kept in touch. It was why Chris handled Zach's real estate transactions, even though Chris typically handled retail and office buildings. With their history, they knew they could trust each other. And Chris was really hoping Zach would pull through for him this time.

The phone rang four times before Zach picked up. "Chris! How's it going?"

"Not great, man. I'm in a bit of a pickle. Got a minute to talk?"

"Sure. What's up? Still having trouble with the Pine Valley buildings you asked me about?"

Chris sighed. "Yeah, and unfortunately the situation has gotten a bit more urgent." He filled Zach in on the situation with Townsend.

"Hmm. While I appreciate your conundrum, I'm surprised you're taking it so hard. I don't remember that kind of thing being a consideration for you in the past."

Chris cringed. He had to admit he usually focused on the paperwork, the sale, and the money. He didn't usually consider the aftermath. Sometimes his clients had him look into community pushback, but it wasn't really his area of expertise. He was a transaction guy, a numbers guy, not a touchy-feely guy. It had served him well up until now. "I guess you're rubbing off on me."

Zach laughed. "I would be happy to take credit, but I suspect something else is going on here."

"What can I say? Pine Valley has had a strange effect on me."

"Hmm. Is that all?"

"What else would it be?"

"Nothing. Forget I said anything. I'm not sure how I can help, though. I already told you I don't know any small-town commercial investors."

"I know. I was hoping you might know someone who knows someone, or have leads on a billionaire philanthropist or something."

Zach laughed again. "Billionaire philanthropists don't usually buy commercial spaces just so someone else can't."

Chris sighed. "Yeah, I know. I'm grasping at straws here. I don't want these business owners getting evicted just so some guy can make a buck."

"I hear ya. Let me think about it. I'll dig into my contacts, make a few calls, see if anyone owes me any favors."

"I appreciate it, Zach."

"Any time. And I don't blame you about Pine Valley. It has definitely grown on me, too."

"I hear it has that effect on people."

"I'll be in touch."

Chris disconnected the call feeling both hopeful and unproductive. While he hoped Zach would turn up something, he couldn't count on it. He had to get to work.

Chapter 22

By the time Natalie woke up, it was lunch time. Startled that she had slept so long, she scurried to brush her hair and teeth and get herself tidy. Then she headed down to the cafe.

Joey and Sylvie were helping customers, and McKenna, a very part-time staff member who filled gaps in the schedule, had apparently been called in. She was prepping sandwiches in the kitchen.

"No Chloe?" Natalie asked Joey between customers.

He shook his head. "Nope."

"I told you to wake me if she didn't show."

Joey shrugged. "McKenna was available, and you obviously needed the sleep."

Natalie sighed. "Thanks."

"Hello, sleeping beauty," Sylvie greeted her with a smile. "Feel better?"

"Yeah. Thanks. Just had a rough night."

"Happens to all of us," Sylvie said, turning to help another customer.

Natalie greeted McKenna and thanked her for coming in, then washed her hands to help with orders. She was grateful for her team, but she couldn't help but worry. What would happen to them all if the cafe was evicted? She supposed they would just find jobs elsewhere, but would they be valued? Would they feel appreciated?

What would happen after the inspection?

Natalie tried to focus on helping customers during the lunch rush, and by the time traffic had dwindled, she was even more grateful that Joey had let her sleep.

"Thanks for your help today, everyone. It was a busy day." They had about a half hour before closing, but they currently only had one couple sitting at a table near the front. "McKenna, thank you again for coming in. You were a big help."

"Of course. Did you want me to stay to help clean up?"

"No, it's okay. I know you've done a lot in the kitchen already. I'm going to have to touch base with Chloe, but are you available tomorrow if she can't come in again?"

"Probably for at least part of the time."

"Okay, great. Tomorrow is going to be a weird day because the building inspector is coming in. I'm honestly not sure what to expect. Joey, I know you have deliveries to make. Same time, same place tomorrow?"

"You got it, boss."

"Thanks. And thanks for letting me sleep this morning. I needed it."

He gave her a fake salute, then headed to the back room, taking off his apron as he walked.

Sylvie was wiping down counters.

"Now that it'll just be you and me, I was hoping you wouldn't mind chatting for a bit?" Natalie was nervous. But it had occurred to her as she overthought everything during the lunch rush that Sylvie could be a valuable resource. She had been a business owner, and, while their situations were very different, she had gone through major life changes when they decided to sell the motel. At the very least, she could offer some insight, business owner to business owner.

Sylvie smiled knowingly. "I had a feeling you would want to discuss things at some point. You have been so stressed about the building and the business."

Natalie sighed. "I have been. And Courtney next door thinks I'm overreacting, but I've never been one of those people who just waits for things to happen, you know? I want to be prepared, just in case the new owner makes it difficult or impossible for us to stay here."

Sylvie nodded. "I completely understand. It is incredibly difficult when circumstances are out of your hands."

"Exactly. And with Courtney, it's just her. And she lives somewhere else. She would have to get a job, or move her business somewhere else, but she wouldn't be starting from scratch."

"While you have the staff to consider, and your apartment to consider, in addition to the business. I get it."

Natalie's shoulders sagged in relief. "So you don't think I'm overreacting?"

Sylvie pondered for a moment. "I think you are being cautious, and proactive, and doing your best to plan for any eventuality. That's not overreacting. It's just being prepared."

"Thank you. At least someone doesn't think I'm crazy."

"You are not crazy. But you are putting a lot of pressure on yourself."

"I know."

"So, if you don't mind my asking, what is the current status?"

A customer walked in then, followed by another, and Natalie and Sylvie became occupied with helping customers for a few minutes before they had another lull.

"I had looked into buying the building, to have more control and security," Natalie said when they were alone again.

"That's a big responsibility."

"It is. And I had my concerns, but it ended up being a moot point. The bank wouldn't approve me for the amount I would need."

"Would you have wanted it if they had?"

Natalie shrugged. "I don't know."

"That's okay. Since that's no longer an option, though, what are you considering now?"

Natalie took a deep breath. "That's where I'm stuck. I'm not sure what my options are. From what Chris – the listing agent – has said, the prospective buyer who hired the inspector might have his own tenants to bring in, which means some, if not all, of the current tenants would be getting evicted."

"Don't you have leases?"

Natalie nodded. "I do. And I'm sure the others do, too."

"That should protect you then, no?"

"From what I read online, it should, at least until the end of the term. I looked over the lease agreement, and I didn't see anything that made it sound like the new owner could kick us out. But for the cafe, the lease is up for renewal at the beginning of next year."

"Oh dear. What about your apartment?"

"That's a separate lease, since it wasn't available when I first opened the cafe. I have another year on that one."

"So at the very least, you wouldn't lose both at once."

Natalie shook her head. "No, I shouldn't. Unless I'm missing something in the lease agreement or there's some other detail I don't know about."

"Okay. That's something, at least. And there's no guarantee the new owner won't renew your lease."

"It doesn't sound like he will."

"Okay. So you're looking for a backup plan in case things go south."

"Exactly."

"Well, if the lease is up, and the new owner wants you out, you'll have to leave. But Pine Valley isn't known for its large number of vacant retail spaces."

"Exactly. And if other business owners are in the same boat, we would be fighting over the few available options, assuming some are even available at the time."

"So you would be looking at leaving Pine Valley if you want to keep your business."

Natalie could feel tears welling in her eyes. "And I really don't want to do that. Pine Valley is my home. Not to mention I would be starting from scratch."

"I understand. It would be difficult to move, start over. We'll consider that a last resort, then."

"But what are my other options? Ride it out? Hope my lease gets renewed?"

"That is an option. But I know that can be nerve-wracking. There has to be something else."

They lapsed into silence, thinking, until another customer walked in. They greeted and helped a few last-minute customers, then locked the door and started cleaning.

"I know the bank didn't approve you to buy the building, and I know you had your doubts."

"Yes. I don't think I would want to be a landlord, and the building is really expensive."

"But if it was just you, you would like to own?"

"That would be ideal, I think. I wouldn't have to worry about this kind of situation happening again, or that I would get kicked out. But I wouldn't have to be a landlord, either. I could just worry about my own space, my own stuff."

"There would still be building maintenance and all that to worry about," Sylvie reminded her.

"Of course. But I'm not worried about that. I can handle little stuff myself, and if the cafe can keep going as it has been, I can afford the big stuff."

"Do you think the bank would approve you for a smaller amount?"

"Linda, the bank manager, did say to let her know if I found a less expensive property. It was really about the downpayment, I guess? I didn't have enough to put down compared to the amount I would have to borrow. Everything else looked good."

Sylvie nodded once. "Then the solution is simple. We just need to find you a less expensive property."

Chapter 23

Chris was getting nowhere fast. He looked into recent sales of commercial spaces in small towns. He reached out to business associations. He touched base with the Pine Valley town hall. He pursued every possible idea he had to find a better investor. And he was striking out at every turn.

His cell phone rang, and Chris glanced at the screen before answering.

"Zach, please tell me you have something."

"What a greeting."

"Yeah, yeah. I'm in no mood."

"Rough day?"

"Zach, I have tried everything. Either people aren't answering their phones, or they can't help me. And I am running out of time."

"You have time. The inspection starts tomorrow. We both know it will take at least a couple of days with all the properties. Then a couple of days for the report. More, with the holiday in there. You need to calm down."

Chris felt anything but calm, but he ran a hand through his hair and tried to take a deep breath. "I know. I'm just kicking myself for not doing more earlier."

"You were distracted."

"Yeah."

"I just don't know by who."

Chris could feel the heat rising under his collar. "What do you mean?"

Zach laughed. "I know Pine Valley has a certain charm, but not this much. So who is she?"

Chris thought about denying it, but maybe it would be good to discuss it with someone who got it. He sighed. "Fine. Her name is Natalie. She owns the cafe."

"And the cafe is in one of the buildings being sold, right?"

"Yeah."

"And you're concerned that she'll be booted?"

"It's certainly a possibility. Her lease is up for renewal in January, and this buyer has other companies lined up to step in."

"That's a tough break. And I'm guessing she's not the only one."

"Nope. There are at least two other businesses who are up for renewal in the first quarter. And one of the apartment tenants, though I'm less worried about those."

"So you're hoping to find someone who wants to keep everyone as they are."

"Yup. I'm sure everyone expects rent to go up; that's pretty standard. But if they lose their spaces, where will they go? You and I both know Pine Valley isn't exactly full of commercial property for rent."

"It's going to be a tough sell. And you're tight on time."

"You just said I had plenty of time!"

"Not plenty, just some."

"You know, I've even considered buying the places myself. Not the apartment site, but the other buildings."

"Just to make Natalie happy? Man, she's really gotten under your skin."

"Not just to make her happy. But she opened my eyes to some stuff."

"You've got it bad." Chris laughed again. "Fortunately, I may have some options for you."

___ ℓℓ ___

Once Sylvie left, Natalie thought about what she had said. It wasn't as if the thought had never occurred to her. But where in Pine Valley would she find a space to buy? Maybe she should take a walk down to the real estate office. Even if they didn't have any leads, she would get some fresh air, clear her mind. And maybe get some ideas.

Remembering to grab a coat first, Natalie headed out the door. It was a shame Courtney's boutique was closed. She had to see how her date with Josh had gone on Saturday. But at least it would be a good distraction tomorrow when the inspector was poking around.

Natalie walked down Main Street, waving to friends and neighbors, keeping an eye out for any open shop spaces or buildings for sale. If finding something in Pine Valley was a long shot, finding something right on Main Street was even longer, but it didn't hurt to look. Maybe after her trip to the realtors she would explore some of the side streets. There were plenty of small streets and buildings that were still part of the center of town without being on Main Street. She needed to explore all of her options before throwing in the towel or collapsing in a pool of tears.

The real estate office was located on a side street off the other end of Main Street, so Natalie got quite the walk in before reaching the office. She paused on the sidewalk, looking at the pictures of houses available for sale. She had never thought about buying a house before, or any kind of building. She had been focused on building her business. And she was content in her apartment. It was just her, after all. She didn't need much space, and she had everything she needed close by. If she did end up finding a space for the cafe, would it have living quarters for her, too? Or would she still be renting an apartment above the former cafe? That would be weird.

Taking a deep breath, Natalie pushed open the door to the office. She had to know.

"Hello," a woman greeted her with a smile. "Can I help you?"

The woman was seated at a desk that faced the front windows, and Natalie tentatively approached it. "Uh, yeah. My name is Natalie. I was hoping to talk to someone about available properties for sale?"

"Of course. My name is Priya. I am one of the real estate agents here. Why don't we have a seat over here, and we can go over what you're looking for?" The woman gestured toward another desk a few feet away, with chairs on both sides of it. Then she stood up and moved behind the desk.

Natalie took off her coat and sat down in the seat opposite her while Priya pulled out some paper forms.

"Okay. So are you a serious buyer or just browsing for now?"

"Um. Browsing, I guess. Though if the right space is available, I would be looking seriously, if that makes sense."

"No problem. Let's see if we can find something that works for you. Since you said 'right space' instead of 'right house,' I'm getting the impression you're looking for commercial. Is that correct?"

"Yeah. A combination would actually be perfect, with space for me to live either on a second floor or at the back of the building, and then a commercial space at the front. I own the cafe in town, and I'm considering buying instead of leasing. If it's a possibility. Maybe." Natalie was practically shaking with nerves. This was worse than going to the bank. She had been pretty sure that wouldn't pan out. But this? She had no idea.

"Hmm. That will definitely be tricky. We don't handle a lot of commercial properties, simply because there isn't much movement on those here, and multi-use properties are not very plentiful. But let's see what we can find. Why don't we start by having you fill out this interest form, and I'll take a peek at the current listings."

Priya did some searching on the computer while Natalie filled out the form. It had her basic contact info, then went into what she was looking for. Most of it applied to residential spaces, but she supposed that was part of what she wanted, so she filled it out as best she could. By the time she was done, Priya had printed out information about a few listings.

"Okay, so I'm not finding anything currently on the market that quite fits the bill. I only looked in Pine Valley, though. Were you looking to extend your search to other areas?"

Natalie shook her head. "Not right now."

"No problem. I found a few properties that aren't quite right, but with a little work might be options. They are currently listed as residential, but based on where they are located, you might be able to get them rezoned, since there are commercial buildings nearby. They are technically houses, but the floor plans appear to be somewhat open, so you might be able to do some renovation work to get them where you want to be. I'm not sure if that is something you are interested in. You would also likely need to update the electrical system, since I assume you use commercial ovens that would draw more power."

Natalie took a deep breath. As predicted, this wouldn't be a simple solution. But what were her options? She looked at the papers that Priya had placed on the desk. "Can I take these? And think about it?"

"Of course. This is not a quick decision. You need to be sure. Take a look at the specifications, see if you think they could work, and let us know. We can arrange viewings if you would like. And, now that we have your information, we can let you know if anything more suitable comes on the market."

"Thank you. I appreciate it."

"Of course. Is there anything else I can help you with while you're here?"

"No, I think this was it."

"Okay. Thank you for coming in. Here is one of my cards. Let me know if you decide to see one of those properties, and I will be in touch if anything new comes up."

Natalie took the business card offered. "Thanks."

She left the office feeling not exactly hopeful but not despondent, either. Even if not ideal, these were options. And that's what she needed right now.

Chapter 24

The inspector was starting with the largest building, the one that held the cafe. Between the apartments and the businesses, he would likely be working all day, which meant Chris would be spending the day in Pine Valley. Townsend's realtor planned on stopping by at some point in the afternoon to check on the progress, but he was otherwise engaged for most of the day, so Chris was on his own. He was grateful. Having to be sociable with someone who was essentially working against him was not his idea of fun, though it wouldn't be the first time.

Chris led the inspector to the apartments first, since the tenants were all out at work. They had been informed of the inspection, and Chris had the keys, so he hoped they would be in and out without any trouble. The apartments shouldn't take too long. The bulk of the time would be in the businesses and utility spaces. Chris was hoping to spend some quality time with Natalie while the inspector worked, if for nothing else than to tell her about his research the day before. But would she want to see him?

He couldn't wait for this building business to be behind them. He wanted them to get to know each other without this drama and tension hanging over them. Then he could show her who he really was and see if they fit as well as he hoped they did.

But they had a long way to go before then. And he needed to talk to her.

With the time in the apartments being relatively short, Chris stuck around while the inspector did his work. Occasionally the inspector would comment on something he saw, or make a note on his tablet, but otherwise Chris was left alone with his thoughts.

Zach had come up with a couple of contacts who might be able to help. One was a small-scale investor who, like Zach, had interest in revitalizing small towns. The only trouble with that investor was the fact that she was new to the scene and likely didn't have as much working capital as Chris would have liked. It was possible she wouldn't be able to cover the cost of all of the buildings, even if she was interested. The second contact was more of a long shot. He lived out of state and usually focused his investments in Maine, but Zach thought it was at least worth touching base with him, if for nothing else than as a possible source for additional names.

Chris had called both of them and left messages. The investor in Maine had called him back and said he likely wasn't interested but would look at the listings and run them by some other investors he knew. He was still waiting to hear back from the small-town investor. The way Chris looked at it, if that person could cover at least some of the properties, he could perhaps put in an offer on what was left, thereby covering all the commercial spaces in a way that kept Pine Valley intact. That was the hope, at least. Assuming all went well with the inspection, and Colleen Malloy accepted their offers over Townsend's.

Chris ran a hand over his face. If someone had asked him a month ago if he would be bending over backwards trying to sabotage a potential buyer, he would have thought they were crazy. What had happened to him? Was it Natalie's influence, or had he really changed that much so quickly? He should be grateful for a solid offer, a straightforward sale, and a large commission check. Many other times he had been. Why did it matter to him what the buyer did with the property afterward? He wasn't part of this community. He didn't really know these people. It didn't affect his life.

But getting to know Natalie had made the business owners more than names on a piece of paper. They were real people, with real lives that would be greatly affected by potential changes. And if Townsend carried through with his plans and ideas, those real people would have their lives uprooted, and this real town would be forever changed. His eyes were opened now. And he didn't want to close them again.

The inspector finished with the apartments with relatively little fuss. Aside from a few minor concerns, there didn't seem to be much to worry about. So they headed downstairs. Chris let the inspector into the utility room where the HVAC equipment was housed, then wandered back into the hallway. Just as he was about to enter the cafe, his phone rang.

Distracted, he answered without checking the caller ID. "Christopher Parker."

"Chris, it's Alan."

Chris immediately stood up straighter. His boss never called him out of the blue. "Mr. Ryker, hello. What can I do for you?"

Alan sighed. "Well, I admit I'm at a bit of a loss here. You've always been a straight shooter, quick with the sales, a commendable associate."

"I'm happy to hear it, sir."

"However, I hear you've become emotionally invested in some of your current listings, and that concerns me."

Chris swallowed. Of course he was getting emotionally invested. People's livelihoods were at stake. But how had Ryker heard about it?

"I can't have the company's reputation at stake here, Parker. We need everything on the up-and-up. I'm afraid I'm going to need to ask you to relinquish the listings."

Chris closed his eyes and sagged against the wall of the hallway. "I'm at one of the listings now, sir. The inspection is happening. There's a potential buyer already in motion."

"I understand. Eric is driving out to meet you. He'll take over from here."

Eric. Of course. So much for friendship. "I don't suppose there's anything I can say to change your mind."

"Afraid not. The company's reputation is of utmost importance, Parker. You understand."

"Yes, sir."

The call disconnected without a farewell, and Chris put his phone back in his pocket. He supposed in some ways, this was a good thing. He wouldn't have to worry about if he should or should not give Eric the listings, or when. It would make things cleaner if he did decide to make an offer. But the backstabbing hurt. He really hadn't expected Eric to go behind his back like this. And losing the listings made it harder for him to stay on top of the status. It also meant that timing was even more critical.

Chris pushed open the back door of the cafe, more determined than ever to figure things out. They couldn't let Townsend buy the buildings.

Chapter 25

Natalie was helping a customer when Chris entered the cafe with an intense look in his eyes. Shouldn't he be with the inspector? They couldn't be done already, could they?

She finished with the customer in front of her, rang up a second customer, then let Joey take over as she moved to greet Chris.

"What's the matter?" she asked.

"We need to talk."

"Okay." She led him into the back office and closed the door. This seemed important.

"I am no longer the listing agent on the buildings in Pine Valley."

Natalie raised her eyebrows. "Does this mean you've decided to buy them?"

"That is still up in the air. But my boss thinks I've become too emotionally invested and that I'm muddying the waters, so to speak. So he pulled me from the listings."

"So what's your plan?"

Chris sighed and sank into a chair. "That is still up in the air, too. I just found out two minutes ago. I had some things in the works, but I'm not sure how they'll play out, especially since I won't be able to monitor the sale situation as closely."

Natalie sat in the chair next to him. "What did you have in the works, if you're not buying them yourself? Did you find someone else to buy them?"

"Possibly? I have a couple of calls in to investors who might be able to help. Zach White, the guy who bought the motel, gave me their info. He's been good for the town, right?" Chris looked up at her, as if seeking approval.

"Yeah, he's been great. The motel is doing well, and they've been giving me business, so I can't complain."

"Okay, good. I know he's helped other towns. I just wanted to make sure." He looked down then, staring at his hands as he linked and unlinked his fingers.

Natalie examined Chris for a moment. He looked like a lost little puppy, nervous and unsure of himself. It was a far cry from the cocky, self-assured man who had first come into her cafe. "Chris?" She laid a hand on his arm, and he looked up again. "Are you okay?"

He took a deep breath and leaned back in the chair. "I don't know. I've never been pulled from a listing before, so that hurts, especially given my track record. But it hurts more because I'm pretty sure my boss only found out about things because a coworker, Eric, who I thought was a friend, told him. I really didn't expect him to go behind my back like that."

"I'm sorry. Is Eric the one who will be taking over the listings?"

Chris nodded. "Yeah. You'll probably get to meet him today. My boss said he's on his way to take over."

Lovely. Just what she needed: another arrogant man coming in here and trying to take charge. And if he would backstab his own friend, he obviously wouldn't care about the small businesses. He would let Townsend buy the properties without a moment's thought. "Okay, then we need to do everything we can to make sure things go the way we want them to."

"I can't sabotage the listings, Natalie. I still need my job, especially if I hope to get a business loan to buy even one of the properties."

"I wouldn't ask you to sabotage the listings. I'd like to consider myself an honest, ethical person. But we need to figure this out. Legally and ethically."

"What do you suggest?"

Natalie sighed and leaned back in her chair. "I wish I knew. I've been trying to come up with a solution since I first found out about the buildings going up for sale. How long do you think we have?"

"Well, the inspection should take at least a couple of days, possibly three, depending on how involved he gets with the apartment building site. If he thinks soil and water samples are necessary, it could be a little while to get the results back. But with Thanksgiving being on Thursday, he'll probably try to wrap it up before then. Once the inspection is complete, he should have his report back in a couple of days. Then, depending on what he finds, Townsend may or may not put in an offer. If nothing major is found, I think the offer is pretty much guaranteed. And if something is found, he may just offer less money to cover fixing it. I think it would have to be pretty bad for him to change his mind, and from what I've seen of the buildings, I doubt something that bad will come up. There are usually signs."

"Okay. So it sounds like we have at least the rest of this week."

"In this case, the holiday will likely work in our favor. We'll probably have into next week."

"Okay. So maybe we'll see if the people you reached out to get back to you today. And, if not, you can reach out to them again tomorrow. Unless you think it would be better if I did it? Or would that be weird?"

"I can do it. I'll let them know the business owners are on my side, though, looking for support. I'm sure everyone in town would like to keep their businesses intact. Maybe I'll touch base with the other business owners affected, too. I should let them know about the listing agent change anyway. I can do that today, since I had planned on being in Pine Valley all day."

"Okay. Do you think it would be worth it to start a petition or something? Let Townsend know we don't want him here?"

"Not to sound negative, but I don't think it would make much difference. This isn't town property, so the town has limited control over what can be done. Townsend wouldn't be doing anything illegal, and Colleen Malloy is allowed to sell her property to whoever she wants. If Townsend wants to buy it, and Malloy accepts his offer, that's it."

Natalie released a breath. "Okay. Not great, but I get it. And I doubt Malloy wants to drag things out any more than she has to, so she'll take it."

"Exactly."

"Unless we give her a reason not to."

"What are you thinking?"

"I have no idea. But if we can't get someone to offer sooner or more than Townsend, we'll have to think of something."

"Okay." Chris stood up. "I'll get to talking with the other business owners."

"And I'll try to keep an eye on the inspection process and brainstorm ways to shift things in our favor."

"Sounds like a plan." Chris moved to leave.

"Chris?"

He paused and turned to face her. "Yeah?"

"Thanks."

"For what?"

"For doing everything you can. Even if we lose this battle, I appreciate everything you've done to help us."

"What can I say? It's the right thing to do. What you said to me, on our walk that night, it stuck with me. I've been so focused on getting things sold I never thought about what happens after the sale. It's helped me succeed in my career, but I don't want to do that at the expense of others."

Natalie smiled. "I appreciate it. You know, you're not who I thought you were when we first met."

"Yeah, I clean up nice, and I can put on a show to impress anyone."

Natalie shook her head. "This is much more impressive. To me, at least." And before she could overthink it, she kissed him on the cheek and left the office.

Chapter 26

As chaste as it was, Chris could feel that kiss all the way to his toes. It was good to know everything he was potentially sacrificing was worth it. But impressing Natalie wasn't the only thing he was trying to accomplish here. He had to save her business, too.

Chris left the cafe to head to the other buildings, but just as he was about to head toward the side street that held the first one, he saw Eric pull into the parking lot across the street. He changed direction and headed into the clothing boutique first, instead. Closing the door behind him, he tried peeking through the windows to see which direction Eric was heading in.

"Can I help you?" Courtney's voice pulled Chris away from his surveillance, and he turned to face her.

"Hi," he said, attempting a smile. "Sorry, I was just...never mind."

"You're the realtor. Chris, right?"

"Yeah, that's me. But I'm actually no longer the agent selling this building, so I wanted to give you a heads up."

"Is the new agent who you were trying to avoid?"

Chris's face turned sheepish. "Yeah. Sorry. We just...long story. Let's just say I'm not very happy with him at the moment."

"Ooh, drama. I love it. I hope I get to hear the story one day."

Chris attempted a laugh. "Yeah, maybe someday. In the meantime, though, I was also hoping to get your thoughts and opinions on something. As Natalie's neighbor, I'm not sure how much she's told you about what's going on?"

"Well, I know the inspection is happening today, so I'm guessing there's a buyer in place. Beyond that, I know she was toying with the idea of buying the place herself, but I don't think that worked out too well."

"No, it didn't. And, yes, there's a potential buyer who hired the inspector. No offer has been made yet, though."

"Okay. Well, that's what I know. I take it there's something else happening?"

"Let's just say the potential buyer's plan doesn't involve keeping many of the businesses in place. As leases expire, he has new tenants lined up to move in."

Courtney sucked in a breath. "That's not good."

"No, it's not. And I'm trying to find someone else to buy the properties before that happens. That's why I'm no longer the listing agent."

"Got it. So how can I help?"

"Our hands are mostly tied, unfortunately. But I wanted to make sure all the tenants were aware of the situation and could offer backup support as I try to convince a more hospitable investor to buy instead."

"Absolutely. I don't think you'll get anyone who would argue with that."

"I didn't think so. Okay, so that's where things stand. If the new real estate agent comes in, his name is Eric. He'll put on a good show. He's great at getting people to trust him. But don't fall for it, okay? He's just looking to close the deal as quickly as possible."

"Ooh, more drama. You got it."

Chris grinned. "Thanks. If anything changes, I'll let you know."

Then he left the boutique and headed next door to the ice cream parlor. One down, seven more to go.

Natalie watched the slick-looking man cross the street and braced herself for what she expected to be an aggravating experience. He entered the cafe and smiled at her, a smooth smile with a dimple thrown in for good measure.

"Hello there. My name is Eric. I'm with Ryker Commercial Properties. I'm looking for my associate, Christopher Parker. Have you seen him by any chance?"

Natalie looked the guy over and intentionally made an unimpressed expression. "Yeah, he was here. Now he's not." Her voice practically dripped with attitude.

The smile didn't even falter. This guy was good. "Do you by any chance know where he went? Or when he'll be back?"

Natalie shrugged. "Don't know. Don't care."

"No problem. Do you know where I might find the property inspector working here today?"

"Out back somewhere, I think. He was upstairs. Now he's not. Haven't seen him."

"Thank you for your help." Eric tipped his head in thanks, then left the cafe through the front door.

When he was gone, Joey walked up to Natalie and grinned. "I could barely keep a straight face. What was that all about?"

Natalie sighed. "Chris, the guy who was selling the property for Malloy, isn't anymore. He got the boot for being too emotionally invested. And by that I mean, for actually caring about the people who would have to live with the mess left from the sale. That guy's his replacement."

"Gotcha. So we don't like him."

"Nope."

"But we like the first guy."

Natalie sighed again. "Yeah, we like the first guy."

Joey grinned again. "Maybe some of us more than others."

Natalie gave him a playful shove. "Get back to work and out of my hair."

"Sure thing, boss."

Eric disappeared around the corner of the building, and Natalie resumed wiping down counters. It was a good thing none of her regulars had heard her talking to him. They would have thought there was something wrong with her. But they didn't know what had been going on behind the scenes over the last couple of weeks. And she would prefer to keep it that way.

She glanced at the clock on the wall. Business should start picking up for lunch soon. She had no idea what the status was on the inspection. Would he be shutting off power at any point? She knew that was a possibility, but she really hoped they would be closed before that happened. Maybe she should try to find the inspector before things got busy again.

"Sylvie, Joey, I'm going to see if I can find the inspector, get a timeline on things before the lunch rush hits."

"No problem, Natalie," Sylvie replied. "We'll hold down the fort."

Natalie left through the back entrance and tried to figure out where the inspector might be. Seeing the door to the utility room propped open, she headed in that direction.

"Hello?" she asked as she approached the open door.

"Hi there," the inspector replied, standing up from where he had been looking at an electrical panel.

"I'm Natalie. I own the cafe in this building."

"Chuck," the man said, holding out a hand in greeting.

"Nice to meet you," Natalie replied, shaking Chuck's hand. "I was hoping to get an idea of timing. We're moving into lunch time, and I would hate for things to get shut off when we needed them."

Chuck sighed. "Well, I'm almost done here, then I figured I would break for lunch myself before tackling the business spaces. I can start with one of the others if that's helpful."

"That would be great. We close at two, so you can have free rein of the place after that if that works."

"That should be fine. Now, do you have any idea where Chris ran off to? I found something I need to run by him."

Natalie held her breath a moment. Was there something that would hold up the sale? She could only hope. "I think he went to see the other buildings. But he's not in charge of the sale anymore. This guy Eric is. I thought he would have met up with you by now. Maybe he's looking for Chris."

"That's a shame. Well, if you see either one of them, send them my way."

"You got it."

Natalie returned to the cafe, her mind moving a mile a minute. Was there a problem? Or had Chuck just wanted to make Chris aware of something that didn't affect anything? And what kind of impact would it have on the sale?

Chapter 27

Eric caught up with Chris as he was leaving the florist. Chris wanted to run in the other direction, but he knew he would have to face Eric eventually. And, considering how amped up he was feeling after talking with most of the business owners, it might as well be now.

"There you are," Eric said, grinning and attempting to greet Chris with a handshake.

Chris ignored the outstretched hand. "Here I am. Where I'm supposed to be. Shouldn't you be somewhere else?"

Eric put his hand down. "Well, I'm supposed to be with the inspector, but I need the building keys before I can meet up with him. And I'm pretty sure you still have them."

"Yup. I have them. Because it was my listing."

"Which you were considering giving to me."

"Exactly. Considering. There wasn't a need yet. And there might not have been at all."

"You were getting caught up. That's not good for anybody."

"So you saw an opportunity."

"It's not like that."

"You tell yourself that. But it doesn't matter. I'm not going to get into a fight with you, especially not in the middle of town. I've got bigger fish to fry." Chris started walking toward the last of the three buildings.

"Still trying to stop the big bad buyer from taking over? There's nothing wrong happening here, Chris. It's just business as usual. Nothing illegal, nothing unethical."

"Maybe from your perspective. And maybe from Ryker's perspective. But there's a lot wrong happening here, Eric. Because Townsend doesn't care about this town, or the people in these buildings. He just wants to make money."

"And what's wrong with that? From where I'm standing, it looks like you've made plenty of money yourself, in situations just like this. Just because you've had a change of heart doesn't mean everyone else has to suffer."

"Just the little guy, right? Just the people who are out here hustling every day, trying to make a living."

"You and I hustle every day, too. Just because we're not tucked away in little shops in the middle of nowhere doesn't mean we don't deserve to do our jobs, too."

Chris shook his head. "You just don't get it, man. And you probably never will. You want to try and destroy these people's lives? Be my guest." He tossed Eric the set of keys. "But I'm not giving up. Not on this town and these people." And he stepped into the dentist's office that was next on his list.

When Eric reentered the cafe, he did not look happy. Gone was the charming smile, and in its place were stormy eyes.

"Where's the inspector?" he asked Natalie, interrupting a transaction with one of her best customers.

Natalie scowled at him and continued helping her customer. She rang the woman up with a smile, then turned back to Eric in anger. "You may think you walk on water and can do whatever you like around this place, but let me assure you that is not the case. Regardless of who owns this building, this is my establishment, and you will treat me and my customers with respect. Is that clear?"

Eric scowled back at her and didn't reply.

"While I will do what I must in terms of cooperating with the seller, buyer, and inspector, I will not tolerate your rudeness. Until this mess is taken care of, you will be polite, or you will be kicked out of my cafe. Is that understood?"

Eric was silent, the scowl remaining.

"I said, is that understood?"

His scowl deepened, but he gave a single nod in acknowledgement.

"Now, do you want to try that question again?"

He gave a smile that was more of a sneer. "Do you happen to know where I might find the inspector, *ma'am*?"

Natalie matched his snarky smile with one of her own. "Last I saw him, he was in the utility room off the back hallway, *sir*. Oh, and he wanted to see you or Chris about something."

Eric moved briskly to the back of the cafe and disappeared through the back door. Joey came up to her laughing.

"You are totally my hero," he said, patting her on the back.

"Yeah, well, I can't stand that guy."

Sylvie joined them. "I don't know what he did to deserve all that, but you certainly made an impression."

"Let's just say he's a bit of a back-stabbing two-faced creep."

"Okay, then," Joey replied. "Remind me never to get on your bad side."

"I doubt you would ever do anything to deserve it, Joey."

"This is true." He turned to greet another customer and take their lunch order, and Sylvie and Natalie got back to work, too.

Natalie wished she knew what the inspector had wanted to talk to Chris about. She doubted Eric would tell her. But maybe Chris could get information. It sounded like the inspector knew and liked him; he seemed disappointed that he wouldn't be working with him anymore. When Chris got back, whenever that was, she would ask him to do some digging.

About ten minutes later, Eric and the inspector both walked back into the cafe. The inspector greeted Natalie and began perusing the menu, but Eric mumbled that he was going to the diner and left the cafe shortly after. Natalie was grateful. She didn't think she could be civil to him.

By the time Chris returned to the cafe, the inspector was seated with a sandwich and beverage. He seemed an amicable guy, and Natalie had hope that he would be able to help them. Chris greeted her with a smile. She smiled back.

"Productive morning?" she asked.

"Somewhat. All of the business owners are on our side, though that isn't much of a surprise."

"Did Eric catch up with you?"

Chris's mouth turned down. "Unfortunately, yes."

"The inspector wanted to talk to you."

"Does he know I'm not the listing agent anymore?"

"Yeah. He seemed disappointed. And he's probably told Eric whatever he wanted to say, but I'm hoping you could ask him about it, too. Maybe he's got something we can use to discourage the sale."

"It's certainly worth a shot. Wish me luck."

Chris squeezed her hand, and Natalie felt herself grow warm. "Good luck."

They were going to need it.

Chapter 28

"Hey, Chuck. What's going on? I hear you wanted to talk to me."

Chuck looked up from his lunch. "Chris! Wasn't sure if I would see you again. I hear you're no longer representing this building."

Chris pulled out a chair and sat next to Chuck, grimacing as he did so. "No, I am no longer the listing agent. But I'd like to think I still represent its best interests."

"Interesting way of putting it. What's going on?"

Matthew Townsend may have hired Chuck to inspect the properties, but Chris had worked with him on multiple other projects. He was an honest, thorough inspector, and they had been on friendly terms for a while. Chris liked Chuck and knew he could be honest with him.

"Well, I've grown fond of this little town, and while showing Townsend around the properties, I learned that he intends to replace many of the tenants with his own people. Nothing underhanded per se, but not exactly what's best for the town, especially these small business owners. So I've been working to find another buyer who might be a better fit."

Chuck gave a low whistle. "So they kicked you off the listing."

"That about sums it up."

"I'm sorry to hear it. I am glad you're looking out for the little guy, though. I know you usually handle much bigger places than this."

Chris leaned back in his chair. "Yeah, small towns aren't usually my area, but I've found I like it."

Chuck assessed him. "I think it suits you."

"Thanks." After a moment, Chris cleared his throat. "So, if you have any information about the building, I would love to hear it."

Chuck thought for a moment, then leaned forward and looked at Chris. "Okay, here's the deal. I can't give you too many details, especially since I haven't inspected the business spaces yet, but it looks like something's off with the electrical. Some weird wiring that looks jerry-rigged by a not-quite-professional handyman. Everything in the apartments appeared to be functioning without issue, but, honestly, that surprises me. Since this place draws more power than the apartments would with those fancy ovens, the first-floor wiring might be better. But that second floor will need redoing."

"Good to know. I'd appreciate any updates once you've checked out the rest of the spaces."

"You got it. Want me to send you a copy of the final report, too?"

Chris grinned. "That would be great. You know, I'm considering buying one or two of these buildings myself."

Chuck patted him on the shoulder. "I could totally see you doing that. Good for you."

"Thanks. Well, I'll let you finish your lunch. Thanks for the info."

"No problem."

Chris stood up and walked back toward the counter, catching Natalie's eye. He couldn't help a discreet thumbs up as he approached.

They had customers, but Natalie pulled herself away when he reached her. "Good news?"

"Well, yes and no. Apparently there's a problem with the electrical system for the apartments. He still has to check out the businesses, but the second floor at least will need some work."

"Enough to get Townsend off our backs?"

Chris shook his head. "Probably not. It's not cheap, but probably not a deal-breaker. But it should buy us some time, since he'll need an electrician to come out and see what needs to be done so he can have an idea on pricing."

Natalie released a breath. "Okay. And, of course, it's something for any other buyer to be aware of, too, so it might be a turn-off."

"Possibly."

Their gazes met, and neither said anything until Chris looked away.

"Natalie, I was, uh, wondering. Since I'm technically no longer part of the listing, and it's no longer a conflict of interest, maybe we could go out for dinner sometime. We could get to know each other, talk about something other than buildings for sale." He gave a half smile.

Natalie's eyes widened, and she began fidgeting. "Dinner! That reminds me. I have to go talk to Courtney, find out how dinner with Josh went on Saturday." And she took off her apron and hurried around the counter, leaving the cafe in the middle of the lunch rush.

Chris sighed before saying under his breath, "I'll take that as a 'no.'"

Natalie practically ran to Courtney's shop, not even bothering with a jacket, threw open the door, and stepped inside. Courtney and the customer she was helping both looked up in surprise. Natalie took a deep breath, shook her head to indicate it was nothing to worry about, and approached the counter at a much calmer pace.

Courtney finished with her customer, rang him up, then waited until he had left the store before turning to Natalie. "What the heck is wrong with you? Shouldn't you be at the cafe helping your own customers?"

Natalie threw her arms onto the counter and buried her face in them. She felt close to tears, and she didn't know why. "Probably," she mumbled into her arms.

"I can't hear you when you're being ridiculous," Courtney replied.

Natalie looked up. "Probably," she repeated.

"What is going on?"

"Chris asked me out."

"That's great!" Then she saw Natalie's frowning face and wet eyes. "It's not great?"

"I don't know. I mean, I've been so focused on this whole building mess, and he doesn't live here, and what if he becomes my landlord? That would just be weird. And he was so cocky in the beginning, but now he's all nice and trying to help us, and I don't know what to think or feel, and it's just a mess."

"Okay, then. I didn't understand half of that, but it sounded like a bunch of excuses."

Natalie sighed. "Probably. But it's still a mess. And how can I possibly think about going on a date when everything around me might be literally falling apart?"

"It's not literally falling apart."

"I could lose my business, Court. I could lose my home."

"I don't think that's going to happen."

"The business part is a very real possibility. Did you know this potential buyer guy is looking to kick out everyone as soon as their lease is up?"

"Chris mentioned something to that effect. But I have a while left on my lease, so I'm not too worried."

"Well, I don't. My lease is up in January."

"Oh, Natalie."

"And Chris is trying to find another buyer, and he's talked about buying it himself, but I don't know how serious he was, and even if he was serious, that would make him my landlord, and I couldn't possibly date my landlord, even if he did save my business."

"Chris wants to buy the building?"

"He talked about it. But it could have been just talk. And so far nothing else he's tried has panned out, so it might just be getting my hopes up for nothing. I can't let my guard down."

"Okay. Well, stay in here as long as you need."

"Thanks." Natalie rested her head down on her arms again. "Do you remember a month ago when everything was perfect?"

"Yes, things were going well, but nothing's ever perfect."

"I guess." She paused, deep in thought. "Oh!" she said after a moment. "I almost forgot the excuse, I mean reason, I had for running over here."

"It wasn't just to lament the horrible experience of having a handsome man ask you out?"

Natalie shot her a look. "No, it was to ask *you* about the handsome man who has asked *you* out. How did the date go with Josh on Saturday?"

Courtney blushed. "He was so sweet. He closed his shop early just to take me out, and we went to Giuseppe's, and it was amazing. The food was delicious, of course, and we just ate and talked for like two hours. Did you know he's been experimenting with his waffle cone recipe just to try something I suggested?"

Natalie raised her eyebrows. "What did you suggest about waffle cones?"

Courtney brushed her off with a wave of her hand. "It doesn't matter. The point is, he actually listened to me and took what I said into consideration."

"That's great, Courtney. Really. Josh is a great guy."

"He really is." Courtney closed her eyes and hugged herself. "And he walked me home, and he kissed me good night, and it was perfect."

"I thought you said nothing's perfect."

"Yeah, well, maybe I was wrong. Because this was."

"I'm happy for you, Courtney. I really am."

"Thanks." Courtney sighed contentedly, then looked at Natalie again. "You could be happy, too, you know. From what you've said, and from my limited interactions with him, including when he came into my shop this morning, I think Chris is a good guy, too."

"Yeah, I think he is, too."

"Then maybe you need to get over yourself and give him a shot?"

"I'll think about it."

"You're ridiculous."

"Yeah, I know."

"And you should probably go back to the cafe. I've seen like five people walk by heading in that direction. Sylvie and Joey could probably use your help about now."

"Yeah, I know." Natalie stood up and ran her fingers through her hair. Straightening her spine, she took a deep breath. "I can do this."

Courtney laughed. "Yes, you can. You can go run your business and have a conversation with a good man."

Natalie shot her another look. "Yeah, yeah. I'll get out of your hair now."

She left the boutique, walked next door, and looked around. The cafe was busy, but Chris was nowhere to be seen.

Chapter 29

Chris was disappointed with Natalie's reaction, but he did his best not to dwell on it. As much as he wanted to spend time with Natalie, they did have something more pressing to deal with, and he probably shouldn't let himself get too distracted. But what could he do right now that would help? He still hadn't heard from either investor, and he had already touched base with all of the business owners who would be affected by the sale.

Unsure of a destination, Chris just started walking. Maybe if he cleared his head a bit he would come up with some brilliant idea to get them out of this mess. Not wanting to pass Natalie in the clothing shop, he went in the opposite direction, toward the town green. It was chilly out, but there were still kids running around and playing on the playground. Not wanting to intrude, Chris headed to the gazebo and sat on the step at the entrance. He gazed out up and down Main Street.

A month ago – not even a month – he had been content with his life. He had a good job, an active social life, a comfortable apartment. He was living the dream. How had his life gotten turned upside down so quickly?

He thought back to his interaction with Eric that morning. Eric, who he had considered a good friend. Did Eric really think everything was fine? That there was nothing wrong with what Townsend had planned? When had money become more important than people?

But Chris had to admit that not long ago, he would have acted the same way. Not because he didn't think people were important, but simply because it hadn't really registered how his actions affected them. It had taken a spunky, stubborn woman to open his eyes. And he wasn't naive enough to think that anything he said or did would make a difference to Matthew Townsend or to Eric. They had their own priorities.

Sadly, he didn't think his boss would be on his side, either. Alan Ryker expected his agents to handle sales quickly, efficiently, and bringing as much money into the agency as possible. He obviously didn't like how Chris had been handling this situation, and Chris couldn't really blame him. But where did that leave Chris? Even once this mess in Pine Valley had been wrapped up – one way or the other – would he be able to go back to work, proceeding with business as usual? Would Ryker even let him?

Chris made a very good living, and he had money in the bank, but if he no longer fit in at Ryker Commercial Properties, what would he do? If he was still considering buying at least one of the properties in Pine Valley, he was sure any bank offering him a loan would prefer that he was gainfully employed. Could he quit once he got the loan? Would he be able to make the payments if he did? And what kind of financial position would that leave him in? He could forget buying all three buildings. That would definitely be off the table if he lost his job.

He supposed he could get another job. Another agency would probably be willing to take him on, and he probably had clients who would follow him. Did they align with his new moral vision, though? Could he adjust his specialty, work with smaller companies, or leasing companies, or even residential properties? There would be a learning curve, but he was licensed, and he was smart. He could adjust.

This wasn't helping. Now, in addition to worrying about Natalie and the properties, he was having a major life crisis. Wonderful.

With a sigh, Chris stood up and walked back down to the sidewalk. Maybe he should touch base with the local real estate office again. If the sale did go through, there would soon be multiple businesses looking for retail space. It wouldn't be a bad idea to give them a heads up. And maybe see if they had any leads to get a head start.

Just as Chris reached the sidewalk, his phone rang. He didn't recognize the number, but it looked vaguely familiar.

"Christopher Parker," he greeted.

"Mr. Parker, this is Lena Morseau returning your call."

Chris couldn't help but punch the air. It was the small-town investor. "Ms. Morseau, thank you so much for calling me back. I have a possible project for you."

Natalie finished wiping down the tables, then locked the front door of the cafe. She had hoped Chris would return, but she supposed he was giving her space. She hadn't exactly responded well when he asked her out. But what could she do? She didn't feel emotionally equipped to start a relationship right now, not with him, not with so much up in the air.

She was turning back toward the kitchen when she heard a knock on the front door. Turning, she saw Chris peeking through the glass of the door. He lifted a hand in greeting when he saw her.

Natalie took a deep breath and walked back to the door to let him in. "Hey," she said as he walked inside.

"Hey." He held her gaze for a moment before clearing his throat and looking away. "So, I heard from one of the investors I mentioned."

"That's great!"

"Well, yes and no. Though she is trying to invest in small towns to revitalize communities, her focus has been on buildings that are in states of disrepair, or communities that need an overall facelift to encourage residents to stay and grow with the towns. Pine Valley is obviously already a thriving community, and, even if the buildings need some work, they are fully functioning and appealing as is."

Natalie pulled out a chair and sat down. "So she won't be able to help us."

"She seemed reluctant, simply because she didn't think her involvement was necessary. Other communities could better benefit from her limited available funding."

"So she just buys up buildings, fixes them up, and then what? Does she keep them?"

"It depends on the situation. If the towns just needed a boost, sometimes she'll donate the buildings to the town, or she'll sell them to the business owners at a reduced cost to encourage their ongoing success. There are some that she maintains, with the help of a property manager who oversees her existing portfolio."

"But we already have a potential buyer, the buildings aren't crumbling, and the town is doing great, so she's not interested."

"That's the gist. But I explained the situation, how many of the business owners were in danger of losing their spaces, which puts them in a precarious position, and she is willing to come out and meet with us."

"Well, that's something, at least."

"There's a hiccup, though. The only time she's available to come out is tomorrow afternoon, and I'm not available. I have an appointment with my financial advisor to look into my own viable options when it comes to the buildings. I tried to reschedule, but he's not available for another week, and we don't have that kind of time. Are you available to meet with her?"

Natalie swallowed. While she had no problem talking to her friends and neighbors, interacting with the public on a daily basis, she was not a public speaker. And she did not like the idea of the fate of the community resting on her shoulders. But what choice did she have? If she said no, they could lose their one chance to turn things around. "I can try."

Chris sat down next to her and took her hand. "I know it's nerve-wracking. And I really wish I could be here. But if she won't help us, my limited resources might be our only option."

"I know."

"You can do this, Natalie. You are smart, and strong, and you know what's going on here probably better than anyone. And it will be so much more powerful coming from one of the business owners who would be affected, especially one who grew up in this town and knows this community inside and out."

She knew he was right, even if she felt less than confident at the moment. "I'll do what I can."

Chris took a deep breath. "Okay. That's all I can ask. I'll let her know. I'll see if she can get here after the cafe is closed, so you don't have to worry about the business so much, but I don't know exactly what time she was thinking."

"Okay."

"Great. I'll touch base when I have more info." He stood up and pushed in the chair, then left the cafe.

Chapter 30

Wednesday dawned cold and blustery. The inspector had finished with the first building the day before, so it was business as usual at the cafe, but Natalie felt on edge all morning, worried about her meeting with the investor that afternoon. She hadn't heard from Chris except for a quick text that told her Lena Morseau would arrive at the cafe around 3 pm, and that left her wondering about him, too. When was the meeting with his financial advisor? What was he hoping would happen? If the investor wasn't interested, would he be able to bail them out? Was that putting too much pressure on him?

Natalie greeted and prepped and served and smiled, but she felt like she would explode with anticipation. Her staff knew what was going on, so they helped as best they could, but there wasn't anything they could do about the nerves.

"Do you want me to stay for the meeting with the investor?" Sylvie offered as they finished cleaning up.

Natalie considered for a moment but ultimately shook her head. "No, that's okay. I appreciate it, but I don't know how long this will take, and I don't want to keep you from your family." Sylvie usually spent time with her grandkids after school.

"Well, if you need me, I'm just a phone call away."

"Thanks, Sylvie. I really appreciate it."

Sylvie squeezed Natalie's shoulder, then retrieved her coat. "Good luck," she said as she left the cafe.

Natalie took a deep breath. She would need the luck. And what was she going to do for the next hour?

Deciding she might as well work on more holiday cookie dough while she waited, she went into the kitchen and started pulling out ingredients. Of course, that reminded her of the previous weekend, when she and Chris had been working together, and *that* sent her spiraling about Chris.

Natalie felt tears welling in her eyes. She just wanted her nice, simple, happy life back. She wanted her cafe and her apartment and her friends and her peace of mind. This rollercoaster of emotions and uncertainty over the future was just too much.

She wasn't in a cookie mood. Cookies were for happy, cheerful times, when she was hopeful and looking forward to the coming holidays. No, today, she needed to punch some bread dough. She adjusted the ingredients she had out, washed her hands, and started making her favorite bread base. Depending on how the meeting went, she could either go sweet with a cinnamon swirl or savory with rosemary and garlic. But either way, she would have something delicious to enjoy later. Just the thought helped calm her nerves.

She had just set the dough aside to rise when she heard the knock on the front door. She quickly rinsed her hands and went to answer the door, drying her hands as she went.

The woman looked friendly and greeted Natalie with a smile, which helped settle the butterflies in her stomach. "Hello. You must be Natalie. I am Lena Morseau." The woman held out her hand, and Natalie adjusted her dishcloth so she could shake the woman's hand.

"Welcome. Please, come in. It's brutal out there."

"Yes, it looks like winter is on its way."

"It certainly does. Can I take your coat? I'm not sure if you wanted to sit and discuss things here, or if you had wanted to walk around and check out the buildings or town." Natalie gave a nervous laugh. "I don't know how this kind of meeting usually goes."

Lena smiled warmly. "Every meeting is different. Why don't we have a seat and chat for a bit, then we can take a look around?"

"Okay." Natalie gestured toward a set of plush chairs against one wall with a side table between them. "Would you be more comfortable here?"

"That looks great."

"Can I get you something to drink? Coffee? Tea?"

Lena held up a hand and shook her head. "I'm fine, thanks."

"Okay."

They sat down, and Natalie really wished Chris was there to guide things. She didn't do stuff like this. She was better in the kitchen or behind a counter, not representing a town or group of business owners in front of an investor.

Lena removed her coat and rested it over the arm of her chair. "Now, Natalie, from what Chris has told me, you're struggling with the sale of your building and a few other properties in town, is that correct?"

Natalie nodded, wiping her hands on her pants. "Yes. I'm not the owner, but the owner is selling the properties she and her husband own, and the person who's looking to buy them doesn't exactly have the best interest of the current businesses in mind."

Lena nodded. "Chris said he's hoping to replace the current tenants with businesses he brings in."

"That's my understanding. I haven't actually spoken to him, but that's what Chris said."

"Okay. So what you and he are hoping is that I will purchase the properties as an investment and keep the current tenants in place, is that correct?"

It sounded so self-serving when Lena said it, but what could she say? It was the truth. "That is correct."

"Did Chris explain that I usually look for buildings and towns that need help, with dilapidation and safety concerns that affect the overall quality of life for the residents?"

"Yes. And I know we don't really qualify from that perspective. But if all of these businesses are kicked out of their spaces in favor of big companies or whatever, that will definitely affect the overall quality of life for residents moving forward. Not only will the current business owners lose their livelihoods, but many may have to move to start over or they'll just give up. We don't have a lot of available commercial space here in town. And the community we have here will suffer if we lose all these small businesses. We'll lose our identity, our close-knit camaraderie, our sense of self. We'll become just another town with the same businesses you can find anywhere. All in the name of making money and what I'm sure the buyer would call progress."

Lena cocked her head and assessed Natalie. Natalie felt like squirming, but she did her best to sit still. "I can tell you feel very passionately about this."

"Damn straight, if you'll pardon the language. I grew up in this town. There's something special about it. Even after I went to college, I felt the need to come back because I knew that nowhere else would feel like home. We are Pine Valley. We may be small, but we are mighty, and that mightiness comes from our community, our ability to work together and help each other. If we let big investors come in and ruin who we are, we'll all have lost something special."

"Okay," Lena dipped her head in a nod. "Let's take a look around."

Natalie gave her a tour of the cafe, led her upstairs to take a peek at the row of apartments, then back downstairs to visit Courtney and Josh. Then they bundled up and walked to the other buildings, which sat on streets a couple of blocks away.

Lena met with all of the business owners who were available and examined the buildings with a critical eye. When they arrived back at the cafe, they were both chilled, and Natalie made them cups of tea.

"I'm sure Chris explained there's also another property, a residential space that's zoned for an apartment building. There used to be an apartment building on it, but the owner neglected the property, and it collapsed a year or so ago."

Lena's eyebrows raised in surprise. "I was aware of the property but not the story behind it. What happened?"

Natalie brought their tea back to the chairs they had been sitting at earlier and settled into her seat. "The owner of the properties, Don Malloy, is what you would call a hands-off landlord. As long as you paid your rent on time, he left you alone. Unfortunately, that also tended to extend to problems that really needed attention. In the case of the apartment building, from what I understand there was a serious water issue that caused structural damage. And, rather than address the problem when it first happened, he decided to bring someone in to do a patch job and bribed officials to approve the inspection. The repair didn't hold, and the entire building ended up collapsing last fall."

"Oh my. And this is the same person who owns the other buildings?"

Natalie nodded. "Yeah. We haven't had anything like that happen here, though, and the buildings are currently being inspected for the potential buyer I had mentioned. So far, I know there was a minor electrical issue he's found, but I don't know if there's anything else. Chris might have more details. The inspector was going to keep him posted." She took a sip of her tea.

"What happened to the landlord? Is he selling to avoid future issues?"

Natalie shook her head. "He went to jail. Negligence and manslaughter. A man ended up dying from injuries he got in the collapse. Lots of other people got hurt, too."

"Oh my goodness. That's horrible."

"Yeah." Natalie sighed. "The whole town was pretty shaken up." She took a deep breath. "When he went to jail, his wife took over the properties, and she's the one who decided to sell. I think she wants to leave town. Can't say I blame her."

Lena leaned back in her seat and processed for a moment as she sipped her tea. Then she put the mug down and leaned forward. "Okay, Natalie, here's the situation. I am not a solo investor. I created a foundation to help with the revitalization goals I mentioned, to help small towns. The foundation is relatively new, only a couple of years, and there is a board of investors who help me identify and select projects. Even if I decide this is something I would like us to pursue, I would need the board's approval."

Natalie nodded. "Okay."

Lena nodded once. "Based on the history with the landlord, I may be able to make a case that there is concern for the future prosperity of the buildings and town, that there will need to be work done to ensure the structural integrity of all the buildings. But I'm not sure they'll go for it, since it does deviate from our usual objective. What is the current status of the former apartment building?"

"I think Chris said they had cleaned up the site. It still had debris and crime scene tape from the collapse, but it sounds like it's been cleaned up, so it should just be an empty space with a parking lot now."

"Okay. Rebuilding the apartment building may better align with the foundation's vision, but I know that does not help the small businesses who would be affected by the new owner. Let me see what I can do. I'm going to drive around the town a bit, since it is much too cold for more walking, and see what I can figure out. I have the address for the apartment site, but I want to get a feel for the town in general, too. Keep in mind, as a relatively new foundation, we have limited funds for taking on projects. And we have had other proposals presented. The board will be meeting after the Thanksgiving break to determine our next project. I will let you and Chris know what we decide."

Lena stood up and put her coat back on.

"Thank you so much for your time, Ms. Morseau," Natalie said, standing up as well.

"My pleasure. I have enjoyed meeting you and the other business owners and learning about Pine Valley. I do think you have something special here, and it would be a shame for that to be taken away."

"Thank you."

Natalie walked Lena to the front door, and they said their farewells. She had done the best she could. Now all they could do was wait.

Chapter 31

"So here's the deal," Chris's financial advisor Tony said, "most of your assets aren't liquid. They're tied up in stocks, bonds, an IRA. You would need to sell to get cash money you could use for the downpayment, and that doesn't happen instantly. It will take at least a day or two to get everything taken care of, and with the holiday, even longer. And I strongly discourage you from liquidating everything, especially the IRA. While this would be your first property purchase, it's an investment property, not a first home, so you'll get penalized." He took several papers out of a folder on his desk. "I printed out the values of your accounts as of this morning. Of course, the value will fluctuate based on how the market does before you sell, but this will give you a rough idea."

Chris looked over the paperwork, but he was having trouble focusing. How was Natalie doing with the investor? Did he even need to be going through all this? Did he want to? He had been so sure in the beginning, confident in his ability to manage a property as well as he sold them. But there was so much more at stake than he had realized. He had thought it would be easy money, not a lifeline for multiple small businesses and town residents.

He leaned back in his chair. "Okay, Tony, be honest with me. Do you think I should do this? Should I buy these properties?"

Tony leaned back in his own chair. "From an investment standpoint, property is usually a pretty safe bet. They're in a good area, property values are on the rise, and you have reliable, long-term tenants. However, to purchase all three would be stretching yourself thinner than I would recommend. Even if you liquidated everything but the IRA you would have enough for the purchase price on maybe one of the smaller properties. Anything beyond that, and you'll need a business loan. And if the market tanks or your tenants start abandoning ship, you'll end up with high payments that you can't cover. I suggest purchasing one, *maybe* the two smaller ones at most, keeping a cushion in your investment accounts, keep your IRA intact, and sell no more than seventy-five percent of your stocks and bonds. Hopefully over time you'll be able to rebuild the accounts, but in the meantime, you'll have a backup if something happens."

Like if I lose my job, Chris couldn't help but think. Tony was basically just confirming what he had already figured out on his own.

"If you're interested in investing in real estate, this isn't a bad way to start. And if you go with the smaller buildings without the apartments, the maintenance should be relatively straightforward. Residential spaces can bring a lot of headaches."

Those buildings wouldn't help Natalie, though. And as much as he cared about the other business owners and the town in general, Natalie was his top priority, especially with her space being one of the first on the chopping block. But was he ready to take on the responsibility?

"Okay. I'll have to think about what I want to do. In the meantime, though, let's start selling some of these stocks, get some money in the bank. Chances are I'm going to need it for something."

"Okay. If you can give me a target amount you'd like to have in the bank, I'll review the accounts and see what makes the most sense to sell."

They discussed details, then Chris thanked Tony and said goodbye. He needed to make a decision, and fast. He would need to apply for a business loan, and he needed to know how much to ask for. But, more importantly, he needed to figure out if buying a building was what he really wanted to do.

First, though, he needed to see Natalie. He needed to know how the meeting had gone, and he needed to see how she was holding up.

Driving to Pine Valley was the longest half hour of his life. He kept running scenarios through his head, trying to figure out what to do. He understood what Tony had been saying about starting with the smaller buildings. But he also knew that buying the biggest building would have the greatest impact. Of course, it was also the most expensive. And there was no guarantee he would get a business loan to cover the rest of the amount, though he was pretty confident he would get it. As long as he didn't lose his job.

Chris ran a hand through his hair. Part of him hoped the investor would swoop in and save the day, but part of him wanted to be Natalie's knight in shining armor. And he wanted to feel like a part of this town, this community. If he bought the building, he would be forever tied to Pine Valley and Natalie. That was the biggest draw of all.

The cafe was almost dark when he pulled into the parking lot, the only light coming from the holiday garland hung around the dining area. The sun was starting to set, and streetlights with their holiday decorations were starting to turn on. It was still cold and windy, and Chris was reluctant to leave the warmth of the car. But he had to see Natalie. He texted her to see if she was available. To his surprise, she said she was in the cafe.

He crossed the street and knocked on the door to the cafe. Natalie approached the door like a ghost, emerging from the dim light into the glow of the single bulb over the door. She opened the door for him, let him pass, then closed and locked the door behind them. He saw her discreetly wipe her eyes as she turned.

"Hey, have you been crying?" he asked, placing a hand on Natalie's shoulder.

She shrugged and sniffed.

He couldn't help it. He pulled her close and wrapped her in his arms. "I take it the meeting didn't go well?"

She didn't speak right away, but after a moment she pulled back and released a breath. "The woman was very nice, and she seemed sympathetic to our cause. But she had doubts that the foundation would select our project because the buildings and town weren't in dire straits. I guess they focus on places that really need help, not just business owners who don't want to lose their spaces."

"We knew it was a long shot. Did she give a definite 'no?'"

"No, she said the board was meeting after the holiday and that she would be in touch. But it wasn't exactly confidence-boosting." She stepped out of his embrace and wrapped her arms around herself. He immediately felt the loss. "How did your meeting go?"

"About as expected. My advisor doesn't recommend purchasing more than one property, or the two smaller ones at most. He thinks it will stretch me too thin and put me in a precarious position. But we're going to start liquidating my assets so I can try for something, at least."

Natalie walked to one of the plush chairs against the wall. He followed and sat in the chair beside her. Neither suggested turning on more light, and Chris found that he liked it here in the soft glow. It wasn't an intimidating space, and sitting in the dim light with Natalie felt intimate. He wondered if she felt it, too, that closeness, that warmth.

"If I have to move, maybe I'll find a place with a fireplace. I've always wanted a fireplace for the cafe." Leave it to Natalie to look for the silver lining.

"I can start looking for spaces with fireplaces if you want."

"There's no place available in Pine Valley. I've already checked." She sniffled. "Well, no commercial spaces, anyway. I would have to convert a house or something, and I just don't have the energy for that right now."

He nodded, even though she probably couldn't see him. "I get that. For what it's worth, I'm sorry."

"It's not your fault. You've been doing everything you can. I just don't know what to do."

"Me neither."

They sat in silence for a few moments. Chris could hear the ticking of a clock over the counter and the wind blowing against the side of the building.

"I've been doing a lot of thinking today," Natalie said after a couple of minutes had passed. "And I think you should buy the other buildings."

Chris turned to face Natalie, surprised. He could just make out her silhouette in the shadows. "What? Why?"

"Courtney and Josh still have a long time on their leases, so they'll be fine for a bit, long enough to figure something out if necessary. I don't think the apartments will be a problem. So it's just me in this building. There are more people at risk in the other buildings. I know the florist has already been struggling, and their lease expires in February. The Art Spot is just getting settled. I don't know when the lease expires, but it would be hard for Addy to have to move after everything she's been through. I just...I have been so focused on my own problems, that I haven't been looking at the big picture. And, while I would love to save everyone, I need to think about what would make the most sense overall. I have money in the bank. I'll be okay for a little while until I figure out what to do."

"My advisor suggested I start with one of the other buildings, too. He said residential spaces get more complicated."

"Well, there you go then."

"But, Natalie, you're the one I care most about. You're the one who made me want to do all this in the first place. You showed me how special this little town is, and how important it is to look out for the little guy. How could I possibly abandon you?"

"It's not abandoning me if I'm telling you to do it, Chris."

"I won't let you be a martyr, Natalie. You deserve better than that."

"I don't deserve more than anyone else. I'll figure it out."

He didn't know what else to say. She sounded so hopeless, so resigned to her fate. He had to believe there was still a way out of this. "I'm not giving up," he said finally.

She didn't respond for a while. Then she took a deep breath and stood up. "Well, I'm exhausted. I think it's time for me to head home."

"Okay." He stood up, too. He knew when he was being dismissed. "Do you have plans for Thanksgiving tomorrow? I assume the cafe is closed?"

"Yeah, we're closed. I might go to Maggie's. Or just hang around binging something on Netflix. I'm not feeling very thankful at the moment."

"Even if we don't find a solution, I'm still thankful for meeting you."

She looked up at him. "Yeah, I guess that part's been pretty decent." He could make out a half smile.

Chris held up a hand and cupped Natalie's cheek. Even if she had turned down his date invitation, she felt something. He could tell. Why was she holding back? After a moment's hesitation, he leaned forward and pressed his lips to hers.

She returned the kiss for a few heart-stopping seconds before pulling back. "I think you should go," she said, her voice raspy.

He took a step back. "Okay. I hope you have a good day tomorrow." And he left the cafe without another word.

Natalie released a gasping sob after the door closed behind Chris. What was she doing? It had been a long, trying day, and she was letting her emotions get the better of her. She had too much going on right now to even think about starting a relationship, especially when it probably wouldn't even work out.

She took a few deep breaths, trying to calm herself down. What she needed now was a hot bath and a good cry. Then maybe she could think a bit more rationally about things.

Natalie made sure everything was locked up for the night, turned off the holiday lights, then headed out the back entrance to go upstairs. After the dimness of the cafe, it took her eyes a moment to adjust to the brightness of the hallway, so she closed her eyes and took another deep breath before opening them again and heading for the staircase.

She had almost reached the top when the power cut out. She reached for the railing but couldn't find it in the sudden dark. Crying out, she fell.

Chapter 32

Natalie came to when she heard the sirens. She was lying on the floor of the dark hallway with Maggie by her side. The only light came from a flashlight someone had rested on the staircase.

"Oh, Natalie, thank goodness," Maggie said, clasping her hand. "We were so worried."

"What happened?" Natalie asked, trying to sit up. Her head was killing her.

"Best we can figure, you fell down the stairs. After the power went out, Jordan heard a loud thud and came out to investigate. He found you at the bottom of the staircase."

Natalie looked around and found Jordan standing against the side wall. He held up a hand in a wave. She had never been so glad he was her neighbor.

"He called 911 and then called me."

"Thanks, Jordan," Natalie said.

"No problem."

The paramedics came in through the back door of the hallway with a stretcher. Natalie tried to sit up again, but her head was still pounding, so she laid back down.

The next few minutes passed in a blur as the paramedics checked her vitals and looked her over for any visible abrasions.

"Vitals seem okay," one of them finally said. "But you've got a nasty bump on your head, and you should really get checked out, especially since you were unconscious for a bit."

"Okay," Natalie accepted, then she lay awkwardly while they loaded her onto the stretcher. She turned to look at Maggie. "I hate to ask, but would you mind coming with me?" Her lower lip began to wobble. "I don't know who else to ask."

Maggie squeezed Natalie's hand. "Of course. I was going to offer anyway." She turned toward Jordan. "Jordan, can you please call Richard and let him know I'm going with Natalie to the hospital? I'll give him a call when I get a chance."

"No problem, Miss Maggie," Jordan replied, taking out his cell phone.

The paramedics rolled Natalie out to the ambulance and lifted her into the back. Maggie climbed in after it.

Natalie had never been in an ambulance before. She had never been in the hospital, either. What a day this had turned out to be. She felt on the verge of tears, strapped onto a stretcher, surrounded by intimidating equipment.

"Now, now," Maggie said, patting her hand again. "You'll be okay. I admit you had me worried when we couldn't wake you up, but you'll be fine now."

"Oh, Maggie. It has been such a rough week."

"I know. You had the inspection, and I've seen you gallivanting all over the town with different people. You've been a busy bee."

"You don't know the half of it."

"Well, I'm sure we'll have plenty of time when we're waiting for doctors to catch me up."

Natalie sniffled. Maggie had become one of her closest friends over the last several years, since she had started the cafe after her mother died. Maggie had been a fountain of knowledge and support, and Natalie trusted and respected her more than just about anyone. Maggie had become like a second mother to her. But Maggie's life had been busy and full lately, and Natalie hadn't wanted to burden her with all the drama. Maybe it was time. She could really use a mom right now.

By the time they arrived at the hospital and got settled in a room, Natalie was exhausted. But Maggie had been tasked with keeping her awake until they could run tests, so Natalie did her best to keep her eyes open. Once they completed her CT scan, she should be able to get some rest. She hoped.

"Okay," Maggie said when the admitting doctor had left the room. "I'm guessing we're going to have some time before they'll wheel you in for your test, and you have to stay awake, so let's chat."

Natalie sighed. Where did she even begin?

"Now, I know the building is up for sale. And you said there was a potential buyer, so an inspector was coming. But you haven't given me much detail, so I'm thinking there's something else going on, or at least it's not as straightforward as all that."

"I didn't want to burden you."

"Burden me? I am here for you, sweetie. You are never a burden."

"But you have the diner, and Richard, and the baby. I know you've loved being a grandma, and I didn't want to burst the bubble of your perfect life right now."

"There is no bubble to burst. Nothing is ever perfect."

"Huh. You're the second person to tell me that this week."

"Well, it's true. Life is always full of ups and down, and even something that looks perfect from the outside has its imperfections up close. So, now that we've gotten that out of the way, give me all the dirt."

Natalie laughed softly, then put a hand to her head. It hurt to laugh. "Well, Chris – that's the real estate agent selling the buildings – "

"The one who met up with you that night in the diner. I remember."

"Yeah. Him. Well, he found out that the person who wants to buy the buildings wants to bring in his own tenants and kick all the small businesses out."

"What?" Maggie looked outraged. "Can he even do that? Like, is it legal?"

"Once a tenant's lease is expired, a seller doesn't have to renew. And, unfortunately, at least a few of us are up for renewal very soon."

"Oh, Natalie."

"Yeah. So Chris was trying to find a different buyer for the buildings, someone who wouldn't kick us all out. But he hasn't been having much luck."

"So it's a done deal? This guy is definitely buying the buildings?"

"Not a done deal, but pretty close to it. He hired the inspector, and if all goes well with the inspection, he will most likely put in an offer. And I can't see Colleen Malloy turning down any reasonable offer."

"Okay, so I've seen Chris around, and someone I'm pretty sure was the inspector. Who are the other people you've been gallivanting with?"

Natalie attempted a deep breath. "Chris got in trouble with his boss because he was basically undermining the sale, so he lost the listings. The new guy, Eric, was wandering around yesterday. And earlier today, a potential investor Chris found was checking out the buildings to see if her foundation could help us out." Had it really been just today? It seemed like so long ago.

"I take it she can't help?"

"Another thing that's not set in stone, but it's not looking good."

"No other possibilities?"

"Chris was thinking about buying one of the buildings, but he hasn't decided yet."

"Hmm. Sounds like this Chris guy has been trying pretty hard to help."

"Yeah, he has." Natalie could feel tears welling in her eyes again.

"Why do I get the impression that something else is going on here?"

The tears came in earnest then, and even Natalie's aching head couldn't keep them at bay.

"Oh, sweetie, what is it?" Maggie tried to wrap Natalie in a hug, an awkward attempt at best with Natalie in a hospital bed.

"I like him, Maggie. I really like him. And he likes me too, or at least seems to."

"Then what's the problem?"

Natalie wiped her eyes and sniffled. "Do you remember Jamison?"

"Who?"

"Back when I came home from college. I had a boyfriend. His name was Jamison."

"Oh, yes, that's right. I seem to remember something about him. He didn't stick around long, though."

Longer than Maggie remembered, but not nearly long enough. "We had been together for most of college. We were talking about the future, getting married, kids, the whole bit. He knew that I wanted to come back to Pine Valley, and he said he had no problem with that. It seemed like a great place to raise a family, all that. So after graduation, I came back here, and he and I got an apartment."

Maggie listened in silence, nodding in acknowledgement.

"Jamison had grown up in a city. Not a big city, but certainly a far cry from Pine Valley. And after six months of living together, he decided he couldn't take the quiet. He needed more action, more hustle and bustle or whatever. He gave me an ultimatum, either Pine Valley or him." Natalie swept a hand in front of her. "We both know what I chose."

"That must have been very difficult for you."

"It was. I loved him. I thought we wanted the same things, that we would raise a family and grow old together. But he was just telling me what I wanted to hear."

"That must have been painful. But I'm not sure what it has to do with Chris."

"Chris is used to cities and big suburbs, big companies and hustle and driving fancy cars and dressing up to impress people. That's his life, his world. He might want to help the little guy while he's here, but once the drama of the sale is over, the novelty will wear off, and he won't be happy here. Just like Jamison. I don't want to get my hopes up and fall for a guy who will just leave me."

"Oh, sweetie."

"It is what it is. I'll get over him. It will just take some willpower until he leaves."

"And if he doesn't leave? If he buys one of the buildings and sticks around?"

"Buying a building doesn't necessarily mean he'll be here much. He could just as easily have a property manager handle everything."

"True. But he also isn't Jamison. Maybe you're not giving him enough credit."

"I can't take that chance. It hurt too much last time."

"I get it. I do. And I hate you're going through this."

Silence fell, and Natalie tried to get her emotions in check. While she was glad to get it all off her chest, she hated feeling like this – vulnerable and anxious, waiting for the other shoe to drop. The possibility of losing her cafe was already more than she felt equipped to handle. To think about losing Chris on top of that was just too much.

The doctor walked in to take Natalie for her CT scan, and she was grateful for the reprieve. It was much easier to focus on physical ailments than emotional ones.

<h1 style="text-align:center">Chapter 33</h1>

Chris wasn't close to his parents, and considering they had retired to France, he had no plans to see them for Thanksgiving. In the past he had sometimes gotten together with friends for a day of food and football, but his friend group included Eric, and he was in no mood to spend time with him. That meant Chris had a full day of nothing ahead of him. He would probably put on the game, but that wasn't until later, and he didn't know if he would be able to follow the action anyway.

He found himself wandering aimlessly, unable to settle on anything. He wanted to be with Natalie. He wanted to pick up where they had left off the night before. From what she had said, it didn't sound like she had definite plans for the day. Would she be upset if he called her? Maybe he could text. He had to connect with her in some way; it was the only thing his mind would be happy with. Maybe a simple holiday greeting. She couldn't be upset with that, could she?

Happy Thanksgiving

He threw in a turkey emoji for good measure.

When she didn't reply right away, he began pacing. This was ridiculous. What was wrong with him?

You too

Okay, it wasn't much, but it was a reply at least.

> What are you up to today?

> Apparently spending time in the hospital

Wait. What? She was in the hospital? Was *she* in the hospital? Or was she visiting someone in the hospital?

> What happened???

The dots indicating she was typing lasted way too long. He needed answers.

> Fell down the stairs last night when the apartment building lost power

> Are you ok?

> I have a concussion but nothing major

Thank every heavenly being that had ever existed.

> How long do you have to be in the hospital?

> I could technically be released today but I have nowhere to go. I need to be monitored for 24 hours

> I'll watch you

He hadn't even thought before he typed. It was a no brainer, as far as he was concerned. He had nothing going on. Heck, even if he had a day full of plans, he would cancel them. She needed him.

> I can't ask you to do that

> You didn't ask. I offered

Would it be better to bring her here or take her to her apartment? She would probably want to be around the comforts of home, but could she handle the stairs? His building had an elevator. But she might consider it presumptuous of him to invite her back to his apartment. Not that he would ever even consider taking advantage of an injured woman.

She didn't answer for a long time, and Chris was beginning to think he had gone too far. He had been nervous to even text her in the first place, for crying out loud. Offering to spend the day with her as she recovered from a concussion was a huge step past that.

While he waited, he decided to pack some things into a duffle bag. If she agreed, and they ended up going back to her apartment, he would need some clothes and things for himself. If she didn't agree, he could always unpack them later. He had just stuck a book in the bag and zipped it up when his phone dinged.

ok

It was a long wait for two letters, but they were the sweetest message he had ever received.

on my way. let me know where

Hartford hospital. ask for me at the desk

He had never been so anxious to leave his apartment.

—ele—

Natalie lay staring at the ceiling, wondering what on earth she had gotten herself into. Maggie had stayed with her for a good part of the night, but she always held special Thanksgiving dinner events at the diner, and there was no way Natalie would let her miss it. So she had left around midnight with a promise she would check in when she could.

Without someone to watch her, she figured she would be spending the day in the hospital. She certainly wasn't going to call Courtney or Joey or anyone else and mess up their Thanksgiving plans.

Chris's text had felt like a blessing and a warning. After the emotional roller-coaster of the day before, she didn't know if she could handle spending the day with him. But how could she deny herself the time with him? Maggie had encouraged her to talk with him, discuss her concerns, and see what he was thinking and feeling. It didn't hurt that she really didn't want to spend the day in the hospital.

She told the nurse that she had someone available to pick her up and monitor her, so the paperwork was being filled out while she waited for Chris to arrive. When he appeared in her doorway, she almost burst into tears. The look in his eyes was so tender, so full of concern.

"Hey," he said softly. "How are you feeling?"

"Like I fell down a flight of stairs."

He approached the bed and sat down in the chair beside it. "How are you besides the concussion?"

"Sore. Some bumps and bruises. Nothing to worry about."

"That's good, at least."

"Yeah."

She felt awkward with him. She was so vulnerable right now, both physically and emotionally, and after their kiss the night before she wasn't sure how to act around him. Maybe this had been a mistake after all.

The nurse walked in before she could tell Chris she had changed her mind. She held Natalie's discharge paperwork as she pushed a wheelchair.

Chris's eyes widened when he saw the wheelchair. "Does she really need to use the wheelchair?"

"Just a precaution," the nurse said with a smile. "Policy for discharging patients."

"Oh, okay." He turned back to Natalie. "Do you need help getting up?"

"No, I think I've got it." Natalie swung her legs off the side of the bed and scooted herself forward before tentatively standing up. She felt weak, unsteady, but Chris's hand grabbed her arm and held her up.

"I've got you. Just take it easy."

She looked up and met his gaze. "Thanks." This time she didn't think the dizziness was from the concussion. His look was so intense. She knew it didn't matter what she tried to tell herself. She was already head over heels for this man.

They lowered her into the wheelchair, and Chris took hold of the handles. For better or worse, she was in his hands now.

Chapter 34

With holiday traffic, it took them almost an hour to get to Pine Valley. After a somewhat awkward conversation, Natalie had indicated she would prefer to be home, and Chris didn't blame her. She had brushed off his concern about the stairs, insisting they would just take them slow.

Though Chris had walked around the property multiple times, it had never occurred to him to park in the lot at the back of the building when he came to Pine Valley. Maybe he just wanted an excuse to walk through the cafe. But today he had to choose the shortest path for Natalie, and that meant parking as close to the back door as possible so they could reach her apartment quickly.

He helped her out of the car and tucked an arm around her as they walked into the building. Though she insisted she was fine, he could tell she was shaky on her feet and nervous about going too quickly. Her body was tense, and she focused on her feet as she tentatively stepped through the hallway. At least the power had come back on. At the bottom of the stairs, she took a deep breath and looked up. Then she reached for the railing and took one step at a time.

She was panting by the time they reached her apartment. Chris continued to hold onto her as he took the keys from her trembling fingers and opened the apartment door.

The only times he had been here before were to show Matthew Townsend and Chuck around the building. At the time he had been focused on the task at hand, not the decor or the fact that this was Natalie's apartment. But when he stepped over the threshold, he breathed deeply. Much like the cafe, the apartment was warm and welcoming, filled with comfortable furnishings and pleasantly cheerful artwork. It was Natalie, and he felt instantly at peace.

Chris guided Natalie to the sofa, then returned to close and lock the door. "Can I get you anything? Water or something?"

Natalie closed her eyes and adjusted herself on the sofa. "Water would be good. Glasses are in the upper cabinet to the right of the sink. There's a pitcher in the fridge."

Chris poured them both glasses of water and brought them to the living room area. He placed them on the coffee table, then stood up. "I packed a duffle bag with some stuff I thought I might need. I'm going to go grab it. I'll be right back, okay?"

Natalie began to nod, then winced. "Okay," she said instead.

He grabbed the keys from where he had placed them on the kitchen table and hurried out the door. He didn't want to leave her unattended for any longer than necessary. The nurse had given him a list of things to look out for, and he was determined not to let Natalie down. He returned no more than five minutes later, slightly out of breath from running down and up the stairs. Natalie was exactly where he had left her, lying down with her eyes closed.

"I know you have to rest," he told her, "so I'll try not to bug you. But let me know if there's anything you need. Are you hungry or anything?"

Natalie partially opened her eyes. "Not really. They gave me breakfast at the hospital. But if you're hungry, help yourself to anything in the kitchen. I honestly don't know what I have. I haven't been shopping in a few days."

"I'm good for now. You just rest, and I'll be right here if you need me." Chris settled in an armchair that sat against the side wall beside the sofa. He was glad he had brought a book. He had his phone, too, of course, but he didn't want to make too much noise and disturb Natalie. He settled in to read, occasionally peering over to check on Natalie. After a few minutes, he could see her breathing had deepened into sleep.

Chris took a deep breath of his own. It was going to be a long day, but there was nowhere else he would rather be. Funny how this morning he had been antsy, bouncing from activity to activity, yet here he was, content with sitting still. Maybe he just needed Natalie to soothe his soul.

The day passed slowly and uneventfully. Around lunchtime Chris made himself an omelet since Natalie was still sleeping. When he brought it over to the living room, though, the scent seemed to wake her up. Soon after her cell phone dinged. Groggy, she slowly sat up and blinked her eyes open.

"What time is it?"

"About twelve thirty. Are you hungry?"

"I could eat."

"I made myself some eggs. There were still more in the carton, though. You want some of those? Or something else?"

"Eggs would be fine." She rubbed her eyes and reached for her phone.

"Here, have mine," Chris offered, handing her the plate he hadn't yet started. "Everything okay?" he asked, nodding toward the phone in her hand.

"Thanks. Yeah, it's just Maggie checking in." Natalie typed out a message, put the phone down, and picked up the plate. She took a couple of bites. "Mmm. Either I'm hungrier than I thought or you're a really good cook."

Chris grinned from where he stood back at the stove. "I know my way around a kitchen. But I can't make anything fancy, so don't go asking for cordon bleu or anything."

"Nah, I'm a simple gal. Meat and potatoes, some salad. None of that hoity toity stuff for me."

"Good to know." He finished up his own meal and brought it back to the living room. "I'm not much for fancy stuff either."

"No? You seem like the kind of guy who's used to eating at fancy restaurants and banquet dinners and all that."

Chris shrugged. "I've been to my fair share, but it's not my preferred way to dine. Give me home cooking any day."

Natalie looked at him, assessing him while she took another bite.

"What?" Chris asked.

She shook her head and winced. "Nothing. You're just not what I expected."

"I thought you knew me by now."

"I guess. Kind of. But we're always in the middle of some big drama, so it's hard to get a read on who you really are."

"Well, this is me." It occurred to him he was still wearing the sweatpants and t-shirt he had planned to spend the day in.

"Good to know."

They finished eating in silence, but it didn't feel awkward. Chris thought back to how he had been shortly after they had met, when he had been brainstorming ways to impress her. He never would have guessed that he would be sitting in her living room in sweatpants, eating eggs while she nursed a concussion. So much for impressing her. And yet, she seemed more at ease with him than she ever had. Was it just because of her injury?

"How are you feeling?" Chris asked once they had both finished eating. He picked up Natalie's plate and brought both to the kitchen sink.

"A little better, I think," Natalie said. She adjusted on the sofa but didn't lie down again.

"That's good. I'm not sure what you wanted to do this afternoon. I read that you're not supposed to focus on anything, so no TV or reading or anything, but I could put on some music, if you'd like. Or I wouldn't mind reading to you, if that's something you would be interested in."

"What would you read?"

"Whatever you want. I brought a book with me that I've been reading. I could start that one from the beginning, or if you have something here you'd like me to read, I can."

"What did you bring?"

"Just a classic sci-fi book that I've read a million times."

"Is that what you like to read? Sci-fi?"

Chris shrugged. "I like all kinds of things."

"Okay. There's a bookshelf in the corner with a bunch of my favorites. Take your pick."

Chris selected a suspense novel he had never read and settled back in his chair to read. They spent the afternoon lounging and reading. Chris had never felt so content.

Chapter 35

She could get used to having him in her apartment, Natalie mused as Chris continued to read. He had a soothing presence, and she felt cared for and protected. But he respected her space and her things, not taking over any more than necessary. Yes, it was nice to have him around. Too bad it wouldn't last.

She must have drifted off again, since the next thing she remembered was waking up to a knocking on the door.

"I'll get it," Chris said, getting up before Natalie could attempt to move.

When he opened the door, Natalie could see Maggie in the doorframe. Of course.

"Chris, right?" Maggie greeted with a smile.

"That's me."

"I'm Maggie, from the diner. Do you remember? We met that one time a couple of weeks back."

"I remember. How are you?" He stepped aside to let Maggie into the apartment.

"I'm doing just fine. How's our patient?" Maggie was carrying two plates covered in aluminum foil, and she placed them on the coffee table as she entered the living room.

"Shouldn't you be at the diner serving Thanksgiving dinner?" Natalie asked, adjusting into a sitting position.

"Things were winding down, and I wanted to check on you. I also brought you both a plate. I figured you wouldn't have the energy for making a full Thanksgiving meal."

"Thank you, Maggie, that was very nice of you." Natalie leaned forward and lifted the foil off one plate. "It smells delicious."

Chris stood hovering at the edge of the room, seeming uncertain where he belonged now that Maggie was here. Natalie smiled up at him, and he returned the smile, his shoulders easing.

"Actually, Maggie, since you're here, I was wondering if you could help me with something."

"Of course. What is it, sweetie?"

"I, um, need to use the facilities?" She didn't want to embarrass Chris, but it had been a concern of hers, if she would be able to get to the bathroom on her own. While she was sure he would do what he could, they were certainly not at that point in the relationship for him to help her on the toilet if needed.

"Of course! Do you need help standing?" Maggie held out her arms to support Natalie if needed.

She was able to stand up, wobbling only slightly, but she was grateful for Maggie's arms as they shuffled to the bathroom. "Be right back," Natalie called over her shoulder to Chris.

"I'll be here."

"So," Maggie asked once they were out of earshot of Chris. She lowered her voice. "That's Chris. How has it been?"

Natalie took a deep breath. "Surprisingly okay."

"Has he been taking good care of you?"

"Yeah, he really has. He's been considerate, and gentle." Natalie felt her lower lip tremble. She didn't want to cry.

"Oh, sweetie, that's a good thing."

"I know. But I was afraid of this. The closer we get, the harder it will be to let him go."

"Have you talked to him yet? About your concerns?"

"No, not yet."

"Maybe this is a good opportunity."

"Or it will make things awkward, and he'll want to leave."

They were standing in the bathroom now. "Do you need help with the rest?" Maggie asked.

"I think I'll be okay." The sink was close to the toilet, so she could use it for support.

"Okay. I'll wait right outside the door. Let me know if you need me."

Natalie sat for longer than necessary, trying to regain control of her emotions. She was torn between wanting to savor this time with Chris and wanting to keep her distance. But he had been so sweet, and the look in his eyes whenever he looked at her, with a mix of concern and affection, was wearing down her defenses.

When they returned to the living room, Chris was sitting in the armchair again. The plates remained untouched. *He waited for me*, Natalie couldn't help but think. *Even though he's probably starving.*

They chatted for a few more minutes before Maggie said goodbye and left. Natalie found herself strangely relieved when it was just her and Chris again. They had built a cozy cocoon here, and it was nice to have the place to themselves.

Chris removed the foil from their dinner plates and went into the kitchen to get silverware. "What would you like to drink?"

"I think I should probably stick with water. But there's some soda and iced tea and stuff if you want."

"I'm good with water." He poured two glasses and brought everything back to the living room.

"You know, it didn't even occur to me to ask if this was totally messing up your plans for the day. You probably had something better in mind."

"I had no plans," Chris said, placing the glasses on the table. "And I would have had no problem cancelling them if I did." He smiled at her.

"You don't get together with family or friends for Thanksgiving?"

Chris shrugged. "My parents live in France. I have no siblings. Sometimes I get together with friends, but I wasn't feeling it this year, especially since one of those supposed friends is Eric, and you know the story there."

"I'm sorry. That must be tough."

"Not really. This whole experience has been very eye-opening, and I'm not sorry about any of it."

They began eating.

"Wow, this is delicious," Chris said, taking another bite of turkey.

Natalie laughed softly. "Yeah, she does this every year. At Christmas, too. It's a big hit. I probably would have ended up there if this hadn't happened." She placed a hand on her head.

"You don't have any family or friends to spend Thanksgiving with?"

"My parents are gone. My brother and his family live up in Massachusetts. I've gotten together with them sometimes, but it can be a long day, since I have to be back for the cafe in the morning. I've done Thanksgiving with Chloe, but with everything going on with her parents, I knew that wouldn't work out this year. Courtney goes to Rhode Island to be with her family. Maggie's obviously at the diner. And, yeah, that's about it. I have other people I'm friendly with, but not close enough to spend Thanksgiving."

"Gotcha. Well, then, injury aside, I guess this worked out for both of us." He smiled at her, and her stomach did a flip.

"Yeah, I guess it did." They gazed at each other for a moment before Natalie cleared her throat. "Actually, that reminds me, with my not being at a hundred percent, I should probably give Joey a heads up. I need to make sure he's okay with doing most, if not all, of the baking tomorrow morning. And I should probably reach out to McKenna, too, see if she can help cover breakfast." She didn't want to think about the next day and the return to reality. And Chris leaving.

They finished eating in silence. Once they were done, Chris took their dishes to the kitchen to wash, and Natalie sent text messages to Joey and McKenna. Natalie glanced at the clock on the wall above the armchair. It wasn't very late, but usually she would be getting ready for bed about now. Four o'clock came very quickly.

But with all the napping she had been doing, she wasn't very tired. Her body was sore from the fall, but her head was starting to feel better, and she wanted to savor this time with Chris. What would the evening bring?

Her eyes drifted to the boxes of Christmas decorations sitting in the corner of the room. With Chris in the apartment, the holiday spirit felt like it was trying to emerge. She didn't know how much she would be able to accomplish, but maybe if Chris helped her, they could make at least a little progress in decorating. Then she would have something to remember after he left.

Chapter 36

They hadn't discussed the rest of the night, and Chris felt nervous bringing it up. Technically the twenty-four hours of observation was up, but he didn't feel comfortable leaving Natalie alone. Sure, she had been doing fine all day, but that didn't mean she couldn't take a turn. Plus, if he was being honest, he just didn't want to leave her, regardless of how she was feeling. This had been his best Thanksgiving in a long time.

But just because he wanted to be there didn't mean Natalie wanted him there. And if she was feeling better, she might want her space back. Not to mention that spending the night was a whole different ballgame compared to spending the day. As intimate as their day had been, cozied up in her apartment on their own, night brought a new level of intimacy, filled with pajamas and where to sleep and the quiet stillness of the night. Would it be too intimate for Natalie's comfort? Maybe they should have asked if Maggie could stay.

He finished washing the dishes and was about to return to the living room area when Natalie called out, "If you're interested in dessert, I have some day-old items from the cafe in the bread box."

Chris grinned and called back. "You don't have to tell me twice." He opened the bread box and pulled out a container filled with an assortment of cookies and pastries, then brought the container back to the living room.

They sat and indulged, content in the companionable silence.

After a few moments, Natalie cleared her throat. "I was wondering if you might be willing to help me with something."

"Of course. What do you need?"

Natalie looked down and picked at the blanket on her lap. She looked nervous, or shy. "I, um, usually decorate my apartment for Christmas about now. Well, actually, I usually have things up before Thanksgiving, but this year has not been usual. So I was going to try to do it this weekend, and, well..."

"I would be happy to help. What would you like me to do?"

Natalie gestured toward a pile of boxes against one wall of the living room. "The decorations are in there. I have a tree that would need to be assembled, and then garland and stuff."

"No problem." Chris wiped his hands on a napkin, then stood up and walked over to the boxes. He didn't know the first thing about decorating, but he found he was actually looking forward to this unexpected project. "Start with the tree?"

"That would be good. Not sure I could manage that on my own in my current state, and it is the most important." Natalie attempted a smile, then stood up on shaky legs and walked slowly over to join him, arms out to keep her balance. "The bottom one has the tree."

Chris separated the boxes from the stack, and Natalie gently brought herself to a sitting position on the floor. She opened the box that held the tree.

"It has the pole and the branches. Have you ever put one together before?"

Chris shook his head. His family had always had a real tree, brought in by someone they hired and decorated with the usual assortment of glass balls, shiny garland, and lights.

"The poles go into the base, just like with a real tree. And then the branches go into the notches on the poles." Natalie directed him, helping to pull out the appropriate branches as he needed them. By the time the tree was assembled, she was visibly exhausted. "I think that's going to have to be it for now. But thank you."

"Of course." Chris stood back and looked at the tree he had assembled. "It's looking pretty pathetic, though."

Natalie laughed, then put up one hand to her head with the pain. "The branches need to be fluffed up a bit. That will make it look better."

"Oh, okay." He reached out and tentatively moved a couple of branches apart. It would take some doing, but he could see how it worked. After pulling apart a few branches, he stepped back again and cleared his throat, not wanting to look at Natalie. "At the risk of making things awkward, we should probably discuss what you want to do from here."

"What do you mean?" Natalie asked, still sitting on the floor beside the boxes.

"Uh, about tonight. You seem to be doing okay, so I didn't know if you wanted me to stay or if I should go." He turned to look at Natalie.

Natalie picked at the corner of one of the boxes. "I hadn't really thought about it. I thought you had planned on staying. I mean, you brought a bag and all that."

"I can definitely stay. I did pack things just in case. I just wasn't sure. I mean, the required observation time is over, so I didn't know if you wanted me out of your hair."

"Do you want to go? You don't have to stay if you don't want to."

Chris paused, waiting for Natalie to meet his gaze. Then he knelt down beside her and took her hands in his. "I want to stay. But I don't want to make you uncomfortable. You've seemed to want to hold me at arm's length, so I wasn't sure what you wanted."

Natalie sighed. "Help me up."

He pulled her to a standing position, then placed an arm around her as they walked back to the sofa. Once she was seated comfortably, he returned to the chair beside her.

Natalie leaned back on the sofa and looked down at her hands. "I want to tell you a story."

"Okay..."

"It's about a girl and a boy." She paused, taking a deep breath. "The girl grew up in a small town, and she loved that small town. But she knew she had to go to college to learn what she should to have a secure future. So she did. And while she was at college, she met a boy. And they fell in love. They talked about getting married and buying a house and having a family, all the usual growing up stuff. And the boy knew that the girl wanted to move back to the small town. He assured her that was fine with him, that he would be happy there, and they would do everything they had planned to do."

Natalie paused again, but Chris stayed silent. The story was obviously not over yet. After a few moments, Natalie resumed, emotion clogging her voice.

"After college, they moved to the small town and lived together, starting the life they had planned. But the boy had grown up in a big town, with lots of things to see and do. And he began to get bored. And resentful. And he started dropping hints, subtle at first but then more obvious, until finally he made the girl choose. If she wanted to have a future with him, she had to leave the small town she loved so much. She was torn. She loved the boy very much, but she realized that she wouldn't be happy someplace else, and he wouldn't be happy in the small town. So the boy left, and the girl stayed. And she built a life she loved and was happy for a while."

Another pause. Natalie wouldn't look at him, continuing to look down at her hands, which were now fiddling with a blanket.

"She was happy for a while," Natalie repeated. "But then another boy came along. And he made her feel things she hadn't felt in a long time. But this new boy also came from a big town, and he already had a big, fancy life. The girl was scared..." Natalie sniffled. "The girl was scared that this new boy would want to leave, too. And she didn't want to fall in love just to have it taken away again."

Natalie fell silent, and Chris took a deep breath. He understood not wanting to get hurt. And he couldn't blame her for questioning if they had a future. He had no idea what the future held, and not just because of the building getting sold. Did he still have a job? Did he still want his job? Was he happy leaving and staying away from Pine Valley? Would he be happy staying here? He had no real assurances to offer. All he knew was that he cared about Natalie. And he didn't want to lose her. But what could he say?

"Thank you for sharing your story," Chris said once he had processed everything. "I understand you're scared, and I don't blame you. That must have been horrible." He sighed. "I don't know what the future holds, Natalie. But I do know I want you in mine, if you'll have me."

She looked up then, meeting his gaze with watery eyes. "I don't know if I can handle that."

Chris took another deep breath. "Okay. Well, then, we'll take things one day at a time. And we'll see if the future becomes clearer. But for now, I'd like to stay. Just as friends, because I care about you and want to make sure you're okay. Would that be alright?"

Natalie nodded slowly. "I'd like that."

"Good. Now did you want to stay up a bit longer, or get ready for bed?"

"I'd like to stay up a bit longer, if that's okay."

"Of course it's okay. I'd stay up with you all night if you wanted."

She gave him a wobbly smile. "I don't think that will be necessary. But maybe we could put on a movie?"

"Are you up to that? With your head?"

"I think so. I'll close my eyes and just listen if I have to."

"Okay." He reached for the remote that lay on the side table between the sofa and chair.

"Do you want to come sit on the sofa with me to watch it?" Natalie asked.

"I'd like that," Chris replied, meeting her gaze. Baby steps. He could do baby steps. And hope that everything worked out.

Chapter 37

Natalie awoke to the beeping of her alarm. She groaned. Joey would be there soon, and she couldn't just leave everything to him. But, while her head was definitely feeling better, her body still ached, and she didn't know how much use she would be. Her doctor had also warned her not to jump into normal activities right away. Her brain needed time to heal, and even if it didn't hurt, she wouldn't have the same focus or mental stamina she was used to.

But she needed to get up. She needed to use the bathroom, and, she realized with a groan, she should really take a shower. Was she up for it? She was definitely *not* going to ask for Chris's help with that. And it was much too early to bother Maggie for help. Could she manage it on her own? She would have to figure it out later because she *really* had to get up.

She slid her feet from the bed to the floor. Wait. How had she gotten in her bed? Last she remembered, she and Chris had been watching a movie on the sofa. Had she fallen asleep? Had he brought her here? She was still in the clothes she had worn yesterday, so at least that wasn't something to worry about. She would have to ask him. But for now, priorities.

She felt a little unsteady on her feet, but with a deep breath and holding her arms out for balance, she was able to make it from her bed to the doorway. From there she could hold onto a wall for at least some support. Once in the hallway, she looked toward the living room.

The tree they had assembled stood against the side wall where they had left it, but it was no longer covered in pathetic scrawny twigs. It had been thoroughly fluffed and now shone with twinkling lights and garland. No ornaments yet, but the light and color made her catch her breath. He must have worked on it after she fell asleep. How long had he stayed up? The thought brought tears to her eyes.

Chris was curled up on the sofa, blanket tucked under his arms. He looked so peaceful. Her stomach fluttered. She could love that man.

But that was dangerous. And she had to focus on the here and now.

Natalie made it into the bathroom and did what she had to do. Now she had to figure out the rest of it. She assessed her shower. She didn't have a bathtub, just a stand-up shower, so at least she wouldn't have to step over anything. And there was a little bar that she usually hung her washcloth on, so at least there was something to hold onto if she got unsteady. She would have to get her clothes, though, and towels.

Taking a deep breath, Natalie finished up in the bathroom. She opened the door to find Chris in the hallway. She stumbled slightly, startled. He immediately reached out to steady her.

"Hey," she said once she had regained her balance. "I wasn't expecting to see you."

"Sorry," he replied, rubbing a hand against the back of his neck. "I heard you get up and wanted to make sure you were okay."

"I'm okay. Just, you know, nature called."

"Yeah, of course. Are you going back to bed now?"

Something about those words, when he was looking at her so intently, made her stomach flutter again. "Uh, no. I was going to attempt to shower so I could go help Joey in the kitchen."

"Do you think that's a good idea?"

"Which part?"

"All of it? Do you feel up to it?"

"I need to shower. I am feeling very grungy. And I can't leave Joey all alone. Even if I can't help much, I can at least guide and maybe help with little things."

"Do you, uh, need help?"

Natalie felt heat rising to her cheeks. "I think I'll be able to manage the shower myself. I was just looking at it, and I should be okay. I just have to get my things. I'll probably need help getting downstairs, though."

"Okay. I'll throw on some clothes while you're in the shower."

Natalie tried not to focus on the shorts and undershirt he was currently wearing as she shuffled to her bedroom to get her clothes for the day. Everything was taking longer. At this rate, Joey would be almost done by the time she got downstairs. It would have to be a short shower. Maybe she should send him a text to give him a status update.

Finding her phone on her nightstand, Natalie sent off a quick text, then made her way to the dresser for clothes. It was going to be a very long day.

By the time Natalie showered and dressed, she was exhausted. But at least she had made it. Now she had to get downstairs.

Chris held one arm while her other hand held the railing, and together they made their way slowly down the staircase.

"Thank you for working on the tree," Natalie said after a moment.

"Happy to help. And it was fun. I haven't had much opportunity to do that kind of thing."

"You don't have a tree?" she asked, pausing to look up at him.

He shrugged. "Not usually. Maybe a little pre-decorated thing if I'm feeling particularly festive."

"Huh." She continued walking. After another moment, she asked, "So, do you have to go to work today?" She needed to take her mind off the excruciating slowness of it all. Plus, she wanted to know how long Chris was planning to stick around.

"The office is open, but I don't have any meetings or anything, so probably not."

"Oh. Okay. What was your plan for the day?"

"That depends on you."

Natalie stopped walking again and looked up at him. "I don't want to take up all your time. There must be something you'd rather do than take care of an invalid."

"Natalie, I can honestly say there is no place I would rather be. But if you would rather be on your own today, that's fine. I know you have other people around, so I'm not going to pressure you."

Natalie wasn't sure how to respond. She wanted him there but already felt guilty for taking up so much of his time. "I think I'll be okay as long as I'm at the cafe."

Chris nodded, and they resumed their pace. "No problem. I'll keep myself busy while you're at the cafe, then I'll touch base this afternoon to see what you want to do. Does that sound like a plan?"

"Okay." At least it bought her some time to make sense of everything she was feeling. And maybe discuss it with someone.

They reached the back door to the cafe, and Natalie pulled out her keys. She could see the light on in the kitchen. Joey was likely hard at work. Guilt rose up again for leaving Joey by himself.

Natalie turned to look at Chris again. "I think I can take it from here." She didn't want Joey to see Chris. That would just bring up too many questions she wasn't prepared to answer.

Chris nodded once. "Okay. If you need anything, call or text. I won't be far."

"Okay." She watched him climb back up the stairs, then she took a deep breath and plastered a smile on her face before entering the kitchen.

She found Joey and a woman she didn't recognize bustling about the kitchen, filling the counters with a variety of baked goods. Joey looked up when he heard her come in.

"Hey! You made it! How are you feeling?"

"A little better. Still sore and running a bit more slowly than I would like."

"I bet. Natalie, this is my sister Cassie." Joey gestured toward the woman who had turned to face them. The woman smiled and waved.

"I would shake hands, but..." Cassie held up her hands, covered in bread flour, and laughed.

Natalie smiled again. "Nice to meet you." She turned to Joey for explanation.

"Cassie's my baking assistant at home, and with you being out of commission, I thought we could use the help." He turned to look at Cassie, then back at Natalie with wide eyes. "Totally voluntarily. You don't have to pay her or anything."

Natalie placed a hand on Joey's arm. "You are an angel." She looked at Cassie again. "And thank you for all your help. I will definitely be paying you."

Cassie grinned. "Whatever you say. I'm just happy to help. I love baking, and I didn't have anything else going on, anyway."

"Cassie's home from college for the weekend," Joey explained. "Mom was going to drag her shopping, but that's not really Cass's thing."

Cassie rolled her eyes. "Shopping with Mom is definitely not my idea of fun. She turns it into this psychotic marathon, determined to get all the doorbusters, even if she doesn't know what she's going to do with them. This was way better."

"Even if you had to get up super early?"

"Nah. I haven't been to bed yet."

"Cassie's our resident night owl."

Natalie raised her eyebrows. "Seriously? Okay then. Well, I'm happy to have the help. I wasn't sure what we were going to do." She put her phone down and washed her hands. "Okay, what's the status? What can I do?"

Joey gave her a pointed look. "You can have a seat and rest."

Natalie sighed. "I can't just sit here and do nothing while you guys are running around like crazy. I can at least spoon jam onto cookies or something."

"Okay, okay. Here. Take this cookie dough and scoop onto the sheet," Joey said, handing her a bowl and baking sheet.

"Yessir," Natalie said with mock seriousness.

They found a rhythm and had full display cases by the time they opened for business. Natalie had never been more grateful for her little community.

Chapter 38

Chris folded the blanket on the sofa, cleaned up the baked goods from the night before, and made Natalie's bed. Then he stood with his hands in his pockets, unsure what to do with himself. He should probably take a shower himself. But then what? Part of him wanted to keep decorating the apartment, but he was afraid that would be stepping on Natalie's toes. He didn't know how she liked things. But he wanted to be nearby in case Natalie needed him, though he had to accept that she had her friends now. They would get her through this day, and the next. And his cozy little day with her would fade into the past. Well, for her at least. He was pretty sure he would never forget it.

He thought back to the story Natalie had told him. She had been hurt before, and there was no way he could guarantee she wouldn't get hurt again. But how could he assure her he wanted her in his life? He had to accept that Pine Valley would forever be a part of her, that she would want to stay here. That meant he would have to stay here, too, if he wanted a life with her. Was that what he wanted? Was he willing to move to Pine Valley, if not now, at some point in the future? If the answer was "no," he was better off walking away now, as much as it may hurt, before they got any deeper.

Maybe that should be his project for the day: figure out what the heck he wanted. At the very least, he needed to decide about the whole building fiasco. Did he want to buy one of the buildings? And, if so, which one? Or ones? Both

Natalie and Tony told him to buy one of the other buildings, but how could he leave Natalie out in the cold, especially if he was trying to make her a part of his life? Was there another solution?

First things first, he was going to take a shower. Then he was going to head to the diner for breakfast. He wanted to give Natalie some space, and maybe if Maggie was there, she could offer some insight. If not, at least he would fill his belly and return the dinner plates. Then he was going to walk around Pine Valley and do some serious introspection.

A half hour later, he was seated at the counter in the diner. Maggie was there, but she had been occupied with tables at the far side of the diner since he came in. The diner was busy. He supposed all of the Black Friday shoppers were out and about and looking for nourishment. He didn't take Pine Valley for a shopping hotspot, but it wasn't that far to major shopping areas.

At some point he would have to look into Christmas shopping, but he really didn't have many people to buy for. His shopping usually consisted of cases of craft beer for his friends, some kind of gourmet food basket for his boss, and a spa gift card for the receptionist at the office. His parents got something he ordered online, shipped directly to them. It was all unexciting, not exactly filled with holiday cheer. But it got the job done.

Looking at all the smiling, laughing faces around him, it occurred to him that maybe it didn't get the job done. It had been a responsibility, and not one that brought him much joy. But maybe there should be more to it. He wanted to get Natalie, at least, something more meaningful. Whatever happened in the future, she was important to him now, and he wanted to show her that. But what?

He was looking at the menu, not really taking it in, when Maggie approached with a pot of coffee. She poured him a mug without asking, then put the pot down. "How's Natalie doing?"

"She's doing okay. Moving slowly, but she seems to be feeling better overall."

"Glad to hear it. Where is she now?"

"At the cafe. She insisted on going to help Joey."

Maggie shook her head. "No surprise there. I hope she doesn't overdo it."

"Me, too."

"So what can I get you?"

"I'd really love some clarity, but I'm guessing that's hard to come by. So maybe just some pancakes and bacon."

Maggie sighed. "Did Natalie talk to you? About what happened in the past?"

Chris nodded. "Yeah. She told me last night. And I don't want to hurt her. But I don't know what the future will bring. I just know I care about her."

"Caring about her is great, but if your lives don't fit, you'll both end up hurt."

"I know. I'm trying to figure things out."

"Good. Natalie is a wonderful person, and she's definitely worth it. But you have to be sure." Maggie patted his hand. "I'll go get your pancakes."

Chris ate and thought and looked around and thought. How could he possibly decide his future in one day? He supposed he didn't have to, but he was feeling so unsettled. He needed to figure out something, at least.

After breakfast, he decided to walk around town. He had never gotten to his exploration the other day, getting sidetracked by Lena Morseau's call. But now he had nothing but time.

Main Street was busier than he had ever seen it. The road was filled with cars, sidewalks filled with people. Holiday decorations were out in full force. He could see that Courtney's boutique was advertising Black Friday specials, and he was sure she wasn't the only one. But amid the hustle and bustle was an undercurrent of joy, and Chris could feel it flow through him. That feeling he had had when he first came to town was re-emerging. This place was special. Was it just the holiday spirit in the air? Or was it like this all year round?

He continued down Main Street, then explored the side streets on either side. Offices were closed, shops were open. Big signs in front of the community center promoted a craft fair that would take place the following day. As he walked, though, he veered farther from the bustling center of town and more into the residential areas. It was quieter here, peaceful. He could see the trees that gave the town its name tucked between the houses, but also further in the distance, surrounding the town like a protective hug. He saw families hanging lights from houses, and the occasional inflatable snowman or Santa.

He saw these things in the big town where he lived, of course he did. But he was usually driving by them, rushing somewhere else. He never took the time to just walk and enjoy it. Even if he didn't end up staying in Pine Valley, he should really take the time to enjoy these kinds of things. He was always in so much of a hurry – to meet a client, check out a property, sign paperwork that would make him more money. He was quickly realizing how hollow his life was, and how much fuller it felt since he had started spending time in Pine Valley. But was this just a wake-up call to live less superficially? Or was it a sign that he was meant to be here? Or maybe it was just Natalie.

When his stomach started to rumble for lunch, Chris headed back toward the center of town. He was almost to Main Street when he saw it.

It was a house, two stories, with a wide front porch and a chimney. Big windows at the front, rocking chairs by the door. And a for sale sign right by the sidewalk.

Chapter 39

Chris had to find out more about this house. It looked perfect for Natalie. Okay, maybe not perfect. If it was a typical house, it wouldn't be set up with the dining space and commercial kitchen, but that could be fixed, right? And if the chimney was connected to a fireplace, she could even have that. It was worth looking into, anyway.

The real estate office was close by, so, putting his hunger aside for the time being, he headed there first. But, in typical Pine Valley fashion, the office was closed. Damn holiday. Actually, it wasn't even a holiday anymore. Why were they closed?

Okay, so the office was closed. He would just look everything up online. Too bad his laptop was sitting all comfy in his own apartment, twenty minutes away. Maybe he could try the library. They had computers, right?

The library was closed, too. Didn't anybody in this town work?

Chris felt frantic. He had never wished to be back home more. Technically, he could drive back home, get his laptop, and drive back. But that would take too long. He needed to figure this out. For Natalie. Something needed to go right.

Why hadn't he brought his laptop? He supposed he hadn't expected to need it. But when was the last time he hadn't had it practically glued to his hip? He had thought all this peace and tranquility was a good thing, but maybe he had gone too far. Now he didn't even have the tools he needed, and he was going to let Natalie down because of it.

He sat down on a bench in the center of town and tried to take some deep breaths to calm his pounding heart. He could probably just look at his phone, but it was so hard to get a feel for a space on such a small screen. Natalie had to have a computer, right? Would she mind if he used it? Or they could use it together, look up the house, dream about the possibilities.

Okay, he needed to get a grip. He took a few more deep breaths. This wasn't the end of the world. With the real estate office closed, it was highly unlikely someone was putting in an offer today. Probably not all weekend. They had time.

Except they didn't. The inspection report would come out next week, and Townsend would put in an offer, and Malloy would accept it, and all would be lost. And instead of coming up with a game plan, he had spent an entire day playing house, and an entire morning wandering aimlessly.

Get it together, Parker, he scolded himself. He was supposed to be figuring things out. That's what the walk had been about. And instead, he was spiraling into a panic attack.

Another deep breath.

The cafe would be closing soon. Then he and Natalie could go online and find what they needed. They could discuss the possibility, weigh the pros and cons, figure things out.

Assuming she wanted him around again. Maybe he was deluding himself. But would she be comfortable by herself? Was she feeling up to being on her own? Or had she already asked someone else to stay with her?

Maybe all the anxiety was from hunger. He really needed to get some lunch. Maybe he could look up the house on his phone while he ate. Then perhaps he could think rationally about everything and come to some decisions.

Because time was running out.

Natalie's ability to help in the kitchen had been limited, simply because she was running slowly, moving at a snail's pace and taking longer to make decisions that would usually be made in a split second. But she could run the cash register. So she had pulled up a stool and sat at the cash register, greeting customers and ringing them up while Joey, Cassie, and McKenna did the heavy lifting. Not perfect, but at least she was there. And she was grateful for Cassie's extra help. The cafe was packed right from the moment they opened. It seemed everyone was out and about today, taking advantage of sales and getting a kickstart to the holiday season.

With the increased traffic, Natalie's energy waned quickly. By the time Sylvie came in at ten, she was ready for a nap. But she wasn't sure she wanted to attempt the stairs on her own, so she just went into the back office and put her head down for a bit. A little power nap would do wonders.

She must have slept much longer than anticipated because the next thing she knew, she was being woken up by a knock on the office door.

If she hadn't been sore before, she certainly was now, with her neck tight from the awkward position and her back screaming with every movement.

Since she didn't get up to answer the door, her visitor opened it themselves, and she saw Chris poke his head around to see her. The grimace on her face must have told him how uncomfortable she was because he rushed over to her and helped her up.

"Why didn't you go upstairs if you needed rest?" he asked, gently scolding her.

"I didn't want to tackle the stairs by myself."

"You could have called me. I would have come over to help you."

"I didn't want to be a burden." Her lower lip trembled, and tears were welling in her eyes, but she didn't know if it was from the pain and discomfort or the feeling of helplessness.

"You are not a burden. But you are injured, and you need to take care of yourself if you're going to get better."

Natalie nodded, not trusting herself to speak.

"I'll let the others know that you're going upstairs. I'll be right back to help you up."

He left the office then, and Natalie stayed standing, holding onto the desk for support. She hated feeling like an invalid. She should be out in the cafe, helping customers, making delicious food, and enjoying the start of the Christmas season. She hadn't even put on her holiday music. She was so thrown off this year, between the building crisis and now her fall. This was supposed to be her favorite time of year, and it had just been a mess. No wonder she felt like crying.

Chris returned after a few moments, and he put an arm around Natalie to support her as they walked out the back door and up the stairs to the apartment. Chris still had the keys from when he had cleaned up earlier, and he opened the apartment with one hand while supporting Natalie with the other.

"Sofa or bed?" he asked as they entered.

"Sofa is fine. I slept enough for now."

"Okay."

He helped her to the sofa, and she looked around. The apartment was tidy, everything they had used the night before put away, Chris's belongings back in his duffel bag. The lights on the Christmas tree were off now, but the garland still sparkled in the sunlight coming in from the window.

"I had actually come into the cafe to grab some lunch, and I got sidetracked when I noticed you weren't out front. Do you mind if I run down and grab something now? Will you be okay?"

"That's fine. I'll be fine."

"Okay. Do you want me to bring you something?"

"Um, yeah. Get me a sandwich and some chips. Joey knows what I like."

"Okay. Be right back."

He left the apartment, and Natalie released a breath. Apparently even just checking customers out was too exhausting for her. At least she wasn't feeling as tired as she had been. She sat on the sofa, looking around, unsure what to do with herself. She should really try to use the bathroom before lunch. Could she make it on her own? Her head wasn't as unsteady as it had been the day before, and once she had started moving, the stiffness and discomfort in her back and neck had gotten better. She should be able to make it, even if the distance from the sofa to the bathroom seemed massive. She could do this.

She had made it to the bathroom and back by the time Chris returned. It had been a slow process, but she had done it. She wasn't as incapacitated as she feared.

"Sorry it took so long," Chris said, closing the door behind him and bringing a bag to the living room. "As I'm sure you are aware, it was quite busy down there."

"I should be down there, helping."

"You should be up here, resting."

Natalie sighed. Arguing was pointless. She knew he was right, as much as she hated it.

They ate in companionable silence. When they were finished, Chris cleaned up the garbage, then came back to the living room and sat next to her. Natalie was surprised. Except for the night before, when they were watching the movie, he had been keeping his distance, sitting in the chair instead of the sofa.

"What's the plan?" he asked, looking at her intently.

"What do you mean 'what's the plan'?" she replied.

"Is someone coming over to stay with you? Do you want me to stay?"

Oh. That plan. "I don't have a plan," Natalie said sheepishly. "I had hoped I would be up to being on my own."

"Do you think you're up for it?"

"I don't know," she answered honestly. "I hate to put you out. I'm sure you have other things you would rather be doing."

"The only things I have to do are make sure you're okay and figure out what the heck I'm doing about our building situation."

"Yeah, that. We do have to figure that out, don't we?"

"Yup. I took a long walk today to try and make some decisions. I found something I wanted to run by you."

"Okay."

"Do you have a computer?"

"Yeah, there's a laptop on the table by the bookcase."

Chris retrieved it, and Natalie turned it on and unlocked it, then handed it back to Chris.

"What are you looking for?"

"A house listing."

"A house?"

"Yeah. I found this house that looked like it could be perfect with a little conversion. And it's right off Main Street, so it wouldn't be too far."

Natalie sighed as Chris pulled up a browser and found the listing. "I had already considered that option."

He looked at her with surprise. "You did?"

She nodded. "Yeah. I visited the real estate office like a week ago to see if they knew of any commercial spaces available. They didn't have any leads but did suggest the same thing, houses to convert. She printed some listings for me to look at. They're probably in the drawer of that table the laptop was on."

Chris stood up again and went back to the table. He found the listings in a folder in the drawer and brought them back to the sofa. "I take it since you hadn't mentioned it that you didn't think it would work out?"

She sighed again. "Between the cost of the house, the cost of all the renovations needed, and the time it would take to complete the renovations, it didn't seem like a practical option. I looked into it a little. It's not exactly a simple or fast process."

Chris's shoulders slumped, and he leaned back on the sofa. "It looked so perfect, Natalie. Big windows, even a chimney with what I guessed was a fireplace. And it had a big porch that I could picture little tables and chairs on in the spring and summer."

Natalie just stared at him. She had been so focused on the negatives, and here he was visualizing a dream. And he had listened to her, about the fireplace. And taken it a step further, picturing her cafe, perfectly fitting in with the little town it was a part of. She couldn't help it. She leaned forward and kissed him.

He seemed surprised but leaned into the kiss. wrapping his arms around her and pulling her close.

Before they could get too carried away, Natalie put her hand on his chest and pulled back. "I – I'm sorry."

"Don't be." He was breathing hard and placed a hand over hers.

"I just...haven't had someone dream for me before."

"I want nothing but the best for you, Natalie. No matter what happens between you and me. I just wish I knew how to get it."

"Me, too."

Chapter 40

Natalie's kiss had thrown him off guard, but Chris was certainly not complaining. If anything, it gave him hope that they could find a way, that Natalie was willing to give him a shot.

But they had a long way to go before then.

Okay, so she hadn't jumped at his idea of converting a house. But she hadn't completely dismissed it, either. She had just stated all the obstacles, and they were reasonable, understandable. What if he were to take on those obstacles for her? Buy the house, pay for the renovations, make it exactly how she wanted it?

Okay, now he was *really* getting carried away. It was one thing to buy a commercial building, with income from tenants and appreciating land value. That was a logical, practical decision that made sense as part of his investment portfolio. But to buy a house with next to no benefit to himself, just to make Natalie happy? That was going too far.

They sat in silence for a moment while these thoughts ran through Chris's head. Then he let go of her hand, and they both adjusted so they were sitting a little farther apart.

"Maybe, uh, in light of what just happened, you shouldn't stay tonight."

"Do you have someone else who can stay?"

"I don't know. But I should be okay. I mean, as long as I go slow, I should be fine. My head isn't bothering me really. It's just a little fuzzy. And my body is just sore. I'm capable of doing things. Plus Courtney is downstairs until the boutique closes, and I have Jordan next door's number if I need help overnight. He's a good guy. He would help, or get Maggie if he couldn't."

Chris was reluctant to leave her on her own. But it wasn't his decision. "Only if you're sure."

"I'm sure." She nodded for emphasis.

He had his concerns, but he had to trust her. "Okay. Do you want me to go now or...?"

"You can stay a little longer. If you want, that is."

"Okay."

They sat in silence for a moment.

"I have a few board games, if you want. Or we could watch another movie," Natalie suggested.

Chris didn't know if he could focus on a board game, but he was definitely up for cuddling with Natalie watching a movie again. "We could do a movie."

"Okay."

They found a movie to watch and got settled on the sofa. Natalie rested her head on his shoulder and closed her eyes. It didn't take long for her breathing to deepen into sleep. But he didn't mind. They had resolved nothing, but it didn't seem to matter as much as it had earlier. They would figure it out.

Natalie woke up near the end of the movie. "Sorry. I guess I was more tired than I thought."

"Don't worry about it," Chris said, gently moving her so he could reach the remote to turn off the movie. "You need the rest."

With the movie off, the apartment was suddenly quiet. Chris could still hear cars moving outside, and people laughing and chatting. It wasn't very late, though it seemed much later with everything that had happened since that morning. He should probably get going before he was tempted to stay over again.

"I should probably go," Chris said. "If you're sure you don't want me to stay again tonight."

"I'll be okay."

He wasn't as sure as she was, but he respected her decision. "Okay. I'll touch base tomorrow to check in. And probably tonight, too," he added with a soft laugh.

"Okay."

"Oh, I still have the keys to the apartment," Chris said, fishing them out of his pocket. "You're going to need those."

"Thanks," Natalie replied, taking the keys.

Chris was reluctant to leave, but he knew the longer he waited the harder it would be. Natalie looked at him with still-sleepy eyes. She looked reluctant, too. But it was for the best. He couldn't offer her what she needed, not yet, maybe not ever. And until he figured that out, he had to acknowledge that it was best to take things slow.

The drive home felt long, too quiet, even with the radio on. And when he arrived at his apartment, he looked around at the clean, modern decor and felt lost. He missed Natalie's cozy home and her warm presence. Her apartment felt lived in, welcoming, inviting. His just looked sad. Was it just the decor? Or was it her presence? Or the whole experience, with the cafe downstairs and the friendly, smiling faces outside?

He tossed his keys in their dish, placed his duffle bag against one wall, and went into his bedroom to change out of his jeans into sweatpants. The night ahead seemed long. How would he fill the hours? He grabbed his laptop and settled onto his sofa. First things first, he was going to order a Christmas tree. And garland. And lights. And ornaments. He had been amazed at much fun it had been, bringing that tree to life. And maybe that would help bring some warmth into this place. At least it would remind him of Natalie.

The options seemed endless. How tall? How wide? Pre-lit or without lights? Blue spruce or pine? He had never realized how much went into picking out a tree, even a fake one. He closed his eyes and thought back to what Natalie's had looked like. That would be his guide. And once he had found everything he needed, he submitted the order and took a deep breath. Yes. That felt *right*.

Now what?

Chris thought back to earlier in the day, his excitement and anticipation over the house he had found. Natalie might not have jumped at his buy-a-house idea, but he still thought it had merit. It didn't hurt to look into it. And maybe while he was researching, something else would jump out at him, some solution he had overlooked. It was something to do, anyway, and something that might bring him closer to solving their dilemma.

The apartment felt empty without him, Natalie thought. She had gotten used to him being there, moving around the space, offering a comforting presence. The tree he had set up was, as she had expected, a reminder of him. But now she was questioning whether that had been a good idea after all. Giving herself a mental shake, she assured herself it would get better. She was just about to get up in search of a snack when her phone dinged. It was Maggie.

> How are you holding up?

> Doing ok. Chris just left

> I didn't realize he had stuck around

> Yeah, just until he made sure I was settled

> Interesting

> Don't start

> I'm just saying. It was nice of him.

> Yes it was, and we're leaving it at that.

> Ok, ok. Do you need anything?

I think I'm ok

How about dinner later?

I hadn't thought that far

Ok. I'll bring you a plate around 6

Thanks, Mags

Any time

Natalie put her phone down, then attempted to stand. At least she knew she would have dinner, and Maggie would probably stick around for a little while to make sure she was all set. She would be fine without Chris. Even if she missed him.

She made it to the kitchen, found a couple of cookies left in the bakery box, then shuffled back to the living room. What was she going to do until Maggie got there?

Natalie spotted the folder with the house printouts, sitting on the coffee table where Chris had left them. It wouldn't hurt to check them out, she reasoned. It would give her something to do, and maybe she would come up with a new solution to their dilemma.

Chapter 41

Natalie hadn't resolved anything by the time Maggie arrived. All she had accomplished was making her head spin, both literally and figuratively. Reading was not a great idea when her head wasn't a hundred percent. But the pictures had looked nice. And she could see how Chris's vision would fit in with what she dreamed for the cafe. But it was too much to take on. Wasn't it?

Maggie knocked on the door, and Natalie made her way over slowly. She would be really glad when she was back to normal.

Maggie greeted her with a sympathetic smile. "How are you feeling?" she asked.

"I'm okay," Natalie replied. "Just moving slowly." She made her way back to the sofa.

"How's the head?"

"Okay as long as I don't overdo it. I was reading earlier, and my head didn't like that, but otherwise it's been okay."

"Hmm. Still sore?"

"Yeah."

Maggie nodded. "Okay. You have a seat, and I'll bring your food over. What else can I do for you?"

"I'm okay, Maggie, really. I appreciate the food, but other than some mild boredom, I'm fine."

"Missing Chris?"

Natalie wasn't sure how to reply to that, so she didn't.

Maggie chuckled. "That's what I thought." She placed the plate of food on the table in front of Natalie, then sighed. "I know you have your concerns, and rightfully so. But it seems to me he's been trying pretty hard to help you."

"He has, and I appreciate it, but that doesn't mean we're meant to be together."

"I'm just saying maybe you should give him a chance."

"I'll consider it."

"Okay."

"So how was your Thanksgiving celebration yesterday?"

They fell into conversation, catching up on news and gossip while Natalie ate her dinner. When Natalie started drooping, Maggie stood up.

"Okay, sweetie, time for you to get some rest. Do you need help with anything before I go? Getting to the bathroom or anything?"

"No, I'm okay. I've gotten pretty good at moving about, even if it is slowly."

"Okay, then. Get some sleep, and I'll touch base with you tomorrow."

"Thanks, Maggie."

Natalie walked Maggie to the door, then closed it behind her. She probably should go to bed. She wasn't sure what Joey's plan was for the next day, but she wanted to make sure she was in the cafe with plenty of time to help however she could, especially if Cassie didn't join him again.

With a sigh, she cleaned up her dinner dishes and began getting ready for bed. As silly as it was, she had been hoping Chris would check in like he had said he might. But he had probably gotten busy with his own life.

Exhausted with the effort it took to get herself situated, Natalie was drifting off when she heard her phone ring. Her heart began to beat faster, and she reached over to get her phone on the nightstand. Chris. She grinned like a schoolgirl and accepted the call.

***

"Hey," Chris said when Natalie answered. "How are you feeling?"

"I'm doing okay. Getting annoyed with how long it takes to get anything done, but otherwise okay. I was just about to go to bed."

"Oh, I'm sorry. I forget you're one of those early-to-bed, early-to-rise people."

"Yeah, it can be annoying."

"Not annoying, just an adjustment. I won't keep you, then."

"It's okay." Was it his imagination, or did she seem anxious to keep him on the line? That was an encouraging sign.

"Okay, if you're sure."

"I'm sure."

"Okay. So what have you been up to?"

"Not much. I tried reading, but my head wasn't up for it. Maggie came over for a little bit. She brought me dinner."

"That's great. I'm glad she checked on you." He didn't have much to say, but he really wanted to keep the connection. Actually, he really wished he was with her right now. But this would have to do.

"How about you?"

"Not much, either. I bought a Christmas tree."

Natalie gave a little laugh. "You did?"

"Yeah. You inspired me."

"I'm glad."

"It gets delivered tomorrow. Hope I remember how to put it together."

"You'll be just fine. You're a pro now."

"Thanks." Silence fell. "I was actually also looking more into the house thing we had been discussing. I know you said it wasn't a good option, but I thought it might spark some ideas if nothing else."

Natalie gave another little laugh. "Actually, I did the same. That's what I had tried reading – the house listings."

Chris sat up straighter. Maybe they were on the same page, after all. "And, aside from it bothering your head, what did you think?"

Natalie sighed. "I don't know. I still think it will cost too much and take too long. But it's a nice dream."

"If you had more time, would you consider it?"

"Maybe."

"I actually had an idea."

"Oh yeah?"

"Yeah. It occurred to me that this whole time we've been making a lot of assumptions. While Townsend was pretty clear with what he planned to do, we've assumed Colleen Malloy would accept his offer."

"You seemed pretty sure she would."

"Yeah, because she's anxious to sell. But maybe she would act differently if she had all the information. I never told her about Townsend's plans."

"I don't see it making much difference. From what I've heard, the town has pretty much shunned her since everything happened with her husband and son."

"What happened with her son?"

"Oh, he decided to follow in his father's footsteps and make some pretty bad decisions. Went on a petty crime spree and caused mischief a few months back. He's in jail now, too."

"Geesh."

"Yeah. I feel bad for her, to be honest. It sounds like all her friends turned their backs on her and she lost her job. I don't think she's going to really want to help out the town after all that."

"You're probably right. But it doesn't hurt to at least let her know, does it?"

"I suppose not."

"I figured I would give her a call tomorrow. I haven't talked to her since before I was taken off the listings, so I figure that would be a good segue into the conversation. Make sure she was being taken care of and all that."

"Okay."

"I'll let you know what she says, okay?"

"Okay."

It sounded like her voice was fading. He should really let her get some sleep. "Okay, I'm actually going to let you go this time. You need your rest. I'll call you tomorrow."

"Okay." Her voice was barely a whisper.

"Good night."

He disconnected the call and put the phone up against his forehead, his eyes closed. As long as they had this building thing between them, if nothing else, he could maintain contact.

Chapter 42

Since Chris's job had him on the road a good amount of the time, he had a bag that contained all of his notes, listings information, and anything else he thought he might need. So he didn't need to go to the office to get Colleen Malloy's contact information. And that was a good thing, since he still didn't feel up to tackling the office.

Not knowing her personal habits, he decided to call her late Saturday morning.

"Hello?" she answered, annoyance in her voice. That was not a good sign.

"Hello, Mrs. Malloy. It's Chris Parker, from Ryker Commercial Properties."

"I heard you weren't my realtor anymore."

"That is correct. Eric is now handling your properties."

"Then why are you calling me?"

Chris took a deep breath. This was not going well. "I wanted to make sure you were all set with Eric, and make sure the transition had gone smoothly."

"I guess. As long as he can sell the properties."

"That was the other reason I wanted to call. I believe you know that an inspector was out earlier this week to check on the properties. There is a serious buyer who will likely be putting in an offer once the inspector's report is complete."

"Good. I'll be glad to be rid of the things."

How best to put this? "I was actually hoping you might consider turning down the offer."

"Why the hell would I want to do that?"

"When I was the listing agent for your properties, I was the one who originally showed this man around the spaces, and he told me a bit about what he was planning for the commercial buildings. He has companies he works with who want to move into the commercial spaces."

"So?"

"So he will be kicking out all of the small businesses that currently rent space in those buildings. He won't renew any of their leases, which means they will have to close down. As I'm sure you know, there aren't exactly a lot of commercial spaces for rent in Pine Valley."

Colleen didn't respond, which gave him an inkling of hope.

"The business owners are very worried about what this means for their futures. Many of them have lived in Pine Valley their entire lives. They don't want to move, but if they can't have their businesses in Pine Valley, they may have to. Or find some other way to support themselves and their families."

"I don't see how that's my problem."

So much for hope. "It's not your problem. You can do whatever you think is best with the properties. I just wanted to make sure you had all of the information, so you could make an educated decision."

"Is there anyone else who wants to buy the buildings?"

"I was working on finding other buyers for the properties before Eric took over. I'm waiting to hear from a couple of possibilities, but no one who is as far along in the process."

"So if I turn this guy down, I could be stuck for a long time."

If he wanted her to have all the info, he couldn't lie to her. "It's possible. But even though I'm not on the account anymore, I'm still working on finding another buyer for you."

Colleen grunted. "I'll think about it." And she hung up.

Chris released a breath. Well, that hadn't gone exactly as he would have liked, but it could have been worse. At least she hadn't given him a hard "no." Maybe her conscience would win. Until then, he would have to keep working on finding someone else. Or deciding what he wanted to do himself.

He put the contact information back in his file folder for the Pine Valley properties. He had other folders in here, too, for other clients. He should really be putting in some work for them, too. But he felt like he couldn't focus on anything else until this situation was resolved. His drive and ambition seemed to have abandoned him. And, hey, he reasoned, it was a holiday weekend. He could wait a couple of days. He chuckled to himself. Pine Valley really was rubbing off on him.

Chris pulled out a sheet of notes from the Pine Valley folder. It was a list of the other parties who had inquired about any of the buildings, before Townsend came on the scene. They hadn't seemed seriously interested, but maybe it was worth touching base with them just to follow up. After all, if they were interested, they should know the properties could be off the table soon. Shouldn't they?

Chris was just debating which one to call first when his phone rang. He looked at the screen and cringed. Eric.

"Christopher Parker."

"What the hell are you doing contacting my client?"

"Hello to you, too, Eric."

"Dammit, Chris, you have got to stop interfering with this sale."

"I just thought Mrs. Malloy should have all the information before she made a decision."

"That's not your call. You are no longer her agent."

"No, but I am an interested party."

"If this sale falls through because of your meddling, I'm suing you for interfering with a sale."

"If she accepts Townsend's offer, I will not interfere. I just wanted to make sure she knew his intentions so she could make an educated decision."

"I'll have your job for this."

Chris closed his eyes and took a deep breath. While he didn't want to be jobless, the thought didn't terrify him as much as it once may have. The only downside would be the difficulty in getting a business loan if it came to that. "You do what you need to do. I won't reach out to Malloy again. But I am within my rights to let other people know about available properties. That is not a crime."

"Why are you doing this, man? Are you seriously willing to jeopardize your career and your future for a few properties in a dinky little town?"

"It's not for the properties, Eric. It's for the people. If Townsend was willing to keep the current tenants, I would have no problem with him buying the buildings. But I can't stand the idea of all those people getting kicked to the curb just so Townsend can make a few bucks."

Eric sighed. "Yeah, well, you may get your wish."

Chris sat up straighter. "What do you mean?"

"Malloy called me to get more information about the potential buyer and his intentions. Apparently, something you said made an impact."

Chris stood up in excitement. "Are you serious?"

"Don't get your hopes up. She didn't say she wouldn't consider his offer. Just wanted info."

It was a start, and he would take whatever he could get. "I appreciate you letting me know."

"You know you've gone too far with this, right?"

Was it too far to want to help other people? "Until I know those tenants are safe, it won't be far enough."

Chapter 43

Though she hadn't been up to kneading bread, Natalie had at least been able to mix up muffin batter and cookie dough. Her arms felt sore, but more from lack of use than any real pain. Cassie had been back to help with the baking, and between the three of them they were able to make enough to handle the day's business. The big holiday craft fair was happening at the community center, so more townspeople were staying in town, rather than venturing out, and traffic was steady all day long.

Natalie found herself growing tired by early afternoon, but not enough that she needed to take a nap. She was grateful that she was making progress. Maybe if she rested that afternoon and evening and relaxed all the following day, she would be back to normal for Monday. Or at least close enough to make her happy. Cassie would be back at school, so it would be up to Natalie and Joey again. And orders for her holiday cookie boxes had been steadily pouring in, meaning she had to get back to work and soon. The batches she had made with Chris that day would hardly make a dent. Maybe she and Joey could put in extra hours next weekend. Though he had been putting in so many hours already lately since he was coming in early to bake. She didn't want to burn him out.

She was back to worrying again. But at least it was about normal business stuff, not the building drama. What happened with the building was pretty much out of her hands at this point. She would have to take it as it came and deal with the aftermath.

Chris came in shortly before two o'clock. Natalie was surprised to see him, though she supposed she shouldn't have been. She was slightly surprised at the butterflies fluttering in her stomach at the sight of him, though. She had missed him.

"Hey," she said as he approached the counter.

"Hey."

"Did you want something? We'll be closing soon."

"Um, yeah," he said, glancing in the case. "I'll have one of those scones."

"You got it."

She rang him up and handed over the plate with his scone.

"Not a takeout bag? I thought you were closing."

"You can stay if you want."

Their gazes held for a moment before Natalie looked away and cleared her throat. "It'll take time to clean up anyway. We were busy, so we weren't able to keep up with things as much as usual."

"Okay. I'll just be over here. And maybe once you're done, we can sit and chat."

"Did you talk to Malloy?"

"I did. And Eric."

"And...?"

"And it's more than a thirty-second conversation. Do what you need to do, and we'll chat."

"Okay."

The butterflies in her stomach were now due to nerves more than anything else. Had there been an improvement in their situation? Was there hope? Or were they still on this hopeless trajectory? Natalie rushed through the cleaning, and by the time she said goodbye to Sylvie and went to join Chris, her stomach was in knots.

"How bad is it?"

She was still standing, unable to relax. Chris took one of her hands and led her to the seat next to him. "Actually, not as bad as it could be."

What the heck did that mean? "What did you find out?"

"I told Mrs. Malloy what Townsend had planned. Then she called Eric, I guess to get more info. That did *not* make him happy. Actually, when I got off the phone with Malloy, it seemed like she didn't care. But according to Eric, it had some kind of impact. What she's actually thinking, though, is anyone's guess."

"So she didn't say she wouldn't accept his offer."

"No, but she's at least considering it. That's something."

Natalie sighed. "So nothing has really changed."

"Change isn't instant, Natalie. No matter how much we want it to be. But we got the ball rolling. Now we just need to see where it goes."

It wasn't exactly the wonderful news she had been hoping for, but at least it wasn't a complete dismissal of her concerns. She supposed, all things considered, it was the best she could expect. "Now we have to wait."

"Yup. Now we wait."

"When is the inspection report going to come out?"

"Not sure. I know Chuck completed the inspection on Wednesday. He was waiting for one test to come back from the apartment site, but otherwise, it's just a question of compiling all of his notes and sending it over. We should have it by the middle of the week."

"And he's going to give you a copy, too?"

"That's what he said."

"And you don't know of anything that would prevent Townsend from wanting the buildings?"

"Just the electrical issue on the second floor, but that's not too bad. Other things have been minor, as far as I know."

"All this waiting is going to kill me."

"I know. Me, too."

"I'm torn between wanting this all to be over and wanting more time so we can come up with a solution."

"I get it."

Natalie sat in silence a moment, looking down and playing with the edge of the table. The knot in her stomach hadn't loosened much. She suspected it wouldn't loosen until they finally had answers. "So, um, have you given any more thought to what you're going to do? About the buildings, I mean? Are you still considering buying one?"

Chris sighed. "I have been running different scenarios in my head, trying to figure out what to do. I can't buy everything, which means I can't help everyone. But how can I pick who to help?" He looked up at her and took her hand again. "I want to help you, most of all. But you told me not to, and my financial advisor is recommending one of the other buildings, and this one is definitely the most expensive, so I have to consider what makes the most sense, especially considering..."

When he didn't continue, Natalie squeezed his hand. "Considering what?"

He looked down again. "This whole situation has gotten my boss pretty upset, and when Eric found out I had called Malloy, he threatened to go after my job. So I don't know if I'll be losing my job, which puts a serious damper on getting a business loan. I don't know if a bank would even approve me for a loan if I have no income besides the rent, even with a sizeable down payment. So the least expensive building might be the most possible. But even that might be a stretch."

Natalie's jaw hung open. "You might lose your job over this? Because you want to help us?"

Chris took a deep breath. "There is a good chance, yeah. And I'm seriously toeing the line with interfering with the sale, too. If I push much harder, I could get into legal trouble, too, if Eric or Ryker press charges."

"Are you serious?" Natalie stood up, wobbling slightly. "That's it. You're off the case. I really appreciate everything you've done, but you cannot destroy your career or your life because of this. We will survive."

Chris urged her to sit back down. "I appreciate your concern. But I will survive, too. I've been in this business long enough to know what I can get away with on the legal front. With regards to the job, I'm actually not too worried. The biggest concern with that would be the loan. I can find another place to work, just not necessarily in time to make a difference for this."

Natalie's head was reeling from all the new information. If she hadn't felt fuzzy before, she certainly did now. "I'm sorry."

"For what?"

"For dragging you into this. If I hadn't pushed so hard in the beginning, you wouldn't have gotten so involved."

"Hey," he said, lifting her chin so she met his gaze. "I don't regret any of it. I'm glad you pushed me. You got me out of my privileged little life and made me see how real people live. I wouldn't trade that for anything."

Her chin wobbled. "I'm glad you can see reality, but..." She didn't know what else to say.

"Hey," he said again. He kissed her gently on the lips. "No regrets."

"No regrets."

Chapter 44

Natalie decided she needed some fresh air and exercise after being stuck inside for the last couple of days, so after their emotional conversation, Chris grabbed her coat from her apartment, and they took a short walk toward the community center to check out the tail end of the craft fair. She seemed to be doing better, regaining her stability and stamina, for which Chris was grateful. He was also grateful his plight had affected her so much. It showed she cared about him, and that mattered more to him than just about anything else.

The air was warm for the time of year, with the sun shining brightly. Natalie tilted her head back to feel the sun on her face, and Chris watched her with a smile. He loved how she could find moments of joy, despite everything that was going on.

Courtney's shop was busy, and even the ice cream parlor was doing brisk business. Chris could see people leaving the community center with bags of purchases, and others with bags labeled with the names of various businesses around town. This was a town that supported each other, enjoyed each other. He wondered if there was a way to bring Mrs. Malloy back into that fold, make her see that the hardships she had been facing were a result of her family's actions, not her. Maybe he could make the town see that Colleen wasn't the bad guy here.

"Maybe we should do something nice for Colleen Malloy," he said suddenly.

"What, to bribe her to turn down Townsend's offer?"

"Hmm. I was thinking more to get her and Pine Valley on better footing, but I can see how that might be seen as a bribe."

"The timing might be a bit suspicious."

"True. I was just thinking about what you said, about how the town has been shunning her. She might decide to accept Townsend's offer just to spite everyone."

"It is a distinct possibility."

"Any suggestions?"

"I'll think about it. I like where your mind is headed. I just don't want her to get the wrong idea. And I don't want *you* getting into legal trouble."

Chris smiled. He liked that she was looking out for him. "I'll give it some more thought, too."

They reached the community center, and Natalie sighed.

"What's the matter?"

"I'm getting tired."

"We can go back."

Natalie shook her head slowly. "It's not that. It's just that I have so much to do, and my body is just not up for it. I need to be sharp, fast, getting stuff done. And all I want to do is lie down and take a nap."

"Well, the cafe is closed tomorrow, right?"

"Yeah."

"Then take the day to relax and do nothing. Maybe you'll feel better on Monday."

"That's what I tell myself, but I can't stand taking a day off and doing nothing when I have so much to do."

"I get it. What do you have to do? Is there anything I can help with?"

Natalie sighed again. "The biggest worry right now is the holiday cookie boxes. Normally I would be spending this whole weekend making cookie dough."

"You got some done before. How much more do you need to make?"

"A lot."

"When do boxes get picked up?"

"It depends on when people requested them to be ready. The first batch goes out in a couple of weeks."

"Okay. Well, are you up to doing any of it?"

"At the moment? Probably not."

"What about tomorrow? If you rested in the morning and did some work in the afternoon? Or vice versa? Even if you worked at a slower pace and didn't get as much done as you usually would, you would feel better for getting something done."

"I guess. I just can't ask Joey to come in again. He's been working so many hours already. Normally Chloe would help, but with her away, it's just a lot."

"Is this your subtle way of asking me to help out again?" Chris grinned.

"What? No!" Natalie looked up at him, startled. "Oh, geesh. I'm sorry. That's what it sounded like, isn't it? I promise, that isn't what I meant."

Chris laughed. "It's okay. I would be happy to help. If you want me to, that is."

"I just feel so bad; the last few days your whole life has been taking care of me."

Chris turned so he was fully facing her. He took both her hands in his. "Natalie. There is literally no place I would rather be than in Pine Valley, taking care of you."

The pink in Natalie's cheeks deepened, and she pulled her hands away. "If you say so." She cleared her throat. "I would greatly appreciate the help, if you are actually willing to provide it. With the cookies, that is."

"It would be my pleasure. Now, should we turn around, or head inside?"

Natalie looked at the smiling faces of people leaving the community center, bags of purchases in hand. "Let's go inside. Just for a few minutes."

"Okay. Just for a few minutes."

The craft fair was starting to wind down, but they took a leisurely stroll around some of the tables. Chris could see handmade blankets and doll clothes, gift baskets and soaps, ornaments and candles. He didn't think he had ever been to such an event, and he enjoyed watching Natalie smile at the vendors, admire the different items, and inquire how they were made. She purchased a few items, gazed longingly at others, and seemed to enjoy the entire experience before reluctantly admitting she was exhausted and wanted to head home. Chris, meanwhile, snagged business cards for every vendor she had expressed interest in, hoping he could find them online. He wasn't used to putting much thought into gifts, but he needed to find something special for Natalie. Something that showed how much he cared.

He meant "for now," Natalie told herself later, once they had said their goodbyes and she was alone in her apartment. The conversation they had had earlier ran on a loop in her mind. *He meant he wants to be in Pine Valley with me for now, not forever.* She had enjoyed their walk together, their time together at the craft fair. She was glad he had come to see her, and glad that he was coming over the following day to help her in the cafe. Even if she couldn't get as much done as she usually could, she would be grateful for what she could accomplish, and grateful for his help.

For now, though, she had just enough energy to heat herself a can of soup and crawl into bed. She was turning off her alarm and allowing herself to sleep in. She wouldn't be surprised if her body woke her up early out of habit, but she would do her best to stay in bed as long as she could. Then she and Chris would have some lunch, and they would tackle the Christmas cookies. It would be a perfect mix of relaxation and productivity, with time with Chris thrown in for good measure.

It would be, quite possibly, the perfect day.

Chapter 45

Natalie woke up to a knocking on her door. She couldn't possibly have slept in long enough for it to be Chris, could she? But, no, it was still dark out. She turned to look at her bedside clock to find that it wasn't glowing. Great. The power was out again.

She grabbed her cell phone from the nightstand and, using her phone as a flashlight, made her way to the front door. She opened it to find Jordan. flashlight in hand.

"Hey, Jordan. What happened?"

"Don't know," Jordan replied. "All the apartments lost power. Weather seems fine, and everyone else on the street seems to have power. I wanted to make sure you were okay."

"Thanks. I appreciate it. Everything's fine on my end. Did you call the power company yet?"

Jordan shook his head. "Not yet. I was just checking on everyone, trying to figure out what the heck happened."

"Okay. Let me go to their website and see what I can find out."

The residents of the other apartments were hovering outside their doors, too. Natalie pulled up the website while Jordan touched base with their other neighbors. As far as she could tell, they were the only ones without power. Great. That meant it was a building issue. Hadn't Chris said something about the electric panel for the second floor being wonky?

Natalie joined her neighbors and sighed. "Looks like it's just us. And the inspector who was out here last week said something about an issue with the panel, so I think we need to call the property manager."

Travis, who lived with his wife Janet at the other end of the hall, started grumbling. "Looks like we'll be out of power for the week, then." Janet mumbled an agreement.

True, the property management company wasn't known for their quick turn-around, but it could be worse. "If it's because of the panel," Natalie said, interrupting the complaints, "then it just affects the second floor. I think we'll still have heat, since the furnace is on the first floor. So it could be worse." She hoped she was right.

"Yeah, well, I don't appreciate living in the dark," Travis continued. Tanya, their other neighbor next to Jordan, agreed.

Natalie sighed. She couldn't blame him for being upset, but she was not in the mood to argue. "I'll call the property manager."

She called the emergency line, explained the situation, and was told someone would be out when they were available. Natalie checked her phone. It was three in the morning. And with it being Sunday, she had no idea when "they" would be available. Would they send someone out of normal business hours? But what else could she do?

She shared the news with her neighbors, who were not exactly thrilled, but, fortunately, they took their grumbling back into their own apartments, leaving just Jordan and Natalie in the hallway. Jordan and Natalie shared a look, then grinned and burst into laughter. Neither knew their neighbors well, but from what they had seen, it didn't seem to matter what was going on; they would find a reason to complain. Maybe it was a good thing Natalie couldn't buy the building. She would not want to be on the receiving end.

"Can I get you a cup of coffee, Jordan?" Natalie asked.

"Nah, I'm good. You wouldn't be able to make it anyway." He grinned again. "Thanks, Natalie."

"No problem."

Jordan put up one hand in farewell and went back to his own apartment.

Natalie entered her apartment and closed the door. So much for sleeping in. Should she try to go back to bed? She was wide awake at this point, it being not much earlier than her alarm would usually go off. She would love to be able to make herself a cup of tea to relax, but with their stoves being electric, as Jordan had pointed out, she wouldn't be able to. No TV to zone out to, no light to do much of anything by.

With a sigh, Natalie walked to her sofa and sat down. She wrapped the blanket around herself and folded her knees up so she could rest her head on them. Then she looked out the window at the quiet town below.

Pine Valley was so peaceful at night. The streets were quiet, windows dark. Holiday lights glowed along Main Street and in the neighborhoods beyond. As she gazed at the stillness, she thought she saw...was it? Yes, the first snowflakes of the season. Natalie grinned. She loved snow. And if it continued, it would definitely put her in the holiday mood for making cookies later.

Natalie adjusted her position so she was more comfortable, then she closed her eyes and drifted back to sleep.

Chris woke to find snow floating past his window. He hadn't known it was going to snow. He wondered if Natalie had seen it. Did she like snow? He would bet she did.

He rolled over onto his back and stared at the ceiling. He would see Natalie that day. They were having lunch and then making more cookies. But how would he fill the time until then? With a smile he remembered the boxes that had been delivered the previous day – his Christmas tree and decorations. He felt like a kid on Christmas morning as he swung his legs out of bed. It would be the perfect activity to pass the time.

By the time he had to leave to meet Natalie, the tree was assembled and decorated. It definitely made the apartment look more lived-in, but it wasn't enough to make it cozy. And setting it up hadn't been nearly as much fun without Natalie's presence. Still, he was glad he had done it. It made him feel connected somehow – to Natalie, to Pine Valley. It was like a little piece of his new life taking over his old one. With a sigh of contentment, he got ready to leave.

Natalie stretched her arms, legs, and neck, and tried to figure out what was going on. The sun was shining through the window now. She looked at her phone where she had rested it on the coffee table. She had slept clear through to lunch. Guess she needed the rest.

The knock that had woken her up sounded again. "Natalie?" she could hear Chris say through the door. "Are you home?"

"Yeah, I'm here," she called out. "One sec."

She wrapped the blanket around herself and made her way to the door.

"Sorry," she said as she opened it.

"Nothing to apologize for. Just wanted to make sure you were okay. Why are the lights off in the hallway?"

Natalie sighed. "We lost power. About three AM."

"Who's 'we'? It seemed business as usual elsewhere."

"Either the building or the second floor. I haven't checked the first floor yet, but the apartments are out."

"Think it's the electric panel?"

"That would be my guess."

"Do you want me to take a look?"

"Do you know anything about electric panels?"

Chris grinned. "Not really, no."

Natalie laughed. "Then I don't think that would help much, would it?"

"I guess not. Did you call the property manager?"

"Yeah. They didn't give me any idea on time frame, just said they'd have someone out when they're available."

"Hmm. Okay. Well, let's check out the first floor, then maybe we can call an electrician ourselves."

"We can try. Not sure how much that would cost, though, or if the management company would like that very much."

"Hmm."

"Let me just get dressed and ready, and we can head down."

He looked her up and down, just realizing she wasn't dressed for the day. "Sorry, did you just get up?"

"Yeah. I fell back to sleep on the couch after the early morning wakeup."

"I'm sorry. Do you want me to go? You should probably rest."

"No, I'm fine. We have things to do, anyway."

Natalie retreated to her bedroom and got dressed as quickly as she was able. She would shower later, after she was thoroughly covered in flour and who knew what else. For now, she didn't want to keep Chris waiting. A quick brush of her hair and teeth, and she was at least somewhat presentable. He had seen her looking worse, she reasoned. She cocked her head at the thought. Hmm. He *had* seen her at her worst, and instead of being scared off, he had been spending more time than ever around town. She filed that thought away for later.

"Okay, let's go," she said when she was done.

Chris held out an elbow for her to take, and they left the apartment arm in arm.

The cafe had power, which was a relief, but before tackling the cookies, they were having lunch across the street at the diner.

The snow that morning had left a dusting of white that gave everything a cheerful wintry look, but many places in town were closed on Sunday, so the streets were quieter than they had been over the last couple of days. Most people who wanted to be out and about were out of town, so the diner was relatively quiet, too. Natalie and Chris sat down in a booth and took out the menus.

Natalie suddenly felt nervous. This felt like a date, and she wasn't sure how she felt about it. *Too late to back out now,* she thought. She just hoped the whole town wouldn't start talking.

Chapter 46

The electrician showed up midafternoon on Sunday, when Natalie and Chris were fully immersed in making cookie dough. Seeing people inside the cafe, the electrician had knocked on that door first.

Natalie let him into the utility room and showed him where the electric panel was. He gave a low whistle. "This panel's a mess," he said. "I'm surprised you had power at all before this."

Natalie sighed. "Yeah, there was an inspector here last week because the building is up for sale, and he said the same thing."

"This whole thing is going to have to get redone. I don't think I could safely get you guys back online with it as it is."

"I'd love to say go for it, but I can't approve that. You'll have to take it up with the property management company or the owner."

The electrician was already taking out his phone.

Natalie didn't want to hear what was sure to be a heated conversation, so she retreated to the cafe. She had work to do anyway.

"What did he say?" Chris asked when she re-entered the kitchen.

"Basically what Chuck said last week. The wiring needs to get redone. And now, before we can get our power back."

"So before the sale."

"Apparently so."

"That will be one less obstacle for Townsend."

"Yup."

"I should let Chuck know. He'll probably want to come out and inspect again once the work is complete."

Chris wiped his hands, took out his phone, and left the kitchen to call Chuck. Natalie sighed, washed her hands, and got back to work. Her energy was fortunately holding up, but this latest development wasn't helping her mental state.

She thought back to her lunch with Chris, instead. She had noticed Maggie giving her occasional knowing looks, but otherwise it had been pleasant, uncomplicated time together. She had learned more about his childhood and interests, and she had shared more about herself. She had enjoyed herself. And it had felt natural to walk back to the cafe to work on their project for the day.

They had fallen into their rhythm quickly this time, each remembering how the other worked from the last time. Natalie was trying not to focus on how easy it was with him, how natural it felt. She couldn't think about that right now.

The electrician came back to the cafe about the same time Chris entered the kitchen. "What's the verdict?" Natalie asked.

"Well, they approved the work, but not the timing. Since it's Sunday, the rate is higher. I'll have to come back tomorrow."

"So we'll be without power for another day."

"Sorry. If I do another patch job, it could be a fire hazard, and I don't want to take that chance."

"I appreciate that."

"I have another job lined up in the morning, but I'll be back as soon as I can."

"Okay. Thanks. I'll let everyone know." That should be a fun conversation. She walked the electrician out and then turned to Chris. "What a week."

"You can say that again. Will you be okay in the apartment without power?"

"Yeah, I'll be fine. I'm pretty sure the furnace is part of the first-floor grid, so it shouldn't get too cold. And I can take care of cooking or whatever down here."

"Climbing the stairs up and down?"

"I'll plan ahead."

"You're already down here."

"I'll be fine," she insisted. Maybe it was the stress, but she was getting aggravated. She didn't want to be seen as an invalid anymore.

He looked skeptical. "If you say so."

"Let's get back to cookies. I want to see if I can get another batch or two prepped before we call it a day."

She whipped up a double batch of sugar cookie dough, wrapped them, put them in the freezer, then collapsed on a stool.

"Okay, I'm pooped."

"You probably overdid it."

"I'll be okay. I feel better knowing I made good progress."

Chris finished wiping down the counters, then tossed the rag in a bucket. "How much more do you have to make?"

"A bunch. Maybe two more days like today should cover it."

"Should I pencil you in for next weekend?"

Natalie gave Chris a pointed look. "You need a life."

Chris gestured around. "This is as good a life as any. A cozy shop, sweet treats, and a beautiful woman to hang out with."

"Yeah, well, you've done too much already."

Chris didn't respond, just walked up to Natalie and took her hand. "This is going to be a rough week. It helps to know I have something to look forward to at the end of it."

"Even if it ends up being a pity party?"

"It won't be. If things don't go our way, we'll take the time to regroup and brainstorm."

Natalie wasn't feeling very positive, but she didn't want to argue. "I should probably go tell my neighbors about the electrician and come up with a plan for the night."

"Are you sure you're going to be okay?"

"Chris, seriously, you need to stop obsessing. I'll be fine."

"Okay. Do you want help going up the stairs?"

Natalie took a deep breath. "I need to do it on my own." It wasn't just the stress. She needed to start weaning herself off from him. He was right: this would be a tough week. And chances were very high that at the end of it, she would have to say goodbye to him.

He seemed to sense a shift in her attitude, because he let go of her hand and stepped back. "Okay. Well, if you need anything, you know how to reach me."

"Yes, I do. I'll let you know what happens with the electrician tomorrow."

"Okay. I'll let you know if I hear anything else."

They said an awkward goodbye, and Natalie watched him disappear out the back door. She sighed. She just wanted to be happy again, to get off this emotional rollercoaster, to not feel torn every time she started feeling settled.

But for now, she needed to figure out dinner so she wouldn't have to worry later. Chris was right that she wouldn't want to go up and down the stairs any more than she had to, not that she would admit it to anyone but herself. Maybe she could find something in the cafe fridge.

A few minutes later, a bag with groceries that would have to be discarded soon hanging from one elbow, Natalie made her way slowly up the stairs. She held firmly to the handrail, not taking any chances. And she was grateful to make it to the top without incident. After stopping at her apartment to drop off the bag, she then made her way down the hall, knocking on each of her neighbors' doors to tell them what she knew about the electricity. None of them were happy, but there wasn't anything they could do about it.

By the time she returned to her apartment, Natalie was exhausted. It would have been nice to just sit and put her feet up, but first she had to make herself dinner. A day-old roll, some deli meat and veggies, and she had a sandwich. She collapsed onto a dining chair and ate, head drooping. Maybe she shouldn't have dismissed Chris's help so quickly. But she had to stop relying on him so much. She had been taking care of herself for years now. She could do this.

Feeling tears welling in her eyes, Natalie grabbed a napkin to brush them away. It didn't do any good to get upset about the situation. She just had to make it through.

Chapter 47

Natalie hated how she had left things with Chris. Knowing that he had done nothing but help her while she had changed her mind more times than she could count made her feel exceptionally guilty. And, as a result, she woke up in a grumpy mood Monday morning.

The power was still out, of course, but she still had to get up and somehow get ready in the dark while still feeling somewhat unsteady. She had to make it down the stairs without falling again, wear herself out getting the baking done, and then what? Without power her options were limited in her apartment, but she had nothing to do around town. She supposed she would just stay in the cafe taking care of business.

Joey seemed to sense her mood, so he gave her a wide berth, working on his portion of the baking at one end of the kitchen while she did hers on the other. McKenna had been willing to pick up extra shifts, so she came in to open, and Joey signaled her that Natalie was not to be messed with. Natalie noticed the signal and sighed. Maybe she should stay in the office. She wasn't suitable company for anyone today.

The electrician came by around eleven. Joey called her out front, and she showed him back to the utility room. She wondered how long it would take, but as long as he got everything taken care of properly, she supposed it didn't really matter. She had just sat back down at her desk when Joey called her out front again. Natalie released a breath. It was just one of those days.

Her visitor this time threw her off guard, though.

"Mrs. Malloy, what brings you by today?"

"I heard about the electricity issue, of course, and I wanted to make sure it was all taken care of." Colleen sighed, then paused before resuming. "Actually, that's not why I'm really here. I...heard about the concerns with the guy who might be buying the place."

Natalie swallowed. "Have you accepted the offer?"

"He hasn't made one yet. Which makes me think now is the time to act."

"Act how?"

Colleen met Natalie's gaze. "I know it didn't directly affect you, but I'm sorry about what my idiot husband did. I know the town hates us, and I don't blame them."

"The town doesn't hate you. They're mad at your husband. And some of them are still mad about your son, too."

"Well, they've taken it out on me."

"I'm sorry for that."

"Yeah, well, I may not be able to change what they did, but maybe I can make things at least a little better." She took a deep breath. "I'll be honest, I can't stay around here anymore. Between the tension and the constant reminders, being unable to start over. I just can't take it. I can't get a job. The bills are piling up. I can't just not sell. I need the money."

"I get it. I do."

"But it sounds to me like the new guy wouldn't be able to do anything if you had a longer lease, at least not for a while."

Natalie's heart began to beat faster. It wouldn't really solve the problem, but at least it would give them more time. "It would definitely help. My lease is up in January, and I admit I've been a bit worried about it."

"I know. And some of the other tenants are in the same boat." She lifted up the bag she had brought in with her. "So I brought new lease paperwork to sign. Decide how long you want to commit to, and I'll sign it."

"Are you sure? It may affect the offer. If he can't bring in the people he wants soon, he may give up altogether."

Colleen shrugged. "I hope that's not the case, but I wouldn't be able to live with myself if I didn't at least try. My family has done enough damage to this town."

Natalie felt like crying. "Thank you. Thank you so much."

"Well, you've done it now."

Chris hadn't known what to expect when he picked up Eric's call, but it wasn't that. "What did I do?"

"Remember that little heart-to-heart you had with Malloy?"

"Yeah."

"Apparently her conscience won out. She just called to tell me that she has extended the leases for all the tenants who were scheduled to expire in the next year."

Chris's jaw dropped open. "She did?"

"Yup. And I don't think Townsend's going to be too happy about it. It wouldn't surprise me if he backed out altogether."

That would just be too perfect, Chris thought. But out loud he said, "I guess we'll have to wait and see."

"Yeah. So thanks."

Chris grinned. "No problem."

He heard Eric swear under his breath then hang up the phone.

Chris felt like dancing, but after a moment's jubilation, he paused. Why hadn't Natalie called him? Was Colleen just planning to renew? It sounded like she had already done it, so that meant Natalie should have been on the list. Had Colleen somehow missed her? Or was Natalie upset with him about something?

She had seemed off the night before. Maybe he had been getting too clingy, too pushy. Maybe she was trying to distance herself from him. But this was about the building. He had thought she would at least discuss that with him.

Should he call her? But that might be pushy, too. Was there a reason she didn't want him to know about it? That didn't make sense.

Chris looked up at the building in front of him. He was sitting in his car, getting ready to go into the bank to discuss a business loan. With this new development, should he still plan on doing that? He ran a hand through his hair. Just when he had been making some decisions, everything changed again.

He still hadn't gone to the office. He figured if he stayed away, it was harder for Ryker to let him go. So he had done research and paperwork at home, made phone calls, touched base with his clients, and avoided anything that would put his job in jeopardy. If he had hopes of getting a business loan, he would need his job. But would this new information be the final straw? Would Eric go to Ryker again, tell him how he'd interfered? Would he get a phone call any minute telling him to pack up his things?

Maybe he should do the loan application now, before that happened. While the longer leases may discourage Townsend from making an offer, there was no guarantee the next buyer wouldn't be just as bad or worse. And Chris didn't know how long the leases had been extended for. This was just a reprieve; it wasn't a solution. But he could offer a solution, to at least some of them.

Chris slid out of his car, grabbed his briefcase, and walked purposefully toward the bank. Just as he was about to open the door, his phone rang. He glanced at the screen. It was Natalie. He took a deep breath. He couldn't do this right now. He needed to make a decision.

Putting his phone on silent, Chris opened the door.

Chapter 48

Natalie's call went to voicemail, and she left Chris a message to call her back.

He had been the first one she wanted to tell, but with the uncertainty she was feeling around him, she decided to head to Courtney's instead. Courtney had been happy for her, excited even, though she had been suspiciously giddy even before Natalie told her the news. If Natalie had to guess, she would say it had a lot to do with the boy next door who had been spending considerable time in the boutique. And, sure enough, Josh walked in shortly after Natalie arrived, and Courtney's smile widened more than Natalie would have thought possible.

Natalie had shared her news, and then, not wanting to stick around for the lovefest, headed back to the cafe. And she knew she had to call Chris. Whatever she was feeling for him personally, he had a vested interest in this, and he had been the one to make it happen.

It wasn't like him not to pick up when she called. Which was ridiculous, she reasoned. Hadn't she just been telling him she needed to do things on her own and he needed a life? And telling herself she needed to wean herself off him? He was probably busy with, oh, I don't know, his job? His other clients? Friends? Hobbies? Anything that would fill his life aside from her and her stupid building?

But she wanted to share this with him. She wanted to discuss the decisions she had made while she had been sulking in the office all morning. She wanted to hear his voice and see his face light up with that special little twinkle he had when he looked at her.

But she had gone to voicemail.

With a sigh, Natalie put on an apron and washed her hands. She needed to punch some more bread dough.

Mission complete, Chris walked out of the bank half an hour later. While it would take a day or two to get a final approval, the bank manager had been quite hopeful that he would get approved for the full amount he had requested: enough to cover the difference between his available funds and the cost of the two commercial buildings.

Now he had to put in an offer, though he wasn't looking forward to calling Eric back. And he had to tell Natalie.

Better to get Eric over with first.

"Are you serious?" Eric said.

"You knew I was considering it."

"Does this have to do with the lease extensions?"

"Why would it? I wasn't planning on kicking anyone out. I would have renewed their leases anyway."

"So why now?"

"It's just how it worked out, Eric. Nothing underhanded. I had been debating, and I finally decided."

Eric sighed.

"What? I would think you would be happy. Two of the buildings are getting sold. Full asking price."

"Yeah, and that's two less for Townsend, which means he may not want the others now, especially with the whole lease fiasco. Ryker wasn't happy about that, by the way."

"I take it you told him."

Eric didn't answer.

"Well, someone will come along for the others. It's just a matter of time."

"If you say so. Townsend won't be happy, especially after he paid for the inspection. And I was just warming him up on some other properties, too. I swear, if you ruin this whole client for me..."

"It's an offer. Colleen Malloy will have to decide. Just draw up the paperwork, Eric."

"Yeah, yeah. I'll send it over in a few."

One thing out of the way, Chris returned Natalie's call.

"Hey," she answered.

"Hey. I hear congratulations are in order."

"You heard about the leases?"

"Yeah, Eric called me to complain."

"Well, I'm not complaining."

"I didn't think you would. How long did you renew for? Eric was vague about details."

"So, here's the thing. I wanted to discuss something with you."

"Okay...what's up?"

"Not over the phone. Would you be willing to come down to Pine Valley? Or tell me where you are, and I can take an Uber."

"You are not taking an Uber. I can meet you. I have some things to discuss with you, too. But I have a couple of things to take care of first. How about an early dinner? I can aim to be there between five and six."

"That would work."

"Okay. I'll see you soon." Chris disconnected the call and took a deep breath. He wondered how she would take the news, about him putting in an offer on the other buildings. Would she be upset? Relieved? And what did she want to discuss with him? He hoped she wasn't telling him to get lost. Now that she had a lease extension, she technically didn't need his help on the building anymore. She would have time to make plans and figure things out.

He hoped he meant more to her than help with the building, but with her up and down attitude, it was hard to say.

Maybe tonight he would have some answers about that, too.

Chapter 49

Natalie felt nervous, which was ridiculous. How much time had she spent with Chris over the last couple of weeks? Why would she possibly be nervous about spending time with him tonight?

But it wasn't about spending time with him. It was about what she wanted to discuss with him. She wasn't sure if she had made a mistake or a wise move. He knew a lot more about this stuff.

It took forever for five o'clock to roll around. And when Chris wasn't there right at five, she began to second-guess herself. Maybe he wasn't coming. Maybe he was mad at her for how she had treated him the night before. But she tried not to panic. He had said between five and six, so there was still plenty of time.

At around five fifteen, she heard the knock on her door and breathed a sigh of relief.

"Hey," he said when she opened the door for him. He looked nervous, too. She hoped he didn't have bad news for her.

"Hey."

He was dressed in a suit and wool coat, but that wasn't anything new. She felt frumpy next to him, though, in her jeans and a sweater.

"I look like I'm wearing rags next to you. Should I change?"

"You look beautiful, but it's up to you."

"I'm going to go change."

Natalie retreated to her bedroom, her heart beating a mile a minute. This felt even more like a date than last time. What was she doing?

A few minutes later, dressed in a knit sweater dress, she rejoined Chris by the door.

He took in her appearance appreciatively before holding out an elbow and asking, "Shall we go?"

Natalie grabbed her coat and took his arm.

He had parked in the parking lot behind the cafe, and he led her to his car.

"We're not going to the diner?"

"Not today. I made reservations at Giuseppe's." He met her gaze. "Is that okay? I should have asked."

Natalie shook her head. "No, it's fine. I'm just surprised." She swallowed. This was definitely a date. "Glad I changed." She attempted a smile.

He grinned at her. "I'm sure you would have been fine either way."

They drove in silence. It was only a few blocks away, but the silence felt awkward, heavy, filled with anticipation. Natalie was glad when they pulled into the restaurant's parking lot.

They were seated promptly, and they didn't speak to each other until they had placed their orders. Chris began fiddling with his silverware. He looked more nervous than she was.

"So, I made a decision," he said after a moment.

"About what?"

"The buildings." He looked up at her then. "I put in an offer on the two smaller buildings."

Natalie's stomach flip-flopped. Was she happy with this news? Disappointed? He wouldn't be her landlord, at least not for however long she stayed in the building. But he was helping other business owners. "That's great."

"Is it? I wasn't sure if you would be upset that I didn't offer to buy yours."

Natalie shook her head. "No. It's fine. I'm glad those other businesses will be protected. Has the offer been accepted?"

"Not yet." Chris gave a small laugh. "It wouldn't surprise me if Eric sat on the offer for a day or two, just to make me suffer. But he is obligated to present all offers to the seller. I just hope Colleen accepts it."

"Me, too. From our conversation earlier, I'm thinking there's a good chance."

"Yes, how did that go?"

Natalie took a deep breath. "It was surprising, to say the least. I definitely did not expect her to walk into the cafe today, especially with an offer like that."

"She just had a change of heart?"

"Well, she apologized for needing to sell the buildings, but I understood. She's in a tough spot. But she wanted to make up for what her husband did. She said he did enough damage to this town, and she didn't want it to get worse."

"I'm glad. How long did she extend the leases for?"

"I can't speak for the other businesses, but for me, she said to let her know how long I wanted it for, and she would sign the paperwork."

"Wow."

"Yeah. I was a bit taken aback. Part of me was tempted to ask for a ten-year lease or something."

"I take it you didn't?"

"I did not." She paused. "This whole situation has made me take a good hard look at things, at what I want and need. I've hated feeling like the rug could get pulled out from under me at any minute. Everything felt so out of my control, and I am *not* the kind of person who likes to be out of control."

Chris chuckled. "I've noticed."

Natalie gave him a pointed look. "When we started discussing other options, about moving and renovating and everything, I realized that I've been resistant to change. I wanted things to stay the same, and I wanted to know what to expect, and I wanted to be able to ensure that they stayed the same."

"You want to move?"

"No. I don't want to move. At least, not out of Pine Valley. This is still my home, my community. I love this town and the people. But by insisting that things stay the same, I was holding myself back. I wasn't letting myself dream."

"So what's your dream?"

She met his gaze then. She wouldn't say that he was part of her dream, but she could discuss the rest of it. "I don't want to buy my building, even if I could afford it. I don't want to be a landlord and be responsible for other people's property. But I do want to be responsible for my own. I *want* to buy a building, for my business and for my home. And if that means buying a house and going through all the rigamarole of getting it rezoned and upgrading the electrical system and knocking down walls, then that's what I'll do. I made the cafe mine, and that won't change if it moves a couple of blocks over, even if it's off Main Street. If anything, I'll be able to make it even *more* mine, setting things up exactly how I want them."

"That's amazing, Natalie. It sounds awesome. Does that mean you turned down the lease renewal?"

Natalie shook her head. "No. I realized that my biggest hesitation, back when we discussed the whole house thing, was the time factor. There was no way I could buy and renovate a property before my lease was up in January, especially with the holidays and everything in between. So I requested a one-year renewal."

"That's it?"

Natalie took a deep breath. "Yes. I didn't want to have to break a lease if it was longer, and part of me knew that if I gave myself too much time, I might never actually accomplish anything. I would get complacent again, settled in the regular routines. This will give me a kick in the pants, so to speak."

Chris leaned back and assessed her. "Wow. I'm impressed."

Natalie wasn't sure if she should be happy or offended by his assessment, but she chose to think positively. "Thanks."

Their food was served then, and they both lapsed into silence as they ate. Natalie was feeling good. A little nervous perhaps, but that was to be expected. She was on the verge of making a big life change. But she couldn't help but feel little flutters of anticipation, too.

And, even if he didn't end up moving to Pine Valley, if Chris bought the buildings, he would at least have a connection. She would see him at least occasionally. Would that be easier or harder? Better not to dwell on it too much. For now, she would just appreciate the time she had with him. She smiled at him over her glass of wine, and he returned the smile. Life sure could be unpredictable.

Chapter 50

Chris brought Natalie back home after dinner and walked her to her door. He thought about kissing her good night, but he wasn't sure how she would take it. While it wouldn't be their first kiss, she seemed to want to maintain distance, and he was trying to respect that. Even if she had looked amazing tonight. And even if they had seemed like they were getting closer over dinner. He still couldn't make her any promises, and she hadn't given him the go-ahead. So he refrained. But, man, was it tough.

He had just gotten back into his car when his phone rang. Had Natalie changed her mind and wanted him to stay? He certainly wouldn't be complaining. But, no, it was Lena Morseau. The board meeting must have ended. Taking a deep breath, he answered the call.

"Christopher Parker."

"Mr. Parker, this is Lena Morseau."

"Hello, Ms. Morseau. How are you?"

"I am doing well. And you?"

"Can't complain. I'll be a whole lot happier if you have good news for me, though." Chris tried to stay upbeat, but his stomach was twisting in knots. While he had put in the offer on the buildings, he would have no problem losing out to Ms. Morseau's foundation.

"Well, my news is more bad than good, I'm afraid. The board met tonight, and we did make some decisions regarding the Pine Valley properties."

Chris stayed silent, holding his breath while he waited for the bad news.

"As suspected, the commercial properties did not really align with the foundation's purpose, despite the possible future impact a new owner may have. There were too many hypotheticals and uncertainties, especially since an offer had not even been made on the properties."

"I understand."

"They were intrigued, however, by the apartment building property."

Chris paused. It would certainly be better than nothing, and further encouragement for Townsend to leave Pine Valley alone.

"The history that Ms. Mitchell shared with me, about the shady landlord and tragedy that occurred last fall, struck a chord, if you will, with many members of the board. And we discussed the situation in depth. Thus far we have focused on commercial and community buildings, ways to have an impact on the greatest number of people. But the idea of constructing a building to assist those who had been rendered homeless, and encourage further growth of the town, was appealing. We have decided to make an offer for that property, if it has not yet been claimed."

Chris grinned. Eric would be upset, but he certainly wasn't. "It has not yet been claimed. As of now, no offers have been made on that property, though I expect one to be in by the end of the week."

"Well, then, we'd better get moving. Can you send the paperwork over for me to sign?"

"I would love to, but I am actually no longer the listing agent on the Pine Valley properties. But I can connect you with the new agent."

Lena paused. "Why do I suspect there's more to the story there?"

"Because there always is. Suffice it to say that I've been doing what I've had to to make sure these properties are handled properly."

"I'm glad to hear it. Actually, that segues nicely into something else I wanted to discuss with you."

"What is that?"

"I know that you usually handle commercial properties, and I'm sure this would be a waste of your talents and experience, but when we decided to pursue the apartment building, we realized we would need someone available to serve as a leasing agent once the building was complete. The other board members and I have other duties and responsibilities, and none of us are well-versed in that sort of thing. I immediately thought of you."

The suggestion threw him off guard. He had never considered working with leases. Up until now, he had thrived on the thrill of the sale. Would he even like it? And was that a full-time gig, or was it temporary? He would have to look into it.

"Can I think about it?"

"Of course. There wouldn't be a need until closer to the building completion, so we have time. If it goes well, though, the board had discussed doing the same in other communities where there is a housing need and available space, so there may be future opportunities, as well."

It was a lot to take in, and Chris wasn't sure how to respond. "I appreciate you considering me."

"Of course. I have been impressed with your character and work ethic. I think you would be a wonderful addition to our team."

"Thank you."

"Of course. Now, if you would please tell me who I need to contact to make the offer on the property, I would be most appreciative."

Chris passed along Eric's information, then said goodbye to Ms. Morseau. Then he shot a text to Eric to give him a heads up.

He looked back toward the building that housed Natalie's apartment. Part of him wanted to run back inside and tell her what had happened. Part of him needed time to process it all on his own. After a moment's hesitation, he decided to head home. He would call her tomorrow to let her know. Maybe by then he would have made some kind of decision.

All during the ride, Chris weighed the pros and cons of Ms. Morseau's offer. He had never done leasing, just selling. He could suck, especially since he was used to corporate types who wanted to be shmoozed. What did he know about renting out apartments? But he would have time to learn, see what he could find out, pick up some tips and tricks. He was sure with a bit of effort he could do it and maybe even excel. But did he want to? The pay would probably be pitiful compared to what he made now. Did that matter?

It would be another link to Pine Valley. He would have his buildings, assuming his offer was accepted, and the leasing agent gig. Maybe he could convince Natalie that he wouldn't just up and leave. He was putting down roots, in a sense. But if he started working in Pine Valley, would he move here, too? It would be a bit of a commute from his current apartment.

And what about when the apartments were all leased? There may be the occasional vacancy, but not enough to keep him on full time. She had said there would be other properties, if all went well. But where would those properties be? Would he have to move again? Travel long distances on a regular basis?

He would have to leave Ryker Commercial Properties, but that part didn't really bother him. With his boss being upset with him, and Chris's own disillusionment with the business, it wouldn't be hard to walk away. But would his new opportunities in Pine Valley be enough to pay the bills? Would he have enough to do, especially between tenant requests and until the building was complete?

Was there something else he could do to fill the gaps?

Chris thought back to his impressions of the local real estate office: professional but friendly. Would there be a place for him there? True, it was a small office in a small town, so there may not be enough work to go around, but it wouldn't hurt to ask.

Then he would really have to move to Pine Valley. Property owner, leasing agent, and realtor? That was too many commitments to be commuting for. And he couldn't forget the most important reason of all: Natalie. He would be on hand to help her with her new building and whatever she decided to do with it. And they could see where a relationship led, without commitment issues hanging over their heads.

Yes, the idea had merit.

Chapter 51

Natalie lay awake much longer than she should have. She had to get some sleep, but she couldn't keep the events of the evening from running on a loop through her mind. Chris was buying the other buildings. Did that mean he would move to Pine Valley or oversee them from a distance? Or hire a property manager and barely be in town at all? Was she crazy for trying to buy and renovate a house? Should she have signed a crazy long lease and given herself some stability? Even if the cafe wasn't perfect as is, it had served her well, and it made her happy. Couldn't that be enough? Should she call Colleen Malloy back and say she had changed her mind? And why hadn't Chris kissed her goodnight? He wanted to; she could tell. And the whole evening had felt like a date. So why hadn't he? Did he think she didn't want him to? She had certainly given him enough mixed signals. Maybe he was scared of rejection again.

By the time her alarm went off Tuesday morning, Natalie felt like a zombie. She still wasn't a hundred percent, and adding very little sleep to the mix did not make for a happy Natalie. But she dragged herself out of bed and into the shower, hoping it would wake her up. It didn't help much.

It should be a typical Tuesday, barring any more unexpected guests or life-altering news, so Natalie started with the baking like she did every morning. Joey tried to perk her up, but after unsuccessfully trying to engage her in gossip, he settled for raising the volume on their upbeat morning music.

The morning passed uneventfully. Chuck came in to reinspect the electric panel now that everything had been corrected. As he left, he told Natalie that he would be sending over his report that afternoon. With Chris's offer made, should she worry? Of course there was still her building to consider, and Chris's offer hadn't been accepted yet, but would Malloy accept an offer from Townsend now? With other options to consider that would at least tide her over until the rest sold?

Maybe it wouldn't be a typical Tuesday, considering her stress levels. Would she see Chris today? He hadn't made any promises, but they were in crunch time. This week the future of all of their lives could be determined. He had said he wanted her as part of his future. Did that still apply?

Chris knew that he couldn't just up and leave his current job without having everything else in place. At the very least, he was still waiting on the business loan approval. So he spent Tuesday morning working on projects and reports for his current clients. He wasn't looking into taking on any more, though, so he should have the afternoon free to work on future plans. He only hoped something would pan out.

By the time he walked into the real estate office in Pine Valley after lunch, he had convinced himself that the whole endeavor was pointless. Even if they had enough business to support another realtor, why would they want someone who didn't know the first thing about selling residential? That was their focus, after all. But he had to try.

He saw three people in the office. Two were on the phone, and one was seated at a desk that served as reception. Taking a deep breath, he approached the reception desk. The woman sitting there had been in the office the last time he stopped in, back when he was new to Pine Valley. It felt like years ago. Had it really been less than a month?

"Hi," he began. "I'm not sure if you remember me. I came in a while back and introduced myself. I was the agent selling the commercial properties in the center of town."

"Of course! I never forget a face. Chris, right?"

"Yeah, that's right."

"I am Megan Sullivan. It's a pleasure to meet you again. How is the sale going?"

Chris gave a wry laugh. "Much more dramatically than I expected, but we're making progress. I'm actually no longer the listing agent."

"Oh. I'm sorry to hear that."

"Oh, nothing to be sorry about." He had to spin this, make it sound like he wasn't on the verge of losing his job. After all, why would they want to be associated with someone who got kicked off listings? "I decided to put in an offer on a couple of the buildings myself, so I had to recuse myself. Conflict of interest and all."

"Well that's exciting!"

"Yeah. I'm still waiting to see if my offer is accepted, but I'm hopeful."

"I hope it works out."

"Me, too."

Silence fell before Megan spoke again. "So, what brings you in? Just giving a status update?"

Chris took another deep breath. "No, actually. I was...I hoped..." He paused. "Are you in charge of this office, or is one of the others the head broker?"

"My husband John and I run the agency. We brought on Priya a year or so ago to help with our whole work-life balance thing. Was there a problem?"

"Oh, no, nothing like that. Actually, well..." He was making a mess of this. How to put into words everything that had been running through his mind? He paused and tried to formulate a coherent thought. "I came into town as a city kind of guy, ready to sell some buildings and make money, just like I had in plenty of other towns and cities around the state. But, well, Pine Valley grew on me. And it's had me reassessing some things about myself and the way I operate. I'm looking to make some changes. One of those changes, hopefully, will be overseeing the two commercial buildings I mentioned. But I don't expect that to be a full-time gig. I was wondering if by any chance you were looking to take on another agent?"

There. That had made sense, didn't it? Without making him sound like a lunatic?

Megan tilted her head to one side and looked at him carefully. He tried his best not to fidget. "Do you have any residential experience?"

Chris shook his head. "Unfortunately, no. I know that doesn't work in my favor. And I know this is a small office in a small town, so I totally understand if you don't have the resources for it to make sense."

"We actually service several of the towns in the area, not just Pine Valley, so our client base is surprisingly large. And growing, actually. And, while most of our clients are looking for residential properties, we have been seeing more people looking for retail spaces and such."

"That's great."

"Let me discuss the situation with my husband, and we can get back to you. Do you have a resume? References?"

"Uh, yes." Chris dug around in his briefcase and brought out the documents he had carefully prepared last night when he was too wound up to sleep. Finding references had been a challenge, but hopefully the ones he had selected would reflect well on him.

"Great. We'll look this over and get back to you. Maybe in a day or two?"

"That would be great. Thank you so much."

"Absolutely. Thanks for stopping in."

Chris left the office still tied up in knots but feeling slightly more hopeful. Maybe things would work out after all. Should he tell Natalie or hold off until he knew more? Probably better to hold off until he had some concrete answers. But he should at least tell her about Lena Morseau's call. He looked at his watch. The cafe would be closing soon. It was the perfect time to sit and chat. And maybe dream a bit about the future.

Chapter 52

Chris saw Natalie at the register, helping a customer. She looked drained, with a smile that didn't quite reach her eyes. Was she feeling okay? Maybe she had slept about as well as he had.

After a moment, she looked up to see him standing in the doorway, and her face transformed. Chris's heart raced. She was happy to see him. That was a good sign, wasn't it?

She finished up with her customer, and he walked up to her. "Hey."

"Hey."

"Are you free after the cafe closes?"

"I should be. Why? Is everything okay?"

"Everything's fine. I heard from Lena Morseau."

"Oh! Okay. Good news?"

"Fifty-fifty, I'd say."

"Okay. Have a seat, and I'll be over when we're done with the closing stuff. Do you want anything to eat?"

"Surprise me."

Her eyes twinkled, and her lips twitched into a smile. "Okay. Turn around."

Chris laughed but did as requested. A few seconds later he heard a plate tap the counter. He turned to find a chocolate croissant resting on a plate. The first thing he had ever ordered from her. He met her gaze. "Thanks. How much do I owe you?"

"It's on the house."

"Thanks."

Their gazes held for a few moments until Sylvie cleared her throat beside Natalie.

"In case you hadn't realized, we still have other customers," Sylvie said softly.

Natalie blushed. "Sorry." She turned to greet her next customer, and Chris left the counter to find a seat.

He opted to sit at the counter that stood in front of the picture window, with stools facing out. The same seat he had been in when he first confessed his feels for Natalie to Chloe. He never would have guessed just how much his world would be turned upside down. But he wouldn't change a thing. Well, except maybe the drama with Townsend. But hadn't that just brought them closer?

He was lost in thought when Natalie sat down beside him. "So what did Lena Morseau have to say?"

He remained facing the window, convinced he would lose his train of thought if he looked at her. "The foundation turned down buying the buildings."

Natalie sighed. "Okay. Well, with you possibly buying two of them, it could be worse."

He looked at her then. "They want to buy the apartment site, though. And build a new apartment building."

"Really? That didn't seem like the kind of thing they did."

"It's not, apparently. But they thought it could be a good direction, to offer housing to help with community growth and all that."

"That's great."

"Yeah."

"You don't sound too happy about it. That's one less property for Townsend, even if it's not the one we were most worried about."

Chris turned to look out the window again. "Lena offered me a job, to be the leasing agent on the apartments when they were built."

"Wow."

"Yeah."

"Is that something you would want to do?"

"I don't know." He looked at her again. "It would be different from anything I've done before, but I don't think it would be too hard to learn. It would have me in Pine Valley more, at least for a while. Would you be okay with that?"

"Why wouldn't I be okay with that?"

"I don't know. Sometimes it's hard to tell if you want me around or not."

Natalie looked away. "I told you why."

"I know. That doesn't make it any easier, though."

"I'm sorry."

Chris took a deep breath. "It's okay. I get it. And I'm working on figuring things out. I have some things in the works, just waiting to see what pans out. I just hope it's all worth it."

"I'm not telling you to change your life, Chris."

"I know."

"And don't go making crazy changes if you're not sure you want them. That doesn't solve anything. Actually, that makes it worse."

"I know. That's why I'm trying to figure it out. So I'm sure."

A tap on the window interrupted their conversation. They both looked up. Colleen Malloy was standing outside. She waved.

Natalie stood up and went to open the door for her. "Hi. I wasn't expecting to see you again so soon," Natalie said. "Is everything okay?"

"Yes. Actually, I was on my way back from the diner. I had to meet with that Eric guy about some offers. I saw the two of you in the window there and thought I should stop by."

Chris and Natalie shared a look. Was Eric just sharing the offers they knew about, or had Townsend made an offer, too? The inspection results were supposed to come in this afternoon. Chris hadn't even checked his email since lunch. If Townsend got the results, he may have called in an offer.

"Please, come in," Natalie said, gesturing toward the dining area. "We were actually just discussing what I assume one of those offers was."

"Thank you." Colleen sat down in the seat Natalie had just vacated and took off her coat. "I know one of the offers, well, two of the offers, came from you, Mr. Parker. I admit, that one surprised me a bit."

"What can I say? Pine Valley grew on me. And it seemed like a good investment."

Colleen sighed and gazed out the window. "Yes, Pine Valley is special. I grew up here, you know. And after we were married, I'm the one who convinced Don to settle here. If I had known how that would play out, well, let's just say I would have done things differently." She turned back to look at Chris and Natalie. "But what's done is done. I can't change the past. I can only do what seems best for the future. I told Eric I needed time to think about the offers, but what I really needed was to discuss them with you, Mr. Parker."

"Me? Why?"

"Because you seem like a straight shooter. And unlike that Eric guy who seems like he's just out for as much money as possible, you seem to have higher priorities."

Chris swallowed. He didn't dare admit that he had been just like Eric not that long ago. "I appreciate that. I have certainly been trying to do what's best with these properties."

"And you think that for at least some of them, what's best is you."

Chris leaned back in his seat. It sounded incredibly egotistical when she put it that way. "I'm not going to pretend that I have it all figured out, Ms. Malloy. I just know that I couldn't let someone else come in here and destroy everything that makes Pine Valley the special place it is."

"Hmm. I did receive another offer on those properties, from the man I'm assuming you were referring to, a Matthew Townsend, I think it was."

"Yes, that's the man I had told you about."

"He offered considerably more than you did."

Chris's shoulders sagged. He had offered the asking price. The trouble was, he knew the asking price had been low. He had tried convincing her to ask for more, but she had been so anxious to sell them, she was willing to start low. No doubt Eric had encouraged Townsend to offer more to outbid him, knowing they were worth more. But if Chris went higher, he wouldn't be able to afford both buildings. "I wouldn't blame you if you accepted the higher offer. I know you've been put in a difficult position, and you need to do what's right for you."

"I had a feeling you would say that. Now, there were other offers on the other properties, as well. I'm not sure if you know anything about those buyers." She looked at some paperwork in a folder she had been carrying. "The apartment building site had an offer from a Lena Morseau. Any idea about her?"

"Yes, actually that was a buyer we were hoping could purchase everything. She runs a foundation to revitalize communities. The only property that aligned with the foundation's mission, though, was the apartment building. She wants what's best for the town and wants to be a part of its continued growth."

"Hmm. Good to know. And then the other offer was for this building here, actually." Chris shared another look with Natalie. Someone else was involved? Who? "A Joshua Macintire."

Natalie's mouth fell open. "Josh? Josh wants to buy this building?"

"Who's Josh?" Chris asked her. "The ice cream parlor guy?"

"Yeah. It has to be. I'm pretty sure that's his last name. But how on earth could he afford this building? His business doesn't even have customers half the year!"

"I guess the other half must be really good."

"So, this Joshua is the owner of the ice cream shop in this building?" Colleen asked. "I thought the name sounded familiar, but I couldn't place it. What are your thoughts on him?"

"Josh is great," Natalie said. "He's smart, and sweet. I thought he thought I was crazy when I was looking into buying it."

"You wanted to buy it, too?" Colleen asked.

"I was considering it. But I couldn't get approved for a high enough loan. I can't believe Josh could."

"Actually, Eric said it would be a cash offer, no financing required."

Natalie could only stare. Chris knew next to nothing about this Josh guy, but if Natalie was in shock, he must be a pretty low-key kind of guy. Where would a guy like that come up with the cash to buy a place like this?

"Okay, so I have two offers for each of the properties. Matthew Townsend made generous offers on all of them, and then I have you, Mr. Parker, Ms. Morseau, and Mr. Macintire, all at asking price."

Chris didn't know how to respond. Since she was hoping to move and start over, it made sense for Colleen to go with the higher offers, even if it wasn't right for the town. They would offer her more security. He wondered if Townsend knew about the longer leases. If so, he must not have been too bothered by them. Chris only hoped he honored them.

"Well, thank you for your insight. I have some thinking to do. I will let Eric know my decision tomorrow, so you should hear soon about what I decide."

"Thank you for your consideration," Chris said.

Colleen stood up, and Natalie walked her over to the door. When she returned to Chris, she asked, "what do you think she's going to decide?"

"I wish I knew."

Chapter 53

With everything undecided, Chris left shortly after Colleen Malloy did, saying he needed to check on some things and figure things out. Natalie wasn't sure what to do with herself, but she knew what she was going to do first. Remembering to grab her coat, she headed two doors down to Josh's ice cream shop.

The shop was empty, which wasn't unusual for the time of year and time of day.

"Hey, Natalie," Josh greeted her as he entered the front of the shop from the backroom. "What can I do for you?"

"Well, you can start by explaining to me how a guy with an empty shop half the year can suddenly afford a million-dollar building."

Josh's face reddened. "I guess you heard about my offer."

"What the hell, Josh? You made me sound like I was crazy for considering buying this place."

"No, I never thought you were crazy. I didn't want to get into business with a bunch of people, and I still don't, but I saw the appeal of owning the building, not having to worry about someone coming in and messing everything up."

"But, seriously, Josh, how? I know it's none of my business, but I cannot fathom how it's possible."

Josh sighed and gestured Natalie toward the side of the counter that held the register, where they could talk without shouting. "Let's just say I'm good at investing. I have a knack with playing the market, and it has served me well. I keep track of all the tech companies, in particular, and I can usually spot the best times to buy and sell."

"So you're an investing genius."

Josh shrugged. "I've done pretty well for myself."

Natalie leaned against the counter. "I guess so. And with all your money, you decide to run an ice cream shop? I admit, I'm having trouble wrapping my head around it."

"I like ice cream."

Natalie burst into laughter.

"So if Malloy told you about the offer, does that mean she's accepting it?"

"Who knows? She said she has to think about it. She wanted Chris's opinion on the people making the offers. She said we'll know tomorrow."

Josh sighed. "Well, at least we'll know soon. Now, can I offer you a cone?"

"Why not? Fill it with that pumpkin caramel concoction you've got going on there."

Josh made her ice cream cone and handed it over. Natalie reached for her wallet, but Josh held up a hand. "I got it. I think I can cover the cost of a cone." He grinned.

Natalie could only shake her head. "Does Courtney know?"

Josh took a deep breath. "Not yet. I've been trying to find the right time to tell her. It's not like I can just blurt out 'oh, by the way, I'm a millionaire.'"

"Well, she'll find out if you end up buying the building."

"See, I've thought of a way around that. I can have Mrs. Malloy say there's a new owner who wishes to remain anonymous. I'm going to have a property management company run things – a better one than what we've currently got – so she'll never need to know. No awkwardness. Perfect, right?"

Natalie gave him a pointed look. "That's the most ridiculous thing I've ever heard. If you want to have a relationship with Courtney, you need to tell her."

Josh sighed. "I know. Let's see what happens with the offer first. Can you keep it to yourself until then?"

Natalie sighed dramatically. "I guess so. It's a good thing I like you."

Josh grinned. "Thanks. I hope you put in a good word for me, since apparently Malloy values your opinion now."

"Well, it was Chris's opinion she wanted, but, yes, I put in a good word for you."

"Thanks."

"No problem. Now I'm going to take this delicious ice cream and return home to ponder my own future."

"Sounds good. See ya."

Natalie started walking back to her apartment, trying to take in everything that happened over the last hour. It had definitely not been a typical Tuesday. But at least she was feeling better than she had that morning. Apparently shocking news was a great wake-up call.

What would it be like to have Josh as a landlord? Well, she didn't think she would have to worry about her lease being renewed if she wanted it. Hopefully she didn't use that as a reason to delay her plans. She would have to make sure she kept herself on track. Maybe she should start tackling her plan now, while she had the motivation. True, she had a lot going on with the cafe and the holidays, but it didn't hurt to get the ball rolling.

Hand paused on the door handle to the building, Natalie decided to take a walk to the bank instead. She needed to have another talk with Linda.

Chapter 54

Chris drove back to his apartment with the radio off, doing his best to figure out what the heck he wanted. He knew Natalie was right, and that she shouldn't be the only reason he was uprooting his life for Pine Valley. He didn't want to grow to resent her like her crummy ex-boyfriend had or make her promises he couldn't keep. He liked Pine Valley. He really did. But he had to be sure.

But how could someone be sure without knowing what the future held?

He hadn't grown up in a little town. He was used to traffic and noise and big buildings and rushing people. The activity had fueled him, pushed him forward in his career, made him successful. He had been happy. Hadn't he?

He thought back to how he had to suck up to clients, had to plaster on a fake smile to try and butter people up. Heck, even the car he was driving wasn't what he would have chosen. It was bought to impress people and show them how successful he was, how successful he could make them. Every day he had had to spend time with people he couldn't care less about. Even his supposed friendships were all superficial. None of his "friends" knew much about him at all. They laughed and joked and drank beer and watched football and talked about who had the hottest girlfriend or who had scored the biggest sale. That wasn't Chris, not really.

Chris didn't like the flashy lifestyle. He didn't flaunt his money any more than necessary. But even if he decided a career change, lifestyle change, was in order, that didn't mean he had to move. Maybe he didn't want the big clients and fake friends, but what about the rest?

Clients aside, he liked his job. He liked the research and details, getting the best deal and finding the perfect fit. If the real estate office in Pine Valley was willing to take a chance on him, he could bring that passion to their work. And to the apartment building, if he accepted Ms. Morseau's offer. That work was a good match.

He didn't have to live in Pine Valley to work there, though. Even if Colleen accepted his offer, and he started working at the real estate office, and he became the leasing agent at the apartment building, there was something to be said for distancing yourself from your work. He knew about Pine Valley now. He could make sure what he did aligned well with the community. That didn't mean he had to live there. Maybe he could see how he felt working there for a while, see how he felt when it was time to go home. Did he dread it? Or did he crave returning to his "normal" every night?

The idea had merit. He could take his time, not rush into anything. It would help him be sure. Natalie might push back from him, but he couldn't let that be the deciding factor.

Something about it didn't settle right, though. It felt half-assed, wishy-washy, like he couldn't commit. There was also something to be said for jumping in with both feet and figuring out the rest later.

The flutter that built in his stomach when he thought of that made him think he had hit on something.

He thought about how he felt when he was in Pine Valley. He thought about the little tour Natalie had given him, when it was dark and cold and yet charming and peaceful. He thought about how his fake smile didn't work in Pine Valley, how the people were genuine and wanted honesty, not buttering up. He thought about how even grumpy Colleen Malloy had wanted what was best for the town.

Even if she ended up going for the higher offer, she had taken steps to make sure the people were protected. Even if she wouldn't be there to see it.

It wasn't just a different place to live. It was a different mindset, a different *way* of living. And that appealed to him. A lot.

But was he ready to jump in with both feet?

Natalie walked into the bank, took a deep breath, and walked toward Linda's office to see if she was busy. Linda was currently meeting with someone else, but she looked up as she saw Natalie approach, smiled, and put up a finger to indicate just a minute.

Natalie took a seat in the waiting area. Her palms were getting sweaty, but, like the previous time she had been here, she figured the worst that could happen would be getting a "no." And considering Linda's positive feedback after her last application, she figured she had a much better shot this time around. There was nothing to be nervous about. That didn't calm her nerves, though.

Linda called her into the office and offered her a seat. Natalie attempted a smile and sat in the chair across from Linda.

"Hello, Natalie. Good to see you again. What brings you in today?"

Natalie took a deep breath. "Well, there have been some changes in my situation since I was last here, and I was hoping to apply for another loan."

"Oh? Were you able to come up with a source for a larger downpayment?"

Natalie shook her head. "No, I'm not going to try to buy the building I'm currently in."

"Ah," Linda said, leaning back in her chair. "You found somewhere else."

"Kind of. I'm looking into maybe buying a house and renovating it."

"Interesting. Do you have a specific house in mind?"

"I've come across a few." Her thoughts drifted to the house Chris had talked about, envisioned for her cafe.

"Are they currently zoned for commercial?"

"I don't know."

"Hmm. Well, I can certainly work on getting you approved for the purchase cost, but the final approval for the loan will depend on the property. It would need to be appraised, and I have my concerns if the building will not meet your needs. I would hate for you to get into debt for something that doesn't work out."

"What do you suggest?"

"Let's get the application started. We can at least find out how much you would be approved for. Then, stop by the town hall. You can find out what would be involved in getting a property rezoned and maybe discuss the likelihood for any properties you're considering. I don't think it's a quick process, and you would probably need to own the property to be able to actually start the process, but they should be able to guide you."

Natalie sighed. "Okay." She knew it wouldn't be simple, but she hoped it would be worth it. Would the year she had given herself be enough if it took a while to just get the zoning approved? Guess she knew how she would be spending her free time this week.

Chapter 55

The call came at nine o'clock on Wednesday morning.

"Okay, man, you win." Eric.

Chris could only grin. That could only mean one thing. "She accepted my offer?"

"She accepted your offer. And every offer except Townsend's."

"I'm sorry."

"No, you're not."

Chris laughed. "No, I'm not. But I'm sorry for you. I know you were hoping for that client."

"Eh. I already had some other properties lined up to show him. I can spin it."

"I'm sure you can." And he could. Eric was nothing if not persistent and thorough. "When are you thinking for closing?"

They worked out details then disconnected the call. Things were falling into place. He had received email confirmation of his loan approval the day before. Now the buildings could officially be his.

He had to call Natalie. No. He would go to see her. Who cared if she was working? Grabbing his keys and coat, he hurried out of his apartment.

He had just pulled into the parking lot next to the diner when his phone rang again. He didn't recognize the number, but it looked local.

"Christopher Parker."

"Hello, Chris. It's Megan Sullivan, from Pine Valley Realty."

Chris's heartrate quickened. "Hello. How are you?"

"I'm doing well, thanks. I wanted to follow up regarding your visit the other day."

"Absolutely."

"Well, I spoke with my husband. We had been considering bringing another realtor into the office, and we agreed that your commercial experience could be an asset, since we've been getting more of a call for commercial spaces and our expertise is in residential. We would need to get you up to speed on the residential end of things, since that is still our primary focus, but if you're up for the challenge, we would love to have you join us."

Chris took a deep breath. What a day. First the buildings, now a job. Things were falling into place nicely. "Wow. That would be amazing."

"I know you're currently working with a commercial agency, and I'm not sure what your current responsibilities are there, so why don't you see how long it would take you to tie up loose ends, and then we can discuss timelines?"

"Absolutely. Thank you so much."

"No problem. We'll talk soon."

They said their goodbyes, and Chris disconnected the call. He hadn't told Natalie about the possibility. He hadn't known how likely it was. But now? Would that be enough to show her he was shifting toward Pine Valley? He still hadn't decided where he would live. But he was getting there.

He looked out his window at the cafe across the street. He had to tell her about the buildings. But maybe he would wait on the job thing. He still had to figure out when and how. At the very least, he should probably wait until after the building closing to leave his current job. He didn't want to put the loan approval at risk.

He took a deep breath. So much was changing so fast. Too fast for him to even catch his breath. Was it too much change? Was he trying to do too much at once? He had gone from not being sure he even wanted to place an offer on a building to suddenly considering uprooting his entire life. It was daunting.

And yet, when he thought about Natalie, and thought about spending his life here with her, he could feel his whole body relax. Even if his mind wasn't ready to make the leap, his body was. And that gave him hope.

He stepped out of his car and crossed to the cafe. He spotted Natalie right away, placing a customer's order into a paper bag. She was laughing, and his breath caught. This woman had changed his life, and he couldn't make himself regret it.

It took her a minute to notice him, but when she did, the smile disappeared from her face. He could see her take a deep breath and say something to Joey, then take off her apron and step out from behind the counter. He hadn't moved from the doorway, stepping to the side only to let customers pass.

Small talk wasn't necessary. "Malloy turned down Townsend's offers."

The expression of pure joy that spread over Natalie's face made him grin. Then her smile faltered. "What about yours?"

"She accepted mine. And Ms. Morseau's. And Josh's."

"That is amazing!" She threw her arms around him, and he held on tight, then spun her around for good measure. "We won!"

Chris put her down and pulled back. "Yes, we won. Of course, now the work really begins, but we're on our way. Dinner to celebrate?"

"Sure."

"I'll pick you up at five."

"Okay."

He left the cafe, pausing outside the doorway to take a deep breath. Then he took a walk to check out the buildings that would soon be his.

Natalie watched Chris walk down the street. So he would be sticking around, at least in some capacity. How did she feel about that?

It was no secret he had turned her life upside down. She had gone from being content with her lot in life, happy with her cafe and friends and community, to feeling anxious and worried and unsure about anything.

But she had started dreaming again.

He had not only made her question how things were but made her think bigger. Of course, if it all blew up in her face, she would totally blame him. But in the meantime? It felt good to dream.

Unfortunately, it wasn't just her cafe she was dreaming about. Chris had highlighted how much she wanted someone in her life. But she couldn't take the chance of being hurt again. If he was going to leave, or just pop in and out of her life when he came to check on his buildings, then it was probably better to keep a distance.

But, oh, how she wanted him in her life. She couldn't help it. He made her feel alive. He made her feel cared for, supported, wanted. Was his buying the buildings a sign that he would stick around? And stick around for how long? How often?

If he never moved to Pine Valley, never committed to being with her full-time, would she be content with a part-time relationship? Would having him in her life just sometimes be enough?

Then again, would she regret letting him go just because he wouldn't move to town?

Natalie sighed. She was glad Townsend wasn't getting the buildings. But even if they had "won," that didn't mean everything had been resolved.

Chapter 56

After the cafe closed, Natalie figured she might as well head to town hall to see what she could learn about the zoning issue. If she put it off, she might end up just giving up altogether. No time like the present, right? She only hoped someone would be there to answer her questions.

She walked into the town hall building and just stood for a moment, unsure where to go. She had never done anything like this before. Who was she supposed to talk to?

"Can I help you?" The voice came from an office to her right, with a cut-out window that faced the lobby. Natalie could see a woman seated behind the window.

"Hi, yes, I'm not sure who I should speak to. I had a question about zoning."

"The zoning commission meets once a month, but if you have general questions, you can try the building department. Down the hall, second door on the left." The woman gestured toward a hallway just past the window.

"Thank you so much."

Natalie took a deep breath and headed down the hall. She had had so many nerve-wracking meetings lately, one would think she should be immune by now, but no such luck.

Finding the correct door, Natalie took another deep breath and pushed it open.

There were two men in the office, working at desks. They seemed busy, so Natalie just hovered inside the doorway, waiting to be noticed. After a few seconds, one of them got up to get something and spotted her.

"Hi, can I help you?"

"Hi. Yeah. Um, I was hoping to find out how someone could go about getting a property rezoned?"

"What property, and what zones?"

"I don't have a specific property yet." Natalie opened the folder she had brought with her. It had the listings Priya had printed for her. "These are some that I'm looking at. They're houses, so I think they're just zoned for residential use. I was hoping to buy one for multiple uses, to have my cafe on the first floor and live on the second floor."

The man slid the papers closer to him and looked through them. "These are all close to the center of town."

"Yes, the streets off Main Street."

"You're good to go."

"What do you mean?"

"Back when this town was founded, there were lots of people doing what you're talking about, having shops and businesses and whatnot and living in the same building. Doctors, lawyers, general stores, all that. The town made it easy and just had everything in the center of town zoned for both residential and commercial. Some buildings were just houses, some just businesses, and some had both, but the land on all those streets can go either way. Or both, as the case may be."

"So I wouldn't have to have any of them rezoned?"

"None of the ones you showed me." He pulled out a paper map of the town and pointed to the center of town with his finger. "This here is Main Street. These streets here – Pine, Center, Woodlawn, Parkview, School, those are all zoned for mixed use." He made a rectangle around the center with his finger. "Anywhere within here, and you're good to go."

"Wow. Okay. That makes things a lot easier. Thank you so much."

"You bet. Good luck."

"Thanks."

Natalie left the town hall feeling lighter than she had in days. Things were finally coming together. Now to decide which building would best suit her needs. That would be the fun part. Natalie got a twinge of giddiness. She had never gone house shopping before.

The real estate office was on the way back to her apartment, so Natalie decided to stop in. The woman she had spoken to before wasn't there, but a man greeted her as she walked in.

"How can I help you?" he asked.

"Hi. My name is Natalie. I had stopped in here a little while and spoken to someone. I think it was Priya? About finding a property. She gave me some printouts and took my information, but I had just been looking. Now I'm starting to think more seriously about it and wanted to stop in. I don't know how this process works."

"Well, welcome back. Let me pull up your information here. What's your last name, Natalie?"

"Mitchell."

"Okay, here we are. It looks like you were looking for a mixed-use building, with commercial on the first floor and residential on the second. Is that correct?"

"Yeah."

"Hmm. Not much available that fits that bill. Nothing in Pine Valley. I have one or two in neighboring towns, if you wanted to take a look."

"I'd like to stay in Pine Valley if possible. Priya had shown me some houses that might work with renovation, so I was looking at those." Natalie took out the listing information. "These were the ones she had printed for me."

The man looked over the printouts. "Yeah, I could see how some of these might work." He put one to the side. "This one actually just accepted an offer, so it's not currently on the market. I'm not too familiar with a couple of these, but the ones I know do have pretty open floor plans on the first floor. What kind of business?"

"Cafe. I own the cafe on Main Street."

"Ah! Of course. I knew you looked familiar. Well, no matter which one you went with, there would definitely be renovation required, even with an open floor plan."

"I know I'll need to update the electrical to accommodate the commercial ovens."

"Yeah, there's that. And if you want more seating, a display case, all that. You're prepared to take on renovations?"

Natalie nodded. "I've started looking into it, so if I can't find something that's just right, I'm prepared to take on the project." She felt tingles of anticipation just saying the words.

"Alright, then. Well, then the next step would be to look at properties. You have some listings here. I'm sure we could find some others. When are you available to visit them?"

"The cafe closes at two, so any time after that during the week. Currently my weekends are occupied with baking prep, so I won't be available on weekends until after Christmas."

"No problem. Weekday afternoons should be fine. Since you started the process with Priya, I will pass along all of this information to her, and I'll have her set up some showings."

"Sounds good. Thank you."

"Any time. She'll be in touch soon."

Natalie left the office and headed back to her apartment. The afternoon was flying by, and Chris would be picking her up soon. But it had been a productive afternoon. Now she just had to wait – to hear back from Priya, to hear back about her loan application. But she could handle that. She felt another tingle of anticipation. She couldn't wait to tell Chris.

Chapter 57

Chris hadn't stepped into any of the businesses in the buildings he would soon own. Instead, he sat on a bench across the street and just stared at them.

Except for his cars, he had never actually owned anything of substance in his life. He rented his apartment, and had been renting since he moved out of his parents' house after college. His watch might be worth something, but that had been a graduation present from his dad, so he didn't count it. He never bought anything expensive, since he just didn't see the point. No risk, no responsibility.

But here he was, soon to be the owner of not one but two commercial buildings, in a small town that up until a year or so ago he had barely even heard of.

The thought was daunting, and not entirely comfortable.

What if he completely messed it up? What if he missed something important, and they burned down or something? Or ended up with some kind of infestation? Or just needed basic maintenance? He didn't know how to do any of that. He was a renter. If something happened in his apartment, he called the superintendent. But now he would be the super. Even if he decided it was too much for him and he hired a property management company, he was still the one responsible.

And these people had been through so much already. Malloy had been a landlord for years, and look at how that had turned out. Chris didn't know what he was doing. The buildings could collapse, and he would be clueless as to how it had happened.

The more he thought about it, the more he started to panic. Was it too late to back out? Technically he hadn't signed the paperwork yet. But what if he did back out? Then Townsend would probably swoop in, and that was exactly what he had been trying to avoid. So he was stuck between a rock and a hard place.

Chris bent over and put his head between his legs. He was gasping for air now, the full weight of what was about to happen sinking in. It wasn't just his life that he would be responsible for now, but the livelihoods of so many people he had come to care about. They were all counting on him, expecting him to save them from eviction, keep their businesses safe and secure. What was he going to do?

He sat there, until his fingers and toes grew numb and the sun started going down. He had to go meet Natalie soon. They were supposed to be celebrating. Chris smiled sardonically. Some celebration. But he stood up, tried to shake feeling back into his arms and legs, and walked awkwardly back toward the cafe. The twinkling holiday lights mocked him. A Santa stood on one corner, ringing a bell to get donations. The bell pierced Chris's skull. Maybe he should just cancel dinner. He wasn't sure he felt up to going out. Or staying in. Or existing, really.

When he knocked on Natalie's door, he didn't know what he would say or do. She opened the door with a smile, but the moment she saw his face, her smile faded.

"What's wrong?"

"Nothing. And everything. And I don't know. I think I've made a terrible mistake."

Natalie gestured for him to come inside. "Mistake about what?"

"Everything. I just... I was so focused on helping people, you know? I didn't think about what it really meant. At first, I thought easy money, and then I thought I had to make sure Townsend didn't get them, and now I think...I just..."

"You don't want to buy the buildings after all."

Chris looked at her, his expression grim. "I don't know what to do."

She looked so sad, it broke Chris's heart.

"But I know I have to. I mean, what's the alternative? Let Townsend come in and kick everybody out? How could I live with myself if I let that happen?"

"Malloy renewed the leases. They would have time now to figure something out."

"Sure, if Townsend doesn't find some BS to get around that."

"So you don't want to buy the buildings, but you don't want Townsend to buy the buildings."

"I don't know what I want."

Natalie pulled out a dining chair and sat down. "I can't make the decision for you, Chris. I told you before I can't be the reason you change your life. Well, a sense of duty probably isn't a good reason, either."

He didn't know how to respond. He knew she was right. But what were his options? Throw these innocent people to the wolves? Suck it up and deal and hope he felt better about it eventually?

He cared about these people, about this town. He wanted to do what was best for them.

Chris thought back to Colleen Malloy's words, about him thinking he was what was best. He didn't, not really. He was just a guy, trying to do what was right. He may have put on a good show, exuding confidence at work, convincing everyone he knew what he was doing. But he was just a regular guy, uncertain and insecure. There were probably much more qualified people out there. He just hadn't found them yet. Could he buy the buildings, then try to find someone else and sell them? Maybe that would work. It would buy him time, at least. Sure, it would cost him in closing fees and all that, but he didn't care about the money. He could always make more money.

"I think in light of the situation, we should skip dinner," Natalie said after a minute had passed in silence.

"Natalie, I..."

Natalie stood up and walked over to where he still stood just inside the doorway. "I can't do this right now, Chris. I have my own things to worry about."

Chris nodded once and turned to go. He hated that he had hurt her.

"Goodnight, Chris," she said.

He stepped into the hallway, and Natalie closed the door behind him. He had never heard anything sound so final.

Natalie closed the door, then slid to the floor and burst into tears. She had known he would break her heart. It was Jamison all over again – making promises and assurances, and then turning his back on all of them. And her.

Stupid, stupid, stupid. She had known better and still fallen for him.

After a couple of minutes, the tears dried up. Natalie wiped her eyes and stood up. Well, she may not be having dinner with Chris, but she still needed to eat. And even if he completely turned his back on the town and the buildings and her and everything, she still had reasons to celebrate. Her cafe was safe, and the path was being laid for her to buy a house, to live out her dream and have more control over her future.

She grabbed her coat and purse. And then, with a deep breath, she straightened her shoulders, lifted her chin, and walked out of the apartment. She didn't need a man to be happy. She could do it on her own.

Chapter 58

Chris didn't want to go home. He didn't even know if he would be up to driving. So he just walked.

It wasn't a great night for walking. The air was frigid, and the wind had picked up, piercing through his coat wherever there was the slightest gap. Chris hardly felt it.

Buying a building would be no big deal, he had thought. It was a great investment. And he could "do commercial in his sleep." Chris scoffed. Sure, if he just cared about the money. He could bring someone in there to run the place and just sit back and collect paychecks. Heck, Don Malloy hadn't even done that much, and he had survived for years. Not that Chris wanted to use Malloy as a role model. But if he could do it, surely Chris could do it.

That whole morals thing seemed to be the sticking point. But he was sure there were many ethical landlords out there, making sure their buildings and tenants were taken care of. Did they feel this enormous weight on them, like one wrong move would have devastating consequences? Maybe it was just because he knew it had already happened here, that negligence had ruined lives. Who's to say he would do any better?

Chris didn't know where he was walking, but he somehow found himself standing in front of the Pine Valley Motel. Not knowing what else to do, he went into the office.

A woman he vaguely recognized stood behind the counter. Why did she look so familiar? He glanced down at her name tag. Lindsay. That's right. The former motel owners' daughter, now the general manager under Zach. She hated him, didn't she? Maybe this wasn't such a great idea.

She looked up when she heard him enter. A smile and greeting were perched on her lips, but they faded. Yup, she hated him.

"Mr. Parker, are you okay?"

He didn't respond. He couldn't. He had spotted a side table that featured a coffee maker and cookies. Natalie's cookies. He would recognize them anywhere. Collapsing onto one of the chairs by the front entrance, he released a sob.

In the background, he could hear Lindsay talking to someone, but he didn't see or hear anyone else. Maybe she was on the phone. It didn't matter. He couldn't do anything but sit there sobbing, staring at Natalie's cookies.

He didn't know how much time had passed when he felt a hand on his arm.

"Hey, buddy," he heard someone say. Chris turned to find Zach standing over him. "What's going on?"

Chris could only stare at him.

"Okay." Zach looked back at Lindsay. "Lindsay, is anyone in the common area right now?"

Lindsay shook her head. "I don't think so, but let me check." She disappeared behind a door and came back a moment later. "No, you're clear."

"Okay, great." Zach tucked a hand under Chris's arm. "Come on, Chris, let's go."

Chris blindly let Zach lead him.

At the back of the motel, where the former owners had had an apartment, there was now a recreation room, with sofas and bookshelves and a foosball table. A Christmas tree sat in one corner, beside an electric fireplace that was flickering merrily. It was cozy, but Chris could hardly take it in.

Zach led him to one of the sofas in front of the fireplace, and they sat down.

"Now, what is going on? You look like some kind of frozen deranged zombie."

Chris's limbs were starting to thaw, and the resulting pain shocked him into coherence. "I've ruined everything."

"I'm sure that's not true. But before we dive into it, let's get you warmed up. How long were you out there?"

Chris shook his head. "I don't know."

"Okay. I'm gonna get you some warm clothes and make you some hot chocolate, okay? In the meantime, take off your frozen coat and wrap yourself in one of these blankets." Zach grabbed a blanket off the back of the sofa and placed it on Chris's lap. "I'll be right back."

Chris tried to take off his coat, but his numb fingers didn't want to work the zipper, so he gave up. He haltingly unfolded the blanket and spread it out over him. His whole body was starting to shake.

Zach returned in a couple of minutes, carrying sweatpants, a sweatshirt and a pair of wool socks. "Okay, buddy," he said, walking over to Chris. "There's a bathroom by the bookcases. You go get changed, and I'll make your hot chocolate." Chris didn't move. "Do you need some help?"

Chris nodded. He felt like he couldn't do anything but sit there.

"Okay." Zach helped him back to a standing position, then, supporting Chris with one arm and holding the clothes with the other, helped him to the bathroom.

It took nearly ten minutes to get Chris changed into warm clothes. He was still shaking, but it seemed to be less violent than it had been, so that had to be a good sign, right?

Zach seemed worn out from the exertion. "Okay, let's get you back to the sofa."

By the time they made it back to the sofa, Zach ended up collapsing right next to Chris.

"Feeling any better?"

Chris nodded. "Yeah, I think so. Though my fingers and toes are not exactly my friends right now."

"That's to be expected. Feel up to telling me what's going on?"

Chris sighed as he did his best to curl into a ball under the blanket. "I put in an offer on two of the buildings, and it was accepted."

"That's great!" Zach said. "What happened with the other properties?"

"A woman and her foundation – that Lena Morseau person you told me about – is buying the apartment site. And the ice cream shop owner is buying the other commercial building."

"Good for him. So it sounds like everything worked out like you wanted it to. What's the problem, then?"

"The problem is that it didn't sink into me until this afternoon how big a deal it is."

"What, buying the buildings?"

Chris nodded.

"Okay...What are you struggling with?"

"Everything. I mean, I wanted to stop Townsend from taking over and ruining these people's lives, but who's to say I'm not going to be just as bad? Maybe I'll totally screw things up and a building will collapse or cave in or whatever, or some horrible disaster will happen, or the place will flood, or something. I mean, how do you do it? You go around buying all these properties, taking on buildings and renovating them and bringing in staff and guests and all that. Don't you worry that something will go wrong?"

Zach laughed. "Of course I do. I'm human. But the best I can do is take precautions so that stuff doesn't happen. I bring in reputable companies for my renovations, don't skimp on safety and all that, get regular inspections. I do background checks on staff, make sure procedures are in place in case of a fire or something. All I can do is try to cover my bases. After that, it's out of my hands."

"And you're okay with that?"

"Depends on the day. But for the most part, yeah. Even if you buy these buildings, it doesn't mean that everything will fall on you. If something happens with the electrical, you bring in an electrician. If something happens with the plumbing, you bring in a plumber. Nobody expects you to handle everything yourself. You've already had the buildings inspected, so you know you're starting with a good foundation. And the tenants will let you know if anything is off." He laughed again. "Trust me, people will let you know if something is off. It's not likely that there won't be signs before something becomes catastrophic. That building collapse last year didn't happen suddenly. It happened because repairs weren't done properly and complaints were being ignored and half-assed patch jobs fell apart."

Chris just sat in silence, trying to let Zach's words sink in.

"Have you ever owned something before? A house or something?"

"No. I've always rented."

"How about your car?"

"Yeah, I've got a car."

"Okay, then. If something starts making a funny noise or doing something it shouldn't, you bring it to a mechanic, right?"

Chris nodded.

"Okay, well, the same applies here. Just with a building, not a car."

"But if my car kicks the bucket, it only affects me. If something happens with the building, it affects other people. It's a lot of responsibility."

"And the fact that you're worried so much about it means you are the perfect person to take it on. Because you will take the proper precautions to make sure that something doesn't happen with the building." Zach leaned back. "Think about it this way: the buildings you're buying are the perfect starter buildings for you. They're one floor with no basement, so no danger of floors collapsing. They're commercial, not residential, so nobody will be homeless if something happens. And you have good, solid tenants already in there. They'll keep an eye on things."

Chris wanted to believe him. He really did. But he still felt uneasy.

"I know it's a big step. But you've got this. Give it some time to sink in. Ask yourself what's the worst thing that could happen, then tell yourself how unlikely that is to happen. Or, if it could happen, come up with a plan to make sure it doesn't."

Chris closed his eyes and took a deep breath. Would it get easier once it had sunk in? He really hoped so. The look in Natalie's eyes haunted him. He had let her down, just like he was trying not to. Was there any way she would forgive him? Probably not if he turned his back on buying the buildings.

"Thanks, Zach."

"Any time. Now was there anything else you needed to get off your chest?"

"A whole bunch of stuff. But right now, I think this is all I can handle."

"Okay. Well, I'm here for you. I'll be in Pine Valley for probably another week or so, so if you need to chat again, just call or swing by."

"Thanks."

"Now, I am late for a dinner meeting, so I have to run. But if you need to crash here tonight, let Lindsay know. I'm sure we have an extra room or two."

Chris nodded. "Okay. Sorry to make you late for your meeting."

"No problem. Priorities, right?"

"Yeah," Chris agreed. "Priorities."

Natalie ended up at the diner, but Maggie wasn't there that evening. It was just as well. Natalie didn't think she was up for a big heart-to-heart right now. She had to focus on her plans for the future, not disappointments from her past. After sitting herself at the counter, though, she decided just to take her meal to go.

She could see Courtney and Josh seated in a booth on one side, and other couples here and there. Families, friends, it seemed everyone had someone. Except her. She was alone.

She knew she had friends. She had people who cared about her. But everyone had someone else, too. Everyone except her.

Okay, she needed to get herself out of this funk. She was letting this mess with Chris affect her far too much. She was going to get her meal to go, head back to her apartment, and look at houses online while she ate. Maybe she would even put on one of those home renovation shows to get her in the mood. That would get her mind off everything but what she wanted to focus on.

Taking a deep breath, she smiled at Jordan, who just happened to be the waiter helping with the counter that evening.

"Hello, Jordan."

"Hey, Natalie. What can I get you?"

"I think I'm just going to get a burger and fries, but I've actually decided to get it to go."

"You got it. Can I tempt you with a piece of pie for dessert?" He grinned.

"Oh, gee, twist my arm why don't you."

"Apple or pecan?"

"Now that is a tough choice. Let's go with the apple."

"You got it. Be back in a few."

While she waited for her food, Natalie tried to reason with herself. Even if love wasn't in the cards for her, she could still have a full life. She had her business and her friends. And soon she would have a house, with a whole big renovation project that would definitely fill up her life, at least temporarily. Sure, she would have liked to be a mom, but she could always adopt. Or foster. If she had a house, she would have more than enough room. Women did it all the time. See? She didn't need a man.

Jordan brought out her bag and her bill, and Natalie paid, then bid him farewell. She had a full night of dreaming and planning ahead.

Chapter 59

Chris woke up in a strange bed, unsure where he was or why. Then the events of the day before came trickling back. His meltdown. His mental crisis. His insecurities poured out first to Natalie, then to Zach. He groaned. What was wrong with him?

He lay there, reliving the disappointment in Natalie's eyes, the compassion on Zach's face. They must think he was a lunatic. Maybe he *was* a lunatic. How could he go from perfectly confident and capable to doubting everything?

No, he had been doubting everything from the beginning. All his wishy-washiness, his indecisiveness. He had just convinced himself that he was doing the right thing, to help the business owners and show Natalie that he could commit. So much for that. He had a lot of ground to cover if he wanted to make it up to her.

But what did he want? What was he going to do? Did he want to walk away, or was he going to see this through? And what about all his other plans, his building a life in Pine Valley? If he gave up on the buildings, would he give up on the new job? The possibility of helping with the apartment building?

Chris groaned and rolled over. He felt like punching the pillow. He had hoped a good night's sleep would provide him with some clarity, but it had been a rough night, and he felt no closer to clarity now than he had yesterday afternoon. And he strongly suspected clarity would not come while he was lying in bed stressing himself out. So he got up, used the bathroom, and tried to figure out where to go from here.

His clothes from the day before were folded on a chair in the corner of the room. He was still wearing the sweats Zach had given him. Well, he might as well get dressed. Then he would try to find Zach and thank him for letting him crash.

By the time Chris went back to the motel office, Zach was nowhere to be seen. He forced himself to look away from the table that now held Natalie's danish on it and instead approached the counter, where Lindsay stood just as she had the night before.

"Well, you're looking better," she said when Chris approached.

"Thanks. What do I owe you for the room?"

Lindsay waved him away. "Zach said not to worry about it."

"I appreciate it. Is he around?"

"He had a meeting this morning. He should be back by lunch, though. Did you need him for something?"

"I don't know. Not really, I guess. We talked last night."

"Yeah. I heard. I didn't mean to eavesdrop, but I couldn't help but hear while I was standing here."

"You must think I'm an idiot."

"No, not an idiot. Just someone who cares, which is more than I can say for a lot of people. And definitely not what I expected from you."

Chris gave a half smile. "Yeah, I know you don't think too highly of me."

"It's not that. I've just been around a lot of people with that slick, charming attitude. My ex-husband, for one. But you treated my parents fairly, and I'm grateful for that."

"How are they doing?"

"They're doing well. Enjoying retirement, though Mom's not exactly retired, since she's working at the cafe, and Dad's not exactly retired since he's been doing odd jobs for just about everyone in town." Lindsay laughed. "But they're happy, and that's what matters."

"I'm glad."

"Thanks." Lindsay paused. "Can I offer you a piece of advice, even if you didn't ask for it?"

"I'll gladly take all the help I can get."

"No one ever feels ready for big responsibilities. I've owned two houses now, I have two kids, and I'm running a motel. There will be times when you panic and are convinced you're doing everything wrong, and there are times when you feel pretty confident. And, of course, times everywhere in between. Nothing will ever be perfect, and the time will never be just right. All you can do is try your best. If it's something you want, and you want to do it right, then you'll be okay. The most important part is caring, and it sounds like you've got that part down."

"Thanks."

"No problem."

"I'm going to get going now, but tell Zach thanks. And thanks again to you, too. I'll bring Zach's clothes back freshly washed."

"You got it. Good luck."

Chris put one hand up in farewell and left the office.

The sun was shining, and the wind had died down, so it didn't feel nearly as cold as it had the night before. It was a good thing, too. Since his car was back at the parking lot behind the cafe, he had a long walk ahead of him.

As he walked, he thought back to everything Zach had said the night before, and everything Lindsay had said this morning. He did care. Maybe too much. But what did he *want*? It had seemed like everything was falling into place. He had the buildings, the job prospect – two job prospects, actually, – and he and Natalie had been getting closer. But he hadn't been able to take that final step, to move to Pine Valley. He had wanted to keep one foot out the door. Was it just cold feet? Was it insecurity? Or was his brain telling him one thing while his heart was telling him another? And which was which? And which was right?

He paused in his walking and closed his eyes, then took a deep breath. He loved it here. He really did. The fresh air, the scenery, the community, the people. But if that was true, why was he having such trouble committing? Why was he making everything into a gigantic issue?

In a perfect world, he would have a job he loved, a home he loved, and a woman he loved. Well, his life as it stood before this whole Pine Valley mess wasn't exactly perfect. He enjoyed parts of his job, but disliked others. He wouldn't say he loved his apartment, though it was okay. And any women in his life were coworkers he wasn't close to or ex-girlfriends he had definitely *not* loved.

In Pine Valley? He had three job opportunities that he might end up loving, though he would have to really give them a try before saying: landlord, realtor, and leasing agent. He didn't have a home here, but he definitely felt comfortable, more like himself here. And maybe home was more than just a place to sleep and eat. Maybe it was a place to belong. And when it came to a woman he loved? Well, that was a no-brainer. He may not have said the words out loud or even to himself, but Natalie was everything he wanted.

So what was holding him back? Fear of failure? Of change? Of disappointing everyone?

Lindsay had said no one was ever ready for big responsibilities. You just had to care enough to try your best. He definitely cared enough. So maybe it was time to jump in with both feet after all.

Chapter 60

Natalie didn't see Chris on Thursday. Or Friday. It was as if he had dropped off the face of the earth. Maybe he really was giving up, turning his back on Pine Valley, and leaving her behind.

Good. Fine. She didn't need him anyway. She was busy baking and serving customers and looking at houses and researching renovation companies. She worried about her fellow small business owners, but they had the longer leases now. They would be fine, wouldn't they? For at least a little while? Well, one of them could have her space when she moved if they needed it.

By the time the cafe closed on Saturday, Natalie was tired. Not just from the usual business, though traffic had been busy. She was tired mentally and emotionally from trying to pretend that Chris hadn't hurt her. But she couldn't cave. She was too busy. There would be time after the holidays to lament what might have been. For now, she had to make more cookie dough. And, actually, start baking some. She had a few boxes scheduled to be picked up in the coming week.

Joey and Sylvie had both offered to help her, but Natalie had waved them off. She needed the time to herself, to crank up the Christmas music and forget about her troubles. She had already taken out all of her ingredients and lined up the empty boxes she would need. She would save the frozen dough for boxes in the coming weeks. For now, it made more sense to just make more dough, bake what she needed immediately, and freeze the rest. So that was her plan.

Natalie locked the door behind Sylvie and turned to head to the kitchen to begin her baking extravaganza. She hadn't quite reached the kitchen, though, when she heard a knock on the door. Turning, she saw Chris peeking through the glass.

Butterflies stirred in Natalie's stomach. What was he doing here? Hadn't he done enough? Did he have to come and ruin her baking time, too?

But she couldn't just leave him standing in the cold. So she unlocked the door and stuck her head out.

"What do you want?"

"Chris Parker, reporting for duty. I'm here to help with cookies."

"I don't need your help." She moved to close the door. Chris stuck his foot in the doorway to keep it from closing.

"Please, Natalie. I know I messed up. Can you please give me a chance to explain?"

Natalie was torn. Even if she was just pushing down her feelings and living in denial, she had been doing just fine. She didn't want him here. But part of her was really glad to see him. And that part let him open the door all the way.

"Say your piece, and then get out of here."

"Okay. Here's the deal." He took a deep breath. "I have never really had responsibilities. I've always rented my apartments, worked for other people. When I thought about going out on my own, I decided it was too much work. And work felt like a game to me, all about finding the matching pieces, getting the best deal, figuring out what the client needed to make them say yes. It was easy and uncomplicated. Sure, the deals could get complicated, but that was all part of the game. Like Monopoly."

"What's your point?"

"My point is: you made me look at things differently. Suddenly it wasn't just the same game I'd been playing. What I did affected other people. It made a difference. And I liked that idea. I wanted to be the hero. I wanted to win this new game. And so I did what I had to, to impress you, to help the other people. But after I won, I realized it's not just a game at all. It's not about being the hero or stopping the bad guy from taking over. These are real lives at stake, real people being affected. And I panicked. I freaked out and realized I'm not ready for that. What if I mess up? What if I do something that's worse than what the bad guy was going to do?" He took a deep breath. "I'm sorry, Natalie. I'm sorry for not being the man you thought I was, for getting your hopes up and then crushing them."

So that was it. He was turning his back on them. Natalie looked down and scuffed the toe of her sneaker on the tile floor. "So that's it?"

"No, that's not it. Because after my meltdown, I took a freezing walk around town and ended up at the motel. And I talked to Zach. And I talked to Lindsay. And I thought some more. And walked some more. And I realized something."

When he didn't continue, Natalie looked back up at him.

"I realized that I *want* to be that man. I want to be the hero, not just because I want to win, but because I want to make a real difference. I care about these people, this town. So when I was doing all that stuff to try to win the game, I was actually also doing stuff that made my life feel more complete."

"So what does that mean? You're going to buy the buildings after all?"

"Yes. I'm going to buy the buildings. But also, after the closing is complete, I'll be leaving my job at Ryker Commercial Properties and starting as a realtor with Pine Valley Realty. And when the apartment building gets built, I'll be the leasing agent for the building. And, hopefully, one of its first tenants."

Natalie's breath caught. Not only was he buying the buildings, but he was building a life in Pine Valley?

Chris smiled and handed her a small gift bag he had been carrying.

"What's this?" Natalie asked.

"Your Christmas present."

"It's not Christmas yet."

"Just open it."

She reached into the tissue paper and pulled out a candle, handmade by one of the crafters she knew in town. The scent was called Home Sweet Home, and the label showed a picture of Pine Valley. Natalie felt tears welling in her eyes. "Are you sure this is what you want?"

Chris took one of her hands in his. "Natalie, I can finally say I have never been more sure of anything in my life."

She sniffed. "And me?"

"And, if you'll have me, I want you by my side through it all. I love you, Natalie."

The tears came in earnest then, and Natalie pulled her hand away to throw her arms around Chris's neck. "I love you, too."

He kissed her, holding her close, for a few moments before pulling back. "Now, how about we make some cookies?"

And Natalie laughed.

Epilogue

Natalie spread the tablecloths over the counter, and Chris and Joey put the prepared platters of sandwiches and cookies on top while Natalie got the carafes of coffee set up.

It was going to be a Christmas party to remember, held on the twenty-third of December, so as not to compete with Maggie's Christmas Eve open house or Christmas Day celebration. She had invited all of her regulars – and anyone else she could think of – as a way to celebrate after the drama and emotional rollercoaster of the last month and a half.

By the time guests started arriving, the holiday lights were glowing, Christmas music was playing in the background, and Natalie felt nothing but joy as she greeted friends and neighbors. The cafe was soon filled with smiling, laughing people, chatting and eating and enjoying the festive atmosphere.

Natalie had just turned to refill a platter of sandwiches when she saw someone enter the cafe. She smiled and walked over to greet the newcomer.

"Mrs. Malloy. I'm so glad you could join us."

Colleen seemed nervous, unsure if she should be there. "Thank you for the invitation. I – I probably won't stay long, but I didn't want to be rude."

"You can stay for as long as you'd like. Would you like something to eat or drink?" Natalie gestured toward the counter.

"Thank you. That would be nice."

Natalie filled the sandwich platter, offered the first pick to Mrs. Malloy, then placed it back on the counter. Then she returned to the dining area, holding a glass and a knife. Tapping the knife against the glass, she asked for everyone's attention.

"Hello, everyone. Thank you so much for coming tonight. As you may or may not know, the last couple of months have been a bit dramatic. Without going into too much detail, suffice it to say we didn't know if the cafe would be here for much longer. There was a very real possibility we would get kicked out in favor of some big company or something. But tonight we can celebrate, because we are still here and won't be leaving Pine Valley anytime soon."

Some of the guests applauded, while others cheered.

"Thank you. We're pretty happy about it, too." Natalie chuckled. "But I wanted to give special thanks to two people today who made it possible. Chris, I know I didn't make it easy, but you refused to give up, and I am very grateful you decided to stick around." She blew him a kiss, and the crowd started laughing and catcalling. "And Mrs. Malloy." The crowd fell silent. "You were stuck in a very difficult position, and this town didn't make it any easier. But when given the choice, you did what was best for all of us, even if it wasn't what was best for you. And I will be forever grateful."

Natalie felt tears welling in her eyes, and she sought out Colleen in the crowd. Colleen was blushing, but her eyes were moist, and Natalie took her hands and squeezed them.

"Thank you," Colleen whispered.

"You were not the bad guy," Natalie replied in a soft voice. "And I'm sorry so many people acted like you were. You will always be welcome here." Natalie hugged her, then backed away as other friends approached to greet Colleen.

Chris came up behind Natalie. "That was very nice of you," he whispered in her ear.

"It was the right thing to do. I do owe her a lot." Chris squeezed her shoulder, and Natalie leaned against him. She couldn't remember ever having been as content as she was right then.

By the time the last guest left, Natalie was exhausted but happy. Everyone had been happy, even Colleen Malloy, by the end of the night.

"I hope people aren't expecting much tomorrow," Joey said as he stacked up the empty platters and brought them to the kitchen. "I don't see either of us getting up very early."

"And that is why I saved some cookie dough from the boxes and prepped bread dough earlier. We can stick to quick and easy tomorrow morning."

"Sounds good to me."

"Good night, Joey. Thanks for your help tonight."

"You got it, boss. See you tomorrow."

He waved goodbye and stepped into the cold night air, leaving just Natalie and Chris in the cafe.

"I think that went well," Chris said, coming up behind her and wrapping his arms around her waist.

"Very well," she said, turning to kiss him.

They held each other for a moment before Chris pulled away. "Okay, as much as I hate it, I should get going." He made a face. "I have my last official transaction for Ryker tomorrow, and I'm not looking forward to it. But I'll see you for dinner after, right?"

"You bet." She kissed him again. "Then I'll have you all to myself."

Chris gave her one last kiss, then headed out the door. Natalie locked it behind him and sighed. She looked around at the cafe that had served countless customers over the years. This would be her last Christmas in this building, and part of that made her sad. But she had just put in an offer on a house – the perfect house with the wrap-around porch and fireplace that Chris had found – and it had been accepted. This time next year, she should be in her new home. And that made her very happy, indeed.

Also by Vanessa E. Kelman

<u>*Pine Valley Series*</u>
Searching for Home
Between the Moments
A Simpler Life

<u>*Fate Trilogy*</u>
Chasing Fate
Accepting Fate
Tempting Fate

<u>*NonFiction*</u>
A Life You Want: Take Charge of Your Life!